THE VIRGINIA CHRONICLES

KAYT MILLER

DEDICATION

To my eighty-two-year-old mom who, after beta reading my book, said,
"You know... I think you need one more sex scene."
I love that woman!

COPYRIGHT

This book is a work of fiction. Names, characters, places, and incidents are the product of the author's imagination or are used facetiously. Any resemblance to actual events, locales, or persons, living or dead, is coincidental.

❋ Created with Vellum

CONTENTS

Chapter 1	1
Chapter 2	5
Chapter 3	17
Chapter 4	23
Chapter 5	29
Chapter 6	35
Chapter 7	39
Chapter 8	43
Chapter 9	47
Chapter 10	57
Chapter 11	61
Chapter 12	65
Chapter 13	69
Chapter 14	73
Chapter 15	79
Chapter 16	91
Chapter 17	95
Chapter 18	99
Chapter 19	109
Chapter 20	119
Chapter 21	131
Chapter 22	135
Chapter 23	141
Chapter 24	143
Chapter 25	151
Chapter 26	165
Chapter 27	171
Chapter 28	175
Chapter 29	181
Chapter 30	185
Chapter 31	191

Chapter 32 197

Chapter 33 201

Chapter 34 205

Chapter 35 211

Chapter 36 217

Chapter 37 223

Chapter 38 227

Chapter 39 241

Chapter 40 253

Chapter 41 259

Chapter 42 263

Chapter 43 273

Chapter 44 281

Chapter 45 287

Appendix: Survey A (For Heterosexual Male Participants) 291

More Books by Kayt Miller 307

Acknowledgments 309

About the Author 311

Thank you! 313

Sneak Peek: One of a Kind 315

CHAPTER 1

"You're a what?" shouts Dave.

"Um, I'm a virgin," I say softly. Now that I think about it, I probably should have warned him about this before we were both naked and panting—well, sort of panting—in my bed.

"A virgin? Aren't you like twenty-one?"

"So?"

"That thing should have been popped a long time ago. What's wrong with you?" he says, pointing angrily at my lady parts.

"Nothing," I sputter. "Nothing's wrong with me." God, what an asshole. To be honest, I'd been seeing a little bit of this asshole side of Dave since we'd started dating a few weeks ago.

"Well, *Virgin*-ia," he says, emphasizing the first part of my name like, you guessed it, an asshole, "you're telling me you want me to take your cherry? Fuck!" he shouts as he paces my tiny dorm room buck naked. "Nuh-uh. No way. If I do, this will all snowball out of control. First, you'll fall in love with me, and when I reject your love, and I *will* reject your love, you'll become a stage-five clinger, and I just don't have time for that. I'm graduating soon. I plan to move out east." He runs his fingers through his receding hairline. "You and I were never going to be long term, Virginia."

I know that. In my heart I know, but I wasn't going into this thinking there was an expiration date. So, I ask the obvious question, not wanting an answer, but I'm a masochist that way. "Why not?"

"Because, Virginia." He sighs. "Look at you." He nods in my direction.

I peer down at my plump body, then back up at him. I know I'm not the best-looking girl on campus, but I've got decent boobs and my butt isn't horrible. Sure, I'd like to scrape off a few inches from my stomach and thighs, but who wouldn't?

"Virginia, you're... you're okay-looking. I just have a picture in my mind of what my life partner—"

"Life partner?"

"Life partner. Mate. Whatever. I have a picture in my head of what my mate is going to look like, and you're not it, Virginia."

"I'm not it?" I ask sort of numbly. "Uh, so what does your mate look like?" *God, why am I doing this to myself?*

"Well, she's blonde. Definitely blonde. And slim," he says, looking at the bulge around my middle.

I pull the white sheet up over my hips and keep tugging until I'm covered up to my neck. Dave doesn't get to look anymore. I want to interrupt, but I don't.

"She's five feet seven inches tall, large breasts, long legs, and—"

I laugh. "Good luck with all of that, *Dave.*" Now it's my turn to be snarky. Dave's nothing special. He's average. Average height, brown hair, brown eyes, dad bod, he's a computer nerd, and he's broke. "You want a trophy wife?"

"So?" he says, bending down to grab his tighty-whities.

Another mark against Dave. No one his age should ever wear those things.

Next, he searches the floor for his athletic shorts and shirt.

After pulling those on, he slips on his flip-flops and walks toward my door, then turns to me. "I'm sorry. I can't do it, Virginia. I'm done. We're done. Good luck with your cherry popping and all that, but it isn't gonna be me that does it. Find some unsuspecting one-night stand and just get it over with. But for fuck's sake, don't tell him you're a virgin. Christ!" he mutters, walking out of my bedroom.

I sit on my bed, clutching my sheet and blinking at the open door. Did that just happen? Did my boyfriend dump me because I'm a virgin?

"God! What an asshole!"

CHAPTER 2

FLOPPING onto my back on our faux Persian rug in our living room, I sigh dramatically. "Why does it feel like something's wrong with me, Peach?"

From her perch on the sofa, Penny "Peach" Marks looks down at me with pity. Stupid, stupid pity. "There's nothing wrong with you, Virginia. There's something wrong with society. Well, maybe not society, but the people our age, millennials. There's just this expectation that everyone will graduate from high school de-virginized."

"*De-virginized?* That's a terrible word."

Peach giggles. "I made it up."

"No! I had no idea," I deadpan. Now it's my turn to giggle. Penny Marks is a dork and my best friend in the entire world. She's the yin to my yang, the bread to my butter, and my... well, you get the idea. Without her, there would have been many times that I would have climbed to the highest mountain peak and stayed there.

"So, tell me again exactly what he said."

I groan out loud because reliving the words *he-who-shall-not-be-*

named said hurts. It's excruciating. I take a deep breath and repeat the words of my ex, Dave. In a voice intending to mimic a slightly deeper one, I repeat, "He said, 'You're a *virgin?*' Like I had leprosy or something."

"Please continue." Peach rolls her hand in the air, encouraging me to continue. She's enjoying this way too much.

I glare at my best friend. "I've told you this story twice. Why do you make me repeat it? It's painful."

"Come on, Virginia, just one more time."

I take a deep breath and start over. "'You're a *virgin?* Jesus, Virginia. You want me to take your, um, cherry?'" I slap my hands onto my lap and push myself to my knees on the way to standing. "And then blah, blah, blah. You know the rest."

"I believe the next part was him shouting and pacing the room. Buck naked."

"If you know this by heart, why—"

"Please?" she says so sugar-sweetly.

I growl. "Fine! He said, 'If I do, this will all snowball out of control. First, you'll fall in love with me, and when I reject your love, and I *will* reject your love, you'll become a stage-five clinger, and I just don't have time for that. I'm graduating soon. I plan to move out east. I don't have time for a clinger.'" I let out a whoosh of air after I repeated that part at double time. How pathetic is it that I remember every word? Yeah. Pretty frigging pathetic.

Once I stop talking, I peer over at Peach, who is blinking slowly and staring with her mouth agape. "No matter how many times you tell me that story, it still shocks me. You two dated for what, a month?"

"Almost. Three weeks."

"And you'd done stuff together? Fooled around?"

"Yes. We did stuff, just not *it*. You know, in retrospect, I should have just kept my damn mouth shut. Would he have even noticed?"

"Possibly, but you don't want it to be like that, do you,

Virginia? You were with him long enough to expect some compassion. Some understanding. You're only twenty-one, for Christ's sake. It's not like you're old, like thirty."

I laugh. "Thirty isn't old, dork."

"Seems old." She shrugs. "Well, screw Dave. Not literally, of course. But who needs him anyway? He was ghostly pale and no fun. The guy never wanted to go outside. He just wanted to sit in front of his computer and program shit. Oh, and play video games. Jeez, girl, how did you end up with a basement dweller?"

"He wasn't a basement dweller."

"Yes, he was."

"Yeah, okay, so he didn't like the outdoors." And he did, in fact, live in a basement apartment. His *parents'* basement apartment. "But he had some good qualities."

"Yeah? Name three."

"Three?"

"Yep. Three."

"Okay, he was nice."

"That's one, barely."

"Two. He was tidy." Peach raises one brow. I take it I'm not giving a convincing enough argument.

"Okay. Two. He was a good kisser." Sort of. Not really. They were a little slobbery. "And three, he, um, he...."

"Can't do it, can you? I'm not even sure I should count number one. Most people are nice."

"Yeah, okay. He was a shit boyfriend. I'm glad he ran out of my room like the Flash when he found out I was a maiden."

Peach spits out the iced tea she'd just sipped. "Maiden? Jesus, Virginia. You read too many Jane Austen books. Maiden?" She giggles.

"I've had a lot of time to ponder all of the synonyms related to virginity. Let's see, there's chaste, virtuous, untouched, maiden, immaculate, sinless, and pure."

"Jesus," she mutters.

"So, now what do I do? I don't want to graduate from college in ten months still a virgin. I can't go on to grad school or into the workforce with this thing hanging over my head. I'm starting to get a little obsessed."

I watch as Peach lies down on our ratty old brown sofa, circa 1985. She's so tall it's almost too short for her. Heck, I bet two of me could lie lengthwise. Widthwise, not so much. One of me fits that way while two of Peach could fit. I can't help noticing how cute she looks today. Even in her casual workout clothes, she looks like she could be on the cover of a magazine. I look down at myself and frown. I'm wearing my oldest pair of yoga pants and an equally old sweatshirt. I'm comfy. And bonus, it hides stuff. Lumpy stuff. Oh, hell, I can't get all obsessy about my body now. It is what it is.

Peach places her hand on her face, rubs her eyes, and sighs. I know this means she's thinking. She calls it meditating and claims most of her best art ideas come when she's meditating. She's an art major here at Iowa State. She wants to be a freelance artist when she's finished, but according to her, that is not a viable option if she intends to have money to live, so she's in the graphic design program. Peach may be flighty and a little crazy (a lot crazy), but the girl thinks things through. "So, the problem is, you need to lose that damn V-card by the end of May, right?"

"Right."

"You know, it's too bad you couldn't advertise."

Now it's my turn to spit out my tea. "Are you nuts?"

"No, hear me out. We both know that hooking up with some random from the bar is out, right?"

"Right."

"You want to be able to vet the person who takes your, um, maidenhood?"

"Now who's reading Austen?" I smirk. I *loves* me a good Jane Austen story just as much as the rest of us.

"Shush and let me finish my train of thought here." Peach taps her finger on her chin. "Okay. You don't want a random to do it. You know, it's a shame you couldn't do a survey to find the perfect guy to do The Deed. Ooh, I know. It could be a dating app or something. You could look for specific things, like for a guy who is willing to pop a nice girl's cherry."

"Okay, first, ew, gross. Second...." I think about her idea. Well, not her *idea*; her idea is skanky. But there's something there. "You may be on to something. I haven't decided on my senior thesis project. I keep going back and forth between 'American Teens and Their Devices'—"

"Yawn."

I laugh at my best friend. "Or," I say loudly, "Advertising and Its Impact on Female Self-Esteem.'"

"Well, those are both topics, that's for sure, but are they *good* topics? Besides, I think those are played out," she says, holding her arm out like she's holding a sword. "You're a sociology major, right?"

I blink at her. Is she actually asking me about my major? "Duh."

"Okay, well, I think you should do a study on virginity."

Now it's my turn to lay my head back and think. I don't need to meditate, but it does help to work things through when my eyes are closed. "One idea could be something about virginity in our generation—the stigma attached to those who aren't 'deflowered' by the time they go to college."

"Mmm-hmm," she contemplates.

"Or it could be broader, like 'What Do Men Want When It Comes to a Mate?'"

"Don't forget about Dave's fucked-up notion that guys—and girls—already have their mate pictured before they even meet them. The expectation is already ingrained in their head."

"Mmm-hmm." She taps her finger on her chin like she's that sculpture *The Thinker*.

"Or it could include that. 'Mate' has two meanings. And more generally, what men want when it comes to mat-*ing*. You know... S-E-X."

"God, please, let's stop saying 'mate.' What are we, wolf shifters?" Peach says, rolling her eyes.

I blink at her because I have no idea what she means. "Wolf shifters?"

"Never mind. Continue," she mutters.

"No, I like the first idea, but I need to expand it. I mean, think about this generationally. When my grandmother was my age, girls were expected to look and behave a certain way. Plus, the stigma of not being a virgin on your wedding night was way worse than my problem today."

"Makes sense why everybody got married so young then. What was she, seventeen?"

"Eighteen."

"I rest my case. Can you imagine marrying some douche from high school when you were eighteen?" She pretends a shiver.

I chuckle. "No. Definitely not. Times have changed, obviously. But even when my mom was my age, it was still taboo to lose the V-card too early. Girls were labeled sluts if they slept around."

"Well, that's still true. Guys are never called sluts."

"Um, I beg to differ. 'Fuckboy' is a contemporary, albeit derogatory, term for a guy who sleeps around." See? I know my stuff. I read things.

"Yeah, but still. It's worse for girls. Guys are still patted on the back when they sleep with a bunch of people." She nods, thinking she spoke a truth. *Halleluiah.*

"It's getting better, though. We can thank the sixties' sexual revolution for some of that, plus the widely accepted knowledge that women need sex just as much as men do."

"Ha! What do you know about needs? You're a V-I-R-G-I-N."

"Shut it, Peach. Why do you think we're having this conversation? I've got needs!"

Peach rolls over in a fit of giggles. "So noted. Now, let's figure this out."

Right. I lay my head back down to think about this idea of merging my sociology senior thesis project with my own, um, problem. "I think I've got two topics going. One is all about the negative aspects of virginity. The other part deals with people's expectations about partners and sex."

"Let's not forget about all of those apps out there now, like Tinder and Ashley Madison."

"You don't have to remind me. Those are all about hookups, and cheating on your significant other if they're using Ashley Madison," I add.

"Yeah, but it's our reality now, Virginia. Guys and women don't need to put any real effort into getting sex. Just open your app and see if there's a willing partner in a two-mile radius. What happened to effort, to the chase?" Peach sighs. "I miss the chase. I miss the times a guy has made an effort to get to know me. And dates? What are those? When was the last time you went on an *actual* date?"

"Never." It's true. I've never been on an actual date. We just meet up places with the guy. I wouldn't even count prom since I went with my girlfriends. "It's like you're asking to turn back time, Peach. Those days are long gone."

She gives me a pouty face. "Maybe they'll come back. Everything comes back eventually."

I roll onto my side and look at Peach. "Okay, back to reality. I like your idea about a survey, and I think I need to focus on mating and how they find potential partners."

"Thinking about what your asshole ex said, I wonder how often people end up with their perfect vision of their mate?"

"I don't know. That sounds like a master's thesis." I wink. I hope to go to graduate school next year, so thinking about future research isn't a terrible idea.

Peach sits up, grabbing her spiral-bound notebook and a pen. "Okay. Survey. Let's write down some sex survey questions."

"A sex survey?"

"Yeah, sex sells. If you want to draw in a lot of surveyors, you need to focus on the sex part of this."

"Participants. Not surveyors."

Peach ignores me and continues. "You could do an online survey."

"I think I'd want to deliver the survey to the participants in person."

"I bet you would, you naughty girl," she says as she does that pervy eyebrow thing.

"You'd better quit doing that; your eyes are gonna stick that way."

She stops immediately, looking horrified. "The survey could be about sex and preferences about partners—you know, looks, personality, careers, et cetera. We could ask about those dating apps, plus we could sneak in a question or two about virginity."

I sit up and grab the notebook out of Peach's hand. "Let's brainstorm on some questions that we could ask. Then I'll narrow them down to fifteen or twenty questions. They need to be qualitative and quantitative."

"Ugh, stop with the sciency talk. Speak English."

"I mean, I need some questions that I can tally statistics about them. Quantitative. Then I need questions about thoughts, feelings, ideas, et cetera. That's qualitative."

"Whatevs. I get it."

I know she gets it. Just because she's an art major doesn't mean she's not well rounded. I know for a fact her grade point average is higher than mine, and she takes just as many science and math classes as me. "Let's get started. Throw some questions out there that could work for a survey. The first few could just be about gender identity, age, major if they're in college and their year, and sexual preference."

"Yeah, no joke, you need to include all of those. We don't live in a two-gender society anymore, and we need to honor that." Peach has a few friends who identify as other than heterosexual. "You'll need to know how many sexual partners they've had."

"Okay. Good. What else?"

"You could ask about relationship status and if they've had long-term relationships."

"How long do you have to be together for it to be considered long term?"

"Six months?"

"That's good. For this survey, it could be six months. Then I think we need to ask questions about personal preferences as it relates to a potential sex partner, like hair color, hair style, body type, height, et cetera."

Peach nods. "You could even ask them to list their favorite body part. You know, some guys like boobs best when another one could be into feet."

I stare at her. "Feet?"

She shrugs. "To each his own. I love a man's forearms. Thick, muscly forearms are the biggest turn-on."

"Gross," I mutter.

Peach giggles again. "Whatevs. Just include it. Trust me."

"Next, we should ask them to rate the qualities they consider important, like faithfulness, being a good kisser, or good in bed, a good listener. Stuff like that."

"Ooh, ooh, I know." Peach has her hand up in the air like she needs me to call on her in class. "If you're going to ask them to rate stuff, ask them things that attract them to a person at first. You know, like seeing someone across the room at a party that makes their heart go pitter-pat."

"So, for you, it'd be some good forearm?" I chuckle. I never knew she was a forearm fetishist.

"Shut it. It's a good idea."

"It is. While we're at it, we can ask them how they've met previous partners. Like at a party, for example."

"Yeah, through friends, those infamous apps, the grocery store, the gym."

"A club, classes, church, weddings."

"Funerals."

"Ugh, gross."

"Hey, don't knock it 'til you've tried it. Sad boys are surprisingly hot."

I roll my eyes at my best friend because there are things about her that really, really concern me. Take that last thing. Funerals? I shake my head and continue to write.

We add a section about personality types, plus how much they use social media in relationships, and ask about masturbation, favorite sexual positions/acts, if they're drawn to certain stereotypes like cheerleader, nerd, or sexy librarian. We also include questions related to dirty talk, and if so, to give or to receive. All in all, it's a very extensive list of questions. Now I just need to write it all out and decide which questions to keep and which to toss, bearing in mind that it should be a valid research study. After that, I'll need to present this idea to my major professor through proper channels to see if I can do this thing. Then I'll figure out how and when I can conduct the survey. But I've got to say....

"Peach, I love this idea. This is going to be fun."

"I hope I get to be there when you're doing the survey. I could catch me a hottie."

I roll my eyes at my best girl. She has no problem "catching hotties." She's a hottie herself. She can't walk out onto the street without a guy hitting on her. She doesn't even realize it's happening, I swear. She's oblivious to the fact that her five-foot-nine body is amazing. She's into exercise and fitness, though she's not stick thin—she's got muscles on her long legs and toned arms.

Couple the rockin' body with the fact that she looks strikingly like Julianne Hough from *America's Got Talent* a la *Dancing with the Stars* and you've got a knockout. It's her cute yet sexy face framed with her light blonde hair cut in a short pixie style that makes her so endearing. I love this girl. It's odd that she has no idea what she does to men. Sweet Peach.

CHAPTER 3

FOR SEVERAL WEEKS, Peach and I work together on fine-tuning the survey questions for all participants. Sometimes we work at home, one time we hung out at the library, and other times, like today, we work over our lunch, sitting at the Memorial Union food court. I take a bite of my double cheeseburger with fries (don't judge) as Peach talks and nibbles on her big salad.

"We've got a problem. Answers for some of these questions won't be the same for both men and women, Peach."

Setting her fork down, she places her elbows on the table and rests her chin on her hands. Peach is getting serious. "Like what? Which question? Give me an example."

"Everything up to question number eight works no matter what your gender. After that, I ask specific questions about physical appearance, like which hairstyle they prefer on a potential sex partner—long and straight, long and curly, shoulder length and straight, et cetera." I sip my Coke before continuing. "Unless we're talking about Fabio, we can't ask women that question in the same way. I mean, guys can have long hair, but they're more likely to have short hair."

Peach taps her finger on her chin as she thinks. "Who's Fabio?"

"Never mind," I mutter, ashamed to admit I know who he is.

"It's almost like you need two surveys," she continues without a beat.

I groan at that notion. I don't want more than one survey. "Well, my major prof, Dr. Kellogg, did mention something about a survey segmenting off at some point in the questionnaire based on demographics. That may be what he meant."

"Okay, so you need to find out if that's possible. What else do you need to figure out?" Peach asks, checking her Fitbit.

"Oh, I've kept you too long. I'm sorry. When's your next class?"

She waves me off. "Not for another hour. This is all cool. I love helping."

"Okay, well, I need to do a more in-depth interview with some of the survey participants, like one-on-one interviews. I want to ask them the same questions in different ways to get more verbal feedback. Should I just ask people when they're taking the survey if they'd be willing to talk in person?"

"You could add a question to your survey asking for volunteers for a one-on-one. That would make it private. They may not be truthful with you if they're with a bunch of people the day of the surveys."

I jump up from my seat across from her and hug my best friend. "You're a frigging genius!"

"Okay, Virginia. It's time to spill."

Sitting back down, I pick up my drink. "Spill? Whatever do you mean?" I say before I suck on my straw. She knows me so well after only three and a half years. We started off as roommates in the dorms, and now we live off campus together. She's seen me at my best and at my worst. She knows how my mind works, just as I know hers.

Peach raises her brow. I know that look. She means business.

"Tell me what's going on with this thing. You're too into it for this to be just about your senior project."

I look up at my friend, "Well, here's what I was thinking." I settle back down into my seat. "Remember when you suggested I find a way to choose who pops the ole cherry?"

"Mmm-hmm," Peach hums hesitantly.

"Well, what if I chose the person based on their responses to the survey?"

"Mmm-hmm."

"I'd choose one of the guys who agreed to the one-on-one interview. That way I'd get to know them better and—"

"You want to hook up with one of your surveyors?"

"Surveyors?" I laugh. "It's participants!"

"Don't be a science snob. You're telling me you're doing this entire thing to meet someone who will do The Deed?"

I hate the way she says "The Deed" like I'm going to murder someone. "Um, yeah."

Peach's face lights up like a Christmas tree. "Awesome, Virginia! I knew I'd rub off on you eventually."

I smile back and clap my hands together like a toddler. For a second there, I thought Peach grew a conscience, but phew, we're good. "I know, right?"

"But won't that jeopardize your research?"

I look at her with as serious an expression as I can muster. "This is my senior thesis project. I'm not publishing this stuff. The whole point of this is to learn how to do this type of research while making sure the results are fairly accurate. This isn't going to be a damn book or article in some professional journal."

"Okay. As long as you're sure. I know how seriously you take your major. You want to be a sociology professor, right?"

"Yeah, I do. But this will be fine. Just fine." *Yeah. No worries. I've got this.*

A week later, I'm tapping away at my computer, entering the final survey questions for the big event the next day.

"Are you ready for this whole survey thing tomorrow?" asks Peach.

"I think so. I've gotten final approval from my major professor and the sociology department chair. They were pleased by the final title: 'The Mating Rituals of the Millennial Generation.'"

"That's a good title. It's general enough that you could shape the final paper to work with whatever results you glean from the surveys."

"Wow, Peach. Look at you talkin' all sciency?"

She giggles. "I know. I'm fascinated by everything you're doing. Consider me your research assistant. It'll be okay if I dip into the survey pool too, right?"

"Um, before or after they've taken the survey?"

"After, of course."

"I suppose. Anyway, I wanted to tell you about the actual survey." I turn the laptop around so she can see the program and format of the survey. "Dr. Kellogg helped me out with that issue of gender and different questions. There are several really good online survey-building tools out there. We found one that let me design the survey to take the participant in different directions." Honestly, I'm only interested in the statistics provided by male heterosexuals. This segmented type of survey is perfect, but I don't want to exclude any of the other sexual identities or genders.

"How does it work?"

"It works like this." I set the program to Preview so we can see what our participants will see tomorrow. "The very first question is 'What is your gender?' with three possible answers: male, female, or other."

"Other? Okay, I'm glad you included that, but it seems harsh to call them '*other*.'"

"Dr. Kellogg said it would be okay for this since I'm not doing a survey or research about gender identity."

"What happens after that?"

"So, if you choose 'female,' the survey will take you to questions directed at only females. The questions are the same in all of the surveys, like how we talked about hair styles, but with different choices. Once they choose their gender, they get a particular set of questions directed at that demographic. I also ask about sexual preference, which will take them to yet another survey. So, I've got Survey A through Survey F depending on sexual preference and sexual orientation."

"That's cool. It saves you from sifting through all of the same surveys to pull out the questions from one group or another." Peach looks pretty pleased with herself.

"*Exaaactly*. Ooh, plus I've added that last question asking for volunteers for a one-on-one interview. So, are you ready to sit at a table all day and attract men?"

"Like bees to honey, baby. Like bees to honey."

That's no lie. With Peach's looks, she'll draw more guys to the table than I ever could. It's all good. I can use all the help I can get.

CHAPTER 4

It's finally here—survey day.

Peach generously volunteered to skip all of her classes to help me, "For science." *Yeah, right.* We've decided to set up outside of the Memorial Union, one of the four main buildings that surround central campus. It's a hub of activity on a normal day, but on Friday, it's even busier thanks to the bookstore, restaurants, and study rooms.

Peach and I get to our spot extra early. Since most classes start at eight in the morning, we start to set up at six thirty. To get as many surveys taken as possible, we've set up a table with signage that is sure to attract the attention of passersby. I made a bright red banner to hang in front of the table that simply says S-E-X. Because sex sells. What college student in their right mind would not stop and check that out? Plus, research has shown that red is the color of love and the most attractive color. Red represents energy, vibrancy, strength, and virility. People are drawn to it like a beacon.

For the survey part of this, I've checked out ten iPads from the library and uploaded the survey software I've chosen to use. The software will calculate all of my information and give me the ability to sort through data and compile the short-answer and written comments. It's amazing. All I need is at least one hundred people to participate.

By seven thirty, Peach and I are set up and ready to go. It's a slow start, with only a few people checking out our banner. It may be too early for our student body. We chose a Friday because everyone is happiest on Friday (yep, research says), but at Iowa State, that's also the day after most off-campus parties. Affectionately named Thirsty Thursday, many of our dedicated student body drink themselves into oblivion and end up hungover to beat the band on Friday.

"I forgot about all of the hangovers," I complain to Peach.

"Yeah, everyone looks like they just slid out of bed in the clothes from last night and slithered to class." She smirks. Peach is a morning person. She gets up at the ass-crack of dawn to work out and then drinks a minimum of three cups of coffee to get the day going.

"I sure hope it picks up. It's eight thirty, and nary a survey is done.

"Nary a survey? What are you now, a pirate?"

"Aye, matey," I say in my best pirate voice.

Peach cackles, "Dork."

Another twenty minutes pass, and we've *finally* drawn some attention. The first round of classes has ended, and people are trickling out of the campus buildings. Several guys spot our table —and probably Peach—and stride right up to her asking her for S-E-X. Yeah, it's going to be one of those days.

"So, you ladies want sex?" asks a guy in red and yellow striped overalls and no shirt. That look is usually reserved for tailgate parties and sporting events, but Friday works, I guess.

Peach flutters her eyelashes. "We're doing a sex survey. Men confuse us, so we've got questions," she says, winking.

Ugh.

"Well, let us help you. We're pretty easy." He winks right back.

"And if this helps me get to know *you* better, I'm all for it," he says, looking directly at Peach.

"You're so sweet," she coos as she stares at him for just a bit too long.

I look at her and mouth, "That guy?"

"He's cute," she whispers, pointing to her forearms.

I can't help but giggle. I guess if you like frat guys who wear overalls and no shirt to class, then he's the one for you. When he finishes up, he hands her back the iPad, pulls a card from the pocket on his chest, and hands it to her while saying, "Here. Call me."

"You've got a card?" I deadpan.

"Of course. I'm a professional."

The three guys around him crack up with laughter. "A professional asshole," one of them mutters.

Ignoring all of that, Peach slides the card into her bra. "Thanks. I'll give you a jingle."

"Great! I'll look forward to it, beautiful." Winking one more time, he turns and walks away, looking back once as he makes his way to Fraternity Row.

Oh, geesh. "Seriously? Him? He's so cocky." I lean over to read the card. "His name is Ryan Reynolds?"

"Apparently."

"What's it say below his name?"

"It says, 'Much hotter than the other one.'"

I giggle. "That is pretty funny."

She shrugs. "Yeah, it is. He's adorable. Oh, and he's not cocky; he's confident."

"Whatever floats your boat, Peaches."

As the morning progresses, more and more men hit on Peach. After she sweetly turns them down, she explains the survey. They each grab a tablet and begin. The survey should take about five minutes from start to finish, unless they're really concentrating on responses. Then I'd say closer to ten minutes. Once the participants finish, they hand over the tablets. Several of the guys try to get Peach's number, but she just smiles and says she'll see them around and she's "got important sciency stuff to do."

By one o'clock, there's a lull in traffic and my butt is numb. I grab two iPads, deciding to step away from behind the table to stretch my legs while also trying to drum up some more participants. Walking across the street, over to central campus, I squeeze between two tall hedges to get to the open area. As I press my body through the pine getting pricked and poked along the way, I nearly fall over someone's feet. I'm able to correct myself before I fall flat on my face, or worse, on top of them.

"Oh, sorry," I say to the guy lying on the grass, baseball hat over his eyes.

He slides his hat back and blinks up at me.

Whoa, the guy is gorgeous. I wait for him to reply, but he says nothing.

"I said I'm sorry."

"Mmm-hmm."

Mmm-hmm? That's all he's going to say? I don't give up easily, most of the time. I scan him quickly. The guy is big. No wonder I tripped on him. Even lying on the ground, I can tell he's tall and broad. His legs are super muscular, at least the part I can see sticking out of his cargo shorts. He's wearing a tight gray tee that says Iowa State Hockey. "Uh, would you like to take my sex survey?"

"Nope."

I move a little closer until I'm casting a shadow over him. "Seriously?"

He slides his hat off his face again. Sure, he's good looking but the fact that he's rather rude is not attractive. "Seriously."

"Please?" I whine. Why am I making a big deal about this?

Sighing, he sits up, holding his hand out to me. Snapping his fingers like some rude guy at a lowly waiter, he says, "Give it to me."

I'm not sure if he wants me to help him stand or... oh, he wants the iPad. I hand it to him and smile. "Thanks. It's for my senior thesis project."

He says nothing as he starts to click. I remain silent, out of courtesy. In less than five minutes, he's finished and handing me the pad. "We done?" he snaps.

"Yep. We're done. Thanks!" I say cheerily. *What an ass.*

Just as I'm about to convince myself that's the reason he's curt, a gorgeous blonde woman bounces up to him and practically flops herself on top of him. "Hey, Bake."

"Hey, sweet cheeks," he says, reaching back cupping her ass with his palm.

With a giggle, the perfect blonde wraps her arms around his neck and pulls herself up for a kiss.

Ugh. Typical. Guys like that drive me crazy. Too perfect, too everything. He's definitely too good for the likes of me. Well, screw that guy. I'm too good for him. With my head held high and my nose in the air, I step away from the obvious public display of affection.

I look back at the blonde's tiny shorts and crop top, then back down at myself. I'm wearing an oversized Iowa State tee with baggy jeans I bought at the thrift store. I shrug—*it is what it is.* Sighing, I squeeze back through the hedges, lamenting. I'd never land a guy like that. I'm too plain. I'm short and overweight packaged in oversized clothing because it's comfortable. I almost always have on Converse tennis shoes in one color or another. I've got five different color choices in my closet: red, yellow, green, black, and hot pink. I've got mousey brown hair that stands stick straight to my shoulder, and I usually wear it in a ponytail at the base of my skull. Plus, I wear thick "nerd" eyewear just to tie all that hot mess together. See? He's out of my league.

On a positive note, I'm guessing his survey will have some good insights on his sex life.

I look back over my shoulder. His big hands are still on the blonde woman's ass but now he's squeezing. "Wow," I whisper to myself. My body is kind of tingly just seeing that. He's hot, for sure, but he's definitely not the kind of guy I want to do The Deed with. He's too advanced for me; he's more of a professional. He's in the big leagues of sex, while I'm looking for more of a minor league player.

I peek back one more time. The blonde is gone and the hockey hottie is looking at me with one arched brow. "Oops." Busted.

Eight hours and two sore bottoms later, we've got over 175 surveys. The majority of them were male participants, but we have a fair amount from women too. Now all I have to do is sort through the information, arrange for the individual interviews, and choose the guy who's going to help rid me of my pesky hymen.

Great! I just grossed myself out.

CHAPTER 5

"Wow! I'm shocked by these surveys," I say as I fill up Peach's beer glass. She and I are sitting at our favorite booth at Cy's Roost, sharing a pitcher and an order of nachos as we go over some of the survey data. It's the same table we carved our names in the night I turned twenty-one.

"What's surprising about them?"

Sipping my beer, I say, "One, I'm blown away by the number of people who volunteered for the one-on-one interview." I suspect a lot of the males think Peach will be interviewing them, but I'll take what I can get.

"Are you *only* going to interview males of the heterosexual variety?"

"Nope. I'm going to let the survey tool choose them. I decided I'd let fate play a role in all of this. Besides, the study would be seriously slanted if I did that. I like the idea of this study and want to know more."

"But about ridding yourself of your pesky hy—"

"Stop!" I say, putting my hand in front of Peach's face. "Don't say it."

"Hymen," she mutters quickly.

Ignoring her, I continue. "I think this research is relevant. And"—I hesitate for effect—"if I happen to find someone who would be perfect for doing, uh, that thing you mentioned, then great. Otherwise, I'll just plan on dying with my hy—thingy intact while alone in my house full of cats."

"You're allergic to cats."

"Fine! Hairless cats. I didn't realize I had to be that specific, Peach."

Ignoring *me*, she says, "Okay, help me out. As a hetero female, tell me something about the men we surveyed. What do they like? What don't they like?"

I stare at Peach.

"For science," she adds smugly.

"Okay." I sigh. "So far, here's what I know in general about that group of participants." I start with the questions and summarize the main points. There's still a lot of data to work through, but I know Peach. All she wants to know is if she's considered hot by these guys. I should have considered that. Her looks and sweet bubbly personality could have swayed the participants. *Hmm, I'll have to think about that.*

"Hello! Earth to Virginia!"

"Oh, sorry. Yeah, so here's the gist. Of our male heterosexual participants, 25 percent were age eighteen and nineteen, and 17 percent were twenty to twenty-one." I flip the page to get to the nitty-gritty. "None of the guys said they were virgins."

"Of course they didn't. Who in their right mind would admit that at their age?"

"Gee, thanks!" I whine. "You're such a dick."

Giggling, she clarifies, "I just meant for guys. They'd never admit that."

"Whatever. Forty-seven percent have been or are currently in a long-term relationship."

"Interesting."

"Uh-huh. The questions related to sleeping with a virgin,

dating, and marrying a virgin were pretty mixed. I'll have to go through that one thoroughly." I turn the page to the 'What attracts you?' questions. "Here we go. Hair color in order of favorite to least favorite: blonde, brunette, black, redhead, blue, purple, pink, et cetera."

"Well, that's not a surprise. Blondes do have more fun." She smirks.

I roll my eyes. "Moving on. Hairstyles," I say, flipping to the next page of my printout. "Long is number one, with long and curly or wavy being first and long and straight second."

"Bummer," grumbles my pixie-haired friend.

"Next is medium curly or wavy, then short, chin length, straight, and so on."

"Do I even want to know where the very short pixie cut is on the list?"

"Probably not. Second to last."

"Whatever, I love my hair," Peach pouts.

I continue. "Body type was athletic first, then average, thin, curvy/voluptuous, I'm not picky, ultra-thin, and full-figured."

"Aren't curvy and full-figured the same thing?"

"I thought so. My guess is these participants saw one term as positive, the other negative. That's interesting. I need to make a note to do more research on that." I jot a note in the margin of the printed stats sheets. "Next was the question about which specific body part attracts you. I had them rank them from one to ten."

"I bet boobs was number one."

"Nope. But it was up there. The numbers on the top five items are pretty close, but here's the order from favorite to least favorite: face, smile, breasts, eyes, legs, ass, mouth/teeth, arms, hands, and last is feet."

"No foot fetishists on this side of the survey? Hmm, interesting," says Peach, tapping her chin.

"What is it with you and feet? Oh, wait, forearms are *your* thing." I giggle.

Ignoring my joke about her fascination with forearms, Peach says, "Keep going. The next one is height, right? I'm tall, so I'm hoping that's the top score."

"Sadly, no it's not, my friend. Short, medium, doesn't matter as long as she's not taller than me, then tall."

"Assholes," she mutters.

"Ooh, this is a good question. I asked them which personality traits attracted them. I'll give you percentages about this one. Intelligence was number one."

"I call bullshit on that one."

"Why?"

"That's the thing they find most attractive? Yeah, right."

"Well, we did survey college guys. That could slant the survey that way." I shrug. "Next was physically fit/active then humor. Moral integrity was fourth with kindness coming in fifth." I flip the page again. "Dependable sixth and the rest were about even after that.

"Weird. You'd think 'good in bed' would be up there."

"Yeah, this one is confusing to me. Perhaps I should have limited the choices. Ten may have been too many, and some terms sort of overlap."

Peach moves over so she can read over my shoulder, pointing to my paper. "This is the question I added to the survey, about attraction when you first meet. Read that one."

"Physical appearance/body type is first. Not a surprise there. Then clothing, speaking voice, personality, how they interact in the particular setting, and the last two are flirting and manners."

"Ha! Manners?"

I shrug. "Good manners are important."

"Not necessarily if guys are trying to hook up. They want bad, bad manners."

"The dating app question is disturbing. Almost all of them have used Tinder in the last sixty days."

"Ugh. Tinder gives dating a bad name," Peach grumbles.

"Don't you use it?"

"Yeah, but I hate myself afterward."

Giggling, I punch Peach in the shoulder. "I need to use the ladies' room," I say with a British accent, standing. "See? I can have manners."

When I return to my seat, Peach is reading through the data. I say, "Your turn. You read."

"Okay. Question eighteen: Do you masturbate? If so, how much?" Looking up at me, she states, "If those guys said anything less than 'Yes, daily,' I'd be shocked."

I know the response to this one by heart. "Yeah, that was number one, but several responded, 'Can't keep track.'"

Peach and I both start to laugh. The beer has kicked in, and we've officially gotten silly.

Gasping for air, she stops laughing and frowns. "Ooh, I just thought of something. Imagine their room. Their bed." Peach shivers. "No amount of bleach...."

"Next!" I shout.

Peach flips to the next page. "Sexual position favorite was missionary." Rolling her eyes, she shouts, "Yawn!" then flips to another page. "Stereotype was 'the girl next door.' Double yawn."

I'm shocked she'd say that. "But, Peach, you're that type."

"Ha! No way. I'm the porn star."

I laugh. "Whatever helps you sleep at night, Peach."

"Next question is about dirty talk." She reads before talking aloud. "The vast majority of guys said, 'Yes, when both parties do the talking.'" Shaking her head, Peach adds, "Show me the guys who said, 'Yes, but only if it's me doing the talking.'"

"I know what you mean." No, I really don't. No one has ever talked dirty to me.

Blinking, Peach says, "No, seriously. Show me those surveys of guys who dirty talk. I want one of them."

"No. I'm not showing you the individual surveys."

"But, Virginia," she whines loudly. "I helped you. I deserve a dirty-talking alpha male as my payment."

"No can do. At least not yet." I fold up the papers. "What about Ryan Gosling?"

"Ryan Reynolds, *biatch*," she mutters. "I sent him a text."

"And?"

Looking at her nails, she attempts to skirt the question. "I thought you had to get to class. You'd better get going. You're going to be late."

"Frick!" I say, grabbing my backpack. Yes, Peach and I are drinking in the middle of the day. In the middle of a school day. It's Friday. Sue me.

Before I leave, I turn and pick up the rest of the printouts. "Better take these," I say, flapping them in front of her. "Wouldn't want them to fall into the wrong hands."

"Whatever," she mumbles.

"And I want to know about Ryan Gosling when I get home!" I shout as I run out the door.

"It's Reynolds, dork!"

CHAPTER 6

As I wait for my class to start, I sift through the papers again. Looking at the twenty-five participants selected by the survey application for the second part of the survey, I pull those pages from the back of the stack and read through the list. It's pretty even, with fourteen males and eleven females. That will be perfect when it comes time to write about all of this.

Since I made it to class a few minutes early, I decide to make contact with the twenty-five. Starting with the first person on the list, I create a text message that briefly introduces me and asks if they are still available for a survey. I copy and paste that text to the remaining twenty-four. If people pull out, I can get replacements from the remaining pool of participants.

Me: *Hi! You signed up for a one-on-one interview related to my sex survey. Send me a quick reply of Y or N to let me know if you're still interested. If Y, I'll follow up with you. Thanks!*

By the time my professor has entered the room, I've gotten three Ys already. By midafternoon, I've gotten twenty more responses, with only one N from a female participant. This is working out great.

After class, I walk past the bus stop and make my way to my job at The Coffee Bean on Welch Ave. As soon as I open the door, the delicious scent of freshly brewed coffee hits me. It never gets old. I've tried almost every coffee concoction we make, and I've loved them all. As I walk to the small back room, I wave at my other favorite person, my coworker Jackson Valmer. "Hey, Jackson."

"Hey, beautiful."

Sighing at his words, I can't help thinking how sweet he is. It's too bad he plays for the other team. Jackson is hot with a capital *H*. He's got long dark hair that hits him in the middle of his back. Ordinarily, he likes to let it flow freely, but he can't at work, so he ties it up into a high bun on the back of his head. His face looks like it was chiseled from stone with his high cheekbones and strong nose. His lips? OMG, his lips are so full and look so soft, I sometimes catch myself fantasizing about kissing him. He isn't super tall, but he's taller than me. Most people are, since I barely get to five-foot-one on the height charts at my doctor's office. Jackson has to be close to five-foot-nine. He's also super in shape thanks to the face he likes the view at the gym. Who doesn't? All those ripped, sweaty guys. Okay, so *I* don't work out at the gym, or anywhere, but I do like the view when I've gone to meet up with Peach.

I step into the back room, stow my backpack in the corner, and grab a dark green apron. Stepping out, I sidle right up to Jackson, bumping him with my shoulder. "Hey, foxy."

"Hey, yourself. Good day?"

"*Meh*. Okay so far. Where do you want me?" Jackson isn't the manager, but he might as well be. Our actual manager is a douchebag, and a lazy one at that.

"The rush will hit in about five minutes, so why don't you man the machines and I'll take orders?"

"Sounds good." I get to work restocking everything I'll need for the after-three o'clock rush. That's when most students head home from their afternoon classes. What can I say? We students need caffeine after a long day listening to lectures and a full night ahead of homework and studying.

"So, how's that sexy survey coming along?"

"Good. Interesting. I'm working on getting twenty-five people to sit down with me for a more in-depth interview."

"I bet you are, naughty girl."

I snicker at his comment. "Ha-ha. Very funny." Jackson knows about my virgin status and that I'm the least naughty girl at Iowa State University. He just likes to tease me.

"No, seriously, do you have twenty-five to interview?"

"Almost. I—" Before I can get another word out, the door flies open and several people walk in. "Time to get to work," I mutter. Once the floodgates open, we'll be busy making complicated coffee drinks for my fellow students for the next couple of hours.

As I work like a demon to make a large iced skinny hazelnut macchiato, sugar-free syrup, extra shot, light ice, no whip, I hear a deep voice above me say, "Hey."

I look up, way up, to see a very good-looking guy peering down at me. I blink at him but then return to my work.

"I said, hey," he says again.

I look up and see him staring at me intently. "Hey? Um, if you need to place an order, Jackson will help you," I say, using my head to point him in Jackson's direction since I've got my hands full with hazelnut juice. Jackson will love helping him; the guy is beautiful and big—two of Jackson's must-haves.

He grunts and moves up to Jackson, where he orders a large black coffee. Weird. Nobody orders a black coffee anymore.

When my shift is over, I hug my friend, remove my apron, and grab my backpack. I've got just enough time to get home and still catch the new episode of *Game of Thrones*. After a long day, I need to relax and get my fill of some Jon Snow, stat!

On the bus ride home, I check my phone, hoping the final two participants have replied. Slumping my shoulders when I see they haven't responded; I decide to give them until tomorrow night before I get replacements for the remaining openings.

By Monday, I have twenty-five confirmed participants scheduled for one-on-one interviews. While I'm nervous to talk face-to-face with people about their sex lives, I'm excited to get to this part of my research. I was able to reserve one of the private study rooms at the library for the days and times I'll need it. It's ideal. It's private, but there's still a window overlooking the main floor of the library.

Since I've got five minutes until my first volunteer arrives, I straighten my pens and papers one more time. It's a nervous habit. I've done it fifteen times already; one more won't hurt.

I look at the questionnaire I finalized with my major professor earlier this afternoon. Besides going over their original responses, I've got additional questions for them. The first section they'll fill out is about themselves, with questions about their full name, address, email address, and phone number, along with their college major and current classes, extracurricular activities, and jobs. Dr. Kellogg told me that biographical information would help supplement their responses to the research questions. If I have good background information about them, I can look at their responses to my questions and analyze it against their other characteristics.

When a knock sounds on the door, I suck in a lungful of air for courage and say, "Come in." When the door swings open, I see my first vic—er, participant. It's a woman. If I had to stereotype her, I'd say she'd fall strictly into the nerd column, just like me. She's wearing horn-rimmed glasses that look authentic, like from the actual 60s. She's also got on a shirt buttoned all the way up to her neck. Her pants are black and polyester, and she's wearing shiny black shoes that lace up. Her hair is pulled back using two barrettes on either side of her head like I used to wear in elementary school.

I clear my throat. "Are you Samantha?"

"Yes. Call me Sam, please."

"Of course, Sam. Please have a seat."

Sam pushes the door closed and sits down on the seat with her back to the window. I planned it that way, so they wouldn't be distracted by people walking by gawking into the room or the few idiots who make faces or hand gestures as they pass.

"Thanks for agreeing to do this, Sam."

"No problem. I'm always willing to help my fellow students with research."

After she completes the biographical information for me, I say, "So, shall we get started?"

"Sure."

"I'd like to go through some of your survey responses and then ask you some follow-up questions. Is that okay?"

"Of course."

"First, I see you're a virgin." I watch her face turn from a pale pink shade to one that's magenta and think she's going to pass out. "Sam? Are you okay?"

"Yeah. I just didn't expect that to be the first question."

"It's one of the things I'm interested in writing about, so...."

"Yes, I'm a virgin," she says, swallowing hard.

"Is that by choice?"

She blinks at me with her mouth agape.

"I mean, are you saving yourself for marriage?"

She lets out a loud guffaw. "No! It's just me, I guess. Who wants to sleep with a nerd?"

"Lots of guys." I don't want to get into any details, but she needs to know. "'The nerd' was the second favorite stereotypical female the guys chose."

"What was first?" she asks, leaning forward.

"The girl next door."

"Fascinating," she says leaning back adding, "I didn't expect that."

"All right, let's move on. You're a sophomore in computer science?"

"Yes."

"You've been in a long-term relationship?"

"Yes. In high school."

"But you didn't consummate that relationship?"

"No. He ended up liking guys."

"Ended up?"

"Well, he was just confused. It happens. We're best friends now."

"Oh, that's cool."

"Uh-huh. Cool," she deadpans.

As I work through the list of questions, I realize I'm a lot like this girl. She's got an air of confidence about her, at least as it relates to her academics. It's just that when it comes to men, she's as clueless as I am.

After the interview, Sam asks, "Will you let me know when you've finished with the research paper? I'd love to read it."

"Of course. I'll make a note to send you a copy."

"Good. I hope it sheds some light on all of this stuff. Men confuse me."

I laugh. "Me too, Sam. Me too."

CHAPTER 8

BY FRIDAY, I'm completely exhausted. My week was filled with classes, work, and interviews with fifteen of my twenty-five survey participants. Since all of them have such different schedules, I've had to work around them by meeting extra early and very late; one male couldn't meet until eleven at night. So yeah, I'm pooped, but I've got to keep chugging along because I've got three interviews scheduled for Saturday, one on Sunday, and the rest next week.

Entering the apartment, I smell something yummy in the air. "You made brownies?" I call out excitedly.

"I did. You've been working so hard. I thought you deserved a treat during *GoT*." (That's *Game of Thrones* for those of you who are out of the loop.)

I move into our dining nook and set my backpack on one of our two kitchen chairs. Leaning in, I peek at the plate of brownies on the table. "Yay! I love you so much!"

"I know. But I've got ulterior motives."

"Uh-huh." Rolling my eyes, I reach for my bag. "Let me change, and then I'll go through the rest of the interview questions before we watch the boob-tube." Taking my bag with me, I step down the hall into my small but cozy bedroom. I opt to change into sweats and an old tee that was already conveniently placed on the floor for me (by me). I remove everything, especially my bra, and dress in the comfy clothes. Pulling the research folder from my bag, I walk back into the living room and plop down on the sofa in front of a plate of warm, gooey brownies that are now on the coffee table. "Yum!"

Peach sits next to me, handing me a glass of milk. She nabs a brownie and says, "We haven't talked all week, so spill. How were the interviews?"

"Well, I think I may have found at least one possible contender to help me with my problem."

"Virginity isn't a problem, Virginia. It's just a state of mind."

I nearly choke on my brownie. "Tell that to my hy—my thingy."

Peach leans down and says into my crotch region, "Hey, you down there. It's a state of mind."

I roll my eyes and giggle. "Moving on. He's really cute in a skater boy kind of way."

"Skater boy? Are there still skater boys? I thought Avril Lavigne took care of that whole thing once upon a time."

"Anyway, he's grunge-like. He had a skateboard with him and was wearing a graphic tee."

"Of course he was."

Bringing my feet up under my butt to get more comfortable, "He likes girls who are more free spirited."

"And? You think that's you?" She snickers.

"I can be free spirited." I chomp down on a second brownie with one eye quirked at Peach. She starts to say something, but I keep right on talking. "He's a junior. I'm calling him Mr. Free Spirit."

"What's his major?"

"He's not sure."

Peach starts to giggle. "Of course he's not sure. Oh, gurrrl, that's not going to end well, but I think you should give it a try."

"His survey says he likes girls with long wavy hair."

"Shocking," she says sarcastically. "Guys are so predictable. I suppose he likes blondes."

"Brunettes."

"Well, that's lucky. You don't need to dye your hair for him."

I look at my best friend and blink. "I hadn't considered that. If this is going to work, I'll probably need to change some things about myself, like hair color, clothing, that sort of thing."

"Don't you think that's a little extreme?"

"It's for science," I say, getting lost in thought. "I could get extensions." Since my hair is barely shoulder length and straight, extensions would be necessary.

"Extensions are expensive, and you're broke."

"I could call my dad. He'd help me."

"Wow, you must really want to do this if you're willing to ask your father for anything. I thought you'd written him off."

"I know. I'll ask him. He may turn me down. Who knows?" My mom and dad divorced when I was ten. He remarried a woman named Tina a month after the divorce was final and moved to Illinois. I see him once a year, maybe, and talk to him about as often. He never sent us any money, and Mom's never forgiven him.

"Back to your potential lovers. Is there anyone else?"

"There was one. I'm calling him Mr. Punk Rocker."

"Mr. Punk Rocker?"

"Yeah. He has dark blue hair and several piercings. I saw the edge of a tattoo on his neck."

"Ooh, a neck tattoo?" Peach says, making a sour face. "I love tattoos, but once they start creeping up on the neck, that's just *no.*"

"He was nice. He likes girls with multicolored hair—"

"Obviously. What's his major?"

"Music."

"A musician? That's trouble."

"He likes dirty talk, but only if it's him that's doing it."

"Oh, well now, that's hot."

"I thought you'd like that."

"So, anyone else?"

"Not yet. I've still got ten more interviews. I think I want one more to add to the mix."

"I bet you do. When did you become such a hoochie?"

I laugh, surprised at her comment. "I'm not going to sleep with all three. I just want to pad the odds in my favor a little bit."

"Good plan."

I hope she's right. "You ready to watch some *Thrones*, baby?"

Peach nods excitedly. "I'll get the lights. You turn up the volume."

"Will do."

CHAPTER 9

I WAKE up bright and early on Saturday to make it into work by six thirty. I'll work until one, then head off to the library for three interviews. It's a busy day, but I like it that way. When I walk into the Coffee Bean, I see our manager, Kip, at the register. With an internal groan, I make my way to the back room to stow my bag.

"Oh, good. You're here," says Kip. "I'm going to let you take over here. I've got a ton of paperwork to get to."

"But—" He doesn't let me finish because he's back in his office in literally seconds. What I was going to say was *But it's Saturday morning. It's going to be busy."* Why bother? He's worthless. I wish Jackson were here.

Sure enough, as soon as I've tied the dark green apron around my waist, the door flies open and a large group of people enters. I do my best, but I can't keep up. I've looked back toward Kip's office several times and called for him twice. I'd run back there to get him if I thought I had time. I don't. People are getting irritated.

"I'm sorry. It's just me here. Just be patient, please."

"This place sucks," grumbles the third guy in line.

"I know," I say under my breath. *Rather, my manager sucks.*

By the time the line is down to a trickle, Kip finally comes out of his office. "Everything okay out here?"

"No! I was slammed. Half a dozen people walked out."

"Well, why didn't you holler?"

"I did!"

He shrugs. "Oops, my bad. Had my headphones on."

I'd love to quit, but I can't afford it. "Yeah, well, maybe you should have your door open when the shop is open."

"Please don't tell me what to do. I'm the manager here. You're my employee."

"Fine," I mutter as I grab coffee beans to refill the grinder. "Whatever."

"Watch that mouth, young lady."

Young lady? Kip's only a couple years older than me. I grumble and keep working.

"I may need you to stay longer today. I've got an appointment—"

"Can't."

"Can't or won't?" he snaps.

"Can't. I've got appointments with participants of my research study. Sorry." *Not sorry*.

At one o'clock, I grab my backpack and push open the door so hard and so fast, I nearly brain a big guy walking into the shop.

"Oh, sorry," I squeak, looking up at a gorgeous guy wearing a white ISU Hockey ball cap.

"S'okay," he mumbles.

Avoiding eye contact with the man, I set off at a fast clip. I make it to the study room just in time and hastily grab three survey printouts and a pen from my bag. Just as I set them on the table, I hear a knock at the door. "Come in."

The door creaks open and reveals a familiar face. Familiar since I nearly broke his nose with the door of the café ten minutes ago. "You? Are you Baker Stark?"

He grunts something that could be taken as an affirmative.

I stand up and gesture toward the chair. "I'm Virginia. Please have a seat."

Baker Stark sits down hard on the wooden chair across from me. He's so tall his knees nearly bump the table. The chair creaks with his weight. I wonder how much he weighs. He's not fat. Oh, hell no. He probably has zero body fat because he's all muscle and brawn. His broad shoulders span way beyond the width of his chair.

I look up at his face to see him staring back with a scowl. Ignoring it, I keep right on looking. Dang, he's so good-looking. His hair is sort of long. He either needs to keep growing it out or get it cut short—it's at that in-between stage. His eyes are dark and broody. It matches his strong nose that reminds me of those Roman statues. I let my eyes move downward to his lips, letting out a little gasp. Nothing loud enough for him to hear, mind you. If I could describe his lips with words, I'd say they were pretty. Is that bad? To call a guy's mouth pretty? Well, his lips definitely qualify. They're full and look soft despite their current flat line of irritation.

Well, I guess that means we'd better get started. Staring time is over. "So, thank you for agreeing to this interview." I hand him the biographical questionnaire and watch him quickly fill it out. "Ready?"

He grunts and gives me a little nod. A man of few words, apparently.

"I'm going to go through your survey, asking you some questions along the way. Is that okay?"

He nods.

Great. Is this how it's going to be? A lot of grunting and nodding? Ugh. "You play hockey for Iowa State?"

"Yeah."

"Is that a thing here? Hockey?"

"Yeah. Club sport."

"Are you any good?"

"Yeah."

"What position do you play?"

"Goalie."

Since it's like pulling teeth to get this guy to respond, I'm moving on. "Your major is kinesiology?"

"Yes."

"What do you plan to do with that?"

"Physical therapy."

Huh. That's interesting. Moving on. "So, you've been in a long-term relationship?"

"Yep."

"How long was the relationship?"

"About a year."

Wow, three words! "When was this?"

"High school."

"How old were you when you started dating?"

He blinks, looking at me like I'm an idiot, then shrugs. "Sixteen or seventeen."

"So, you're no longer together?"

"No."

"Why not?"

He shrugs. "Different colleges."

I think it's safe to say that two or three words may be the most he's able to speak. "Was the breakup mutual?"

"No."

"Who broke up with whom?"

"She with me."

"Were you sad?"

"No."

"So, that's your only long-term relationship?"

"Yes."

"Would you want to be in another long-term relationship?"

He smirks. "You asking?"

"No!" I say, flustered. "I'm just trying to get a feel for your personal feelings about relationships." *Geesh*. I know my face is pink because it got hot in a millisecond. I look through the list of questions and his responses, trying to decide where to go next. "You chose 'other' when I asked you which hair color you preferred."

"Yes."

"You don't have a preference?"

"No."

"Why not?"

He shrugs. "Just don't."

God, this is like pulling teeth. I need to stop asking him yes-or-no questions. "What is it about curvy/voluptuous women that you like? You've chosen that as your preferred body type."

"They're soft."

"Soft?"

"Yeah, soft."

Moving on. "You ranked your favorite body part as a smile?"

"Uh-huh."

"Then legs, face, eyes, ass/behind, mouth/teeth, hands, arms, feet."

"Yep."

"What is it about the smile that made you choose that as number one?"

He shrugs. "I know a fake smile when I see one."

Oookay. "You say height doesn't matter. Why not?"

"I'm six-five."

"And?"

"Do you know any chick taller than six-five?"

Eight words. I'm getting better at this. "Maybe in the WNBA?"

He makes a scoffing noise. "Doubtful."

Note to self, check out the tallest woman in WNBA. "Oh, this is interesting. In the section under 'What attracts you?' you only listed one thing as 'extremely important.'"

He nods and leans forward in his chair, placing his arms on the table.

"The kiss. The rest were 'somewhat important' or 'not important.' Why was the kiss the only one 'extremely important'?"

"The kiss is everything."

"Everything?"

"Hell yeah. The kiss is the ultimate test of compatibility."

"How so?" This is the most animated he's been.

"It just is. The first kiss is the most important kiss."

"Why?"

"Why? Because. It's the most intense, the most exciting. A kiss is the mind, the body... it's *everything*."

I think they're nerve-racking and stressful. "You obviously like kissing."

"I like to fuck too, but I'm not going to fuck someone who can't kiss."

Okay. Graphic much? "Uh, I'll have to take your word for it."

"You don't think so?"

"I don't know."

"You've never been kissed?" He looks at me with a peculiar expression.

"Of course I've been kissed. But this isn't—"

"Stand up." I watch him stand up to his full height. The guy is ginormous.

"What?"

"Please. Stand up," he says softly.

I stand up and watch him slowly walk toward me. "Um," I say, fidgeting back and forth on my feet.

"Can you feel your heart beating faster?"

"Yes."

"I can tell. I can see your heart pulsing in your throat. Your breathing has picked up too. Your chest is moving up and down faster. And it's all because of one thing."

"One thing?"

"Anticipation." He's now standing directly in front of me.

I can't help myself; I look up into his eyes.

His gaze meets mine. "Your pupils have dilated."

"They have?" I swallow, but my mouth is dry.

"Uh-huh," he says, placing his giant hand on my shoulder. "Is this okay? Me touching you?"

"Yeah." God, I sound breathless.

Probably because you are, idiot.

With his other hand, he moves a strand of hair away from my face and pushes it behind my ear.

My body is tingling from his touch.

"I just saw you shiver." He steps closer.

My comfort zone fully invaded, I whisper, "What are you doing?"

"I'm going to kiss you."

"It's not appropriate."

"Appropriate? But it's for your research."

He slides the hand that was on my shoulder to the back of my neck. Leaning down, he breathes in. "Your hair smells nice."

"Thank you. I use baby shampoo."

"I like it."

"Your breath smells good."

Wow, he's full of compliments. "Thank you. I brush regularly."

He chuckles. Running a finger along my lower lip, he whispers, "Your lips are soft."

"Thank you. I use petroleum jelly."

"It does a nice job."

"I know. Uh, so who makes the first move here?"

"I do. I always make the first move."

I suck my lower lip into my mouth and bite down a few times.

"I'm also the only one that gets to bite down on that fucking bee-stung lip of yours."

I whimper at his words. Leaning down, he runs his lips across mine, barely touching them. It was like a breath. "I like to play with the lips, get a taste at first."

I feel him bring his body closer until we're against each other. The hand he used to touch my lip is now around my back, pressing me into him. "I'm going to kiss you now, Virginia."

"Okay," I squeak.

The kiss starts off slowly, with him playing like he said he likes to do. Gradually, I feel more pressure and then his tongue as it sweeps across my upper lip.

"Open for me, Virginia," he says in a husky voice.

I open my mouth slightly and feel his tongue as it enters. I moan the second it touches mine. A chill runs through my body, making my nipples rock hard. I bring the arms that were straight down at my side up and up until they're around his neck. I have to get up on my tiptoes to manage it.

I open my mouth farther and turn my head to the side to get deeper. When he moans, I nearly combust. Holy hell. I've never been kissed like this. Ever. No wonder I'm a virgin. No one has made me feel this much need before. I need sex. I need sex with him. I need his body to do things to my body. Dirty things.

When his big hand moves down to cup my ass, I think I'm going to orgasm. *Yes.* Okay, not really, but I'm damn close. With one arm, he's got me lifted up and against the wall of the study room. I wrap my legs around his waist in time to feel him press his rock-hard length into me. I press myself into him. It's hitting me in the perfect spot. I pull my head back and away, and it thumps the wall. "Oh, God, Baker." *Oh, hells bells, this is amazing.*

When we hear a loud knocking, we pull apart abruptly and look at the window by the main hallway. Several guys are laughing and slapping hands on the window. The guy in front yells through the glass, "Get a fucking room, Bake."

"Fuck," he grumbles, letting me down easy. He's still got his body pressed against mine as he runs his hands over his face back and forth. "Sorry about that. Got carried away."

Attempting to calm myself, I only nod and slide down between the wall and Baker until I'm free. Sitting back down at the table, I clear my throat and pick up the papers. "Shall we continue?"

"Uh, sure." Baker sits down across from me, leaning back in his chair.

I work quickly after that kiss. "So, you masturbate daily?" *Hell and damnation, why did I start there?*

"Yeah. But it'll be more now," he murmurs.

"What was that?"

"Nothing."

"Your favorite position"—*is obviously against the wall*—"is cowgirl?"

"I like them all. But I like to watch a woman's body move above me."

I don't even want him to expand on that one. I'm still pretty frazzled from the kiss. I just need this to be over so he'll leave. "You don't like stereotypes?"

"No."

"You like dirty talk, but only if you're the one doing it?"

"Yes. Want to hear some?"

"Uh, sure?"

He leans forward until his face is only inches from mine. "You kiss like a fucking porn star, Virginia. I don't remember my cock ever being this hard before. It's still rock hard even after we've stopped. There's nothing I want more than to sink—"

"Okay, I get it. You're good at the dirty talk."

He chuckles, leaning back in his chair. "When inspired I am."

Does that mean he's inspired? "Well, I think that's all we have time for today. My next interview will be here any minute."

"I thought this was supposed to last an hour?"

"Twenty minutes, an hour. Whatever it takes."

"You didn't ask me anything on the second sheet," he says, crossing his giant arms across his chest.

"We covered most of it."

Releasing a big sigh, Baker Stark stands up to his full height. As he turns to leave, he stops and says, "I'll be seeing you, Virginia."

I blink at him, then blink some more. No, he won't be seeing me. "Bye," I say quickly. "Have a nice day." *What? Have a nice day?* I'm such a dork.

"Oh, I will. You too."

He moves out of the doorway, pulling the door closed as he goes. When he passes the window, he turns back and winks.

Holy crap! What just happened? I do my best to calm myself, thankful to have almost thirty minutes left until the next participant shows up. My first instinct is to call Peach, but what would I say? "Oh, hey. I just made out with a stranger in the library study room. No biggie." But it *was* a biggie. Sure, I've kissed guys before. Not a lot of guys, but enough to know that *that* kiss was different... special. I think I get why people are crazy about sex now. Not that we had sex, but I *wanted* to have sex. Badly. I could have just dropped my drawers right then and there. *God, when did I turn into that girl?*

The remaining Saturday interviews go without incident. Neither person tries to kiss me. Heck, I can't believe the one guy kissed me. Granted, one was a woman and the other was a man who liked men. I was just relieved to get through them all without making any major mistakes, since I was still sort of frazzled. I don't think my body could take another kiss like the one from Baker Stark.

CHAPTER 10

ON SUNDAY, I oversleep. Probably because I tossed and turned thinking about kissing giant men, one giant man in particular, in the middle of the library while people jeered and laughed. When I finally fell asleep, it was already five in the morning. Scrambling out of bed, I grab some sweats and a semi-clean T-shirt, my backpack, and a bottle of water.

I get to the library late. My only appointment is leaning against the doorjamb doing something on his phone. He's gorgeous. I don't remember him the day of the surveys, and believe me, I'd have remembered him. He has dark hair, and when he peers up at me, I see eyes so blue they remind me of the Caribbean.

"Hey," I say nonchalantly.

Chuckling, my future husband says, "Nice hair. Did you oversleep?"

Ugh! I forgot to brush my hair and my teeth. I shut my mouth and run my fingers through the rat's nest that is my bedhead. "Yeah. Couldn't sleep."

I step into the room as he holds the door for me. Such a

gentleman. "Have a seat." I hold my hand out to shake. "My name is Virginia. Thanks for coming."

He takes my hand in his and kisses the top of it. "The pleasure's all mine. I'm Copeland, but my friends call me Cope."

"Cope. That's cool," I say, gazing at him. He's so damn handsome. He's got a scruff of a beard growing on his chin, but it doesn't detract from his pretty lips. He's got high cheekbones that I'd love to lick. *Huh? What? Lick? God, my mind's in the gutter lately.* "So, shall we get started, Cope?" I say, smiling so big it hurts.

"Absolutely."

"So, it says you've never been in a long-term relationship."

"Well, I had a girlfriend in high school, but do those relationships even count?"

Hmm, I bet the girl from high school thinks it counted. I mean, look at him. I giggle. "I guess not."

"Since then I've just been focusing on school. It's not that I don't want to find a nice girl and settle down, I just haven't found her yet," he says with a pout.

"I get that."

"Besides, I work hard for my grades. I'm the president of my fraternity, Beta Theta Pi, and I have goals."

"What kind of goals?"

"Politics. My dad's a US representative, so I'm expected to follow in his footsteps."

"I see your major is political science."

"Uh-huh. Then law school."

He's so determined and ambitious. That's such an amazing trait for someone his age. The more I read through his list, the more I just know he's the one. I scan the section on the questionnaire about whether he'd sleep with a virgin, finding his "yes." I don't ask him about that, but I do talk to him about the fact that he's chosen "other" for the attraction questions. "You don't have a preference when it comes to hair color, hair style, or body type?"

"Nah. I don't care about someone's appearance. It's what's in here that counts," he says, patting his chest right above his heart. "When I find the one, I know it's just going to hit me. I can't have a predetermined notion of what she's going to look like."

"But if you could choose the hair color, what would you choose?"

"Well, I guess blondes are okay."

"Long hair or short hair?"

"I guess long. I like it when girls put their hair up in that messy thing on the top of their heads, and they wear nerdy glasses. I like intelligent women, so that reminds me of that."

But anyone can wear those nerdy glasses. "Okay, you ranked the features of the female body in this order: smile, face, eyes, mouth/teeth, hands, arms, legs, feet, ass/behind, and breasts. Is that correct?"

"Well, maybe eyes would be first. You can tell a lot by a person's eyes, don't you think? They're the windows to the soul, after all."

"True." That seems a bit off. You'd think breasts or ass would be farther up. Maybe he is looking for his soul mate. "You also ranked the personality traits you like the most as faithful and kind."

"They're the most important."

"What about 'good in bed'?"

"That's something we can work on together after we're married."

"You want to wait for marriage to, uh, consummate your relationship?"

"If possible. When I meet the one, I want to wait."

This guy is too good to be true. He's gorgeous, smart, ambitious, and such a gentleman. I want him! "Your favorite stereotypical woman was 'the girl next door,' then 'the marrying kind,' and third was 'I don't like stereotypes.'"

"I don't like them, no. But the two I listed first and second are okay. They must be sweet girls I could marry and that my mom would be proud to call a daughter."

I nod. "Masturbating? You said no."

"Well, I have done it before. I just try not to. It's wrong."

It's natural, but okay. "You also don't like dirty talk?"

"No! That's disgusting," he says adamantly.

"Missionary is your favorite position?"

I watch him blush. Oh my goodness, this guy is adorable. "The time I had sex, yes. It was missionary."

"Do you ever want to try anything else?"

"Oh, you're embarrassing me, Virginia."

"I'm sorry. I didn't mean to."

Sighing, he admits, "I'd like to try other things, but with the right girl."

"Sounds good." I'm not sure what else to ask him. I don't think he's going to give me much more. "Well, I think that's all I need for today. Thank you so much, Copeland. I've enjoyed talking to you."

"Same here, Virginia. Good luck with your paper."

"Thanks."

He stands and walks out the door.

As he moves, I can't help noticing how firm and round his ass is. "Stop it, Virginia," I hiss to myself. I'm such a damn pervert. One good thing that came out of today was finding my third and final possible deflowerer, and this one is the best of the bunch, my dream man—Mr. Political Science.

CHAPTER 11

IT'S TIME. He should be home from work by now, so I need to do it. I need to call my dad. I rarely take the initiative with him. His phone rings only once.

"Virginia?"

"Hi, Dad."

"How are you, sweetie? Is everything okay? Are you hurt? Do you need help?"

"Yes, everything's fine." God, I'm a terrible daughter. The first thing out of his mouth is concern for me, asking me if I'm okay, hurt. I suck.

"You never call. My first thought is something bad has happened."

"I'm sorry, Dad. No, everything's fine." It's true. If we talk, it's because he's called me.

"How's school? Getting good grades?"

"Yes. School's good. It's why I'm calling, actually." I explain my research project, not all of it, but most of it. I don't get into details about the sex stuff.

When I tell him about my research and the needed funds for

said research, he shocks me. "I've been waiting for you to ask for your money."

"Huh? *My* money?" *What money?*

"I've been putting the money that your mom refused to take in an account for you all these years."

Refused to take money? She told me he was practically a deadbeat dad. "You have?"

"Obviously, your mother didn't tell you. She told me not to tell you or she wouldn't let me see you again."

"What?" I squeak. "Why?"

Dad blew out some air. I could hear the deep sigh. "She was angry with me."

"I know, but that doesn't make any sense."

"I used to put money in my letters to you, but she told me to stop."

"Letters? What letters?" I feel moisture hit my cheeks and realize I'm crying. "I didn't get any l-letters, Dad."

"I wrote to you every week at first. When you didn't reply, I only wrote every month."

I released a loud sob. "Dad. I didn't get any letters."

"Fuck! She told me she gave them to you, but that you didn't care."

I'm crying so hard I can't get any words out.

"Oh, baby. I'm sorry. I thought...."

"N-n-no. She didn't give them to me." I can't believe my mom did that to me—to him. My dad. I'd cry myself to sleep when he'd forget to call me or when he never, not once, invited me to Illinois for the summer or even for a visit. It broke my heart that one minute I was his "little peanut" and the next I was nothing. Mom would hug me and tell me I had her and that was all I needed. Well, she was wrong.

"I'm sorry, Dad." So many years lost.

"I am too, peanut. But now that we know, can we start over? God, I've missed you so much, sweetheart."

The bawling starts all over again. "I've m-missed you too." I can't seem to stop crying.

Once I've calmed down, he asks for my bank account information. "Is this *just* your account?"

"Yeah."

"No one else is listed on it?"

"No." I know he's referring to my mom. "No, she can't access it."

"Good. I'll have your money transferred over tomorrow, so watch your account in the next day or two and let me know when it's safely deposited in there, okay?"

"Okay, Dad."

"I'd like to come visit you. Homecoming weekend is in two weeks, right?"

He knows when my homecoming is? "Yes."

"Can I come?"

"I'd love that, Dad."

"Me too." He sniffles on the other end of the phone. "Thank you for calling me, peanut. I feel happier than I have in years."

"Me too, Dad." *Me too.*

As soon as I hang up, I send a text to Mom.

Me: *Mom, did you keep the letters Daddy sent to me? If so, I want them all. All of them!*

I hope she kept them. When my phone rings, I see it's her. I'm not ready to talk to her so I decide to send a second text.

Me: *Please don't call back. I can't talk to you right now. Just mail me the letters.*

❦

THE NEXT DAY, I log into my online banking and nearly choke on my granola bar. "Holy shit!" My dad has deposited $151,000 into my bank account. I quickly pick up my phone and hit his number.

When he answers, I don't give him a chance to speak. "Dad! That's too much money! I can't take all of that from you."

"It's your money, Virginia. It amounts to one thousand dollars a month for the last ten years. Plus, there's money in there for school. Your mom refused to let me help you with college, so I put the money aside for the day you needed it. I figured I'd give it all to you as your graduation present to help get you set up."

"But you need that money. I can't take all of that."

"It's not my money. It's *your* money. I do well at my job; I've always had it taken directly out of my check and deposited into that account."

"But... I feel like I'm stealing your money, Dad."

"If I had st—uh, stayed, I would have spent way more than that on you." Dad chuckles. "So take it. It would make me the happiest dad in the world if you'd take it and use it the way you need to use it."

"Okay. I will. Thank you, Dad. So, I'll see you in a couple of weeks?"

"Try and stop me. I've already packed my bag," he says, chuckling.

"Love you, Daddy."

"Love you more, peanut. Talk to you soon?"

"Yeah. I'll call you in a day or two."

"Perfect."

I'm so happy my dad and I are talking, but my heart hurts. Mom betrayed me. I may never be able to forgive her for this.

CHAPTER 12

TWO HOURS and one sore noggin later, I've got new hair. I run my fingers through the strands and gaze at my reflection in a Main Street store window as we pass.

Peach stands in front of me, checking out the new do. "It's surprising how much long hair has changed your appearance, Virginia."

"I know, right?" I hardly recognize myself. I didn't change the color; I just had her add about eight inches to the front and ten to the back. "It's surprisingly soft. I can run my fingers through it."

"She said you could curl or straighten it like real hair too."

"It *is* real hair, dork. I can color it too."

"What does it look like pulled up into a ponytail?" Peach reaches out and pulls it back. "Wow, you can't tell."

"I know. It's called Hair Fusion. They literally fuse my hair with the extensions." I flip my hair back over my shoulder and smile. "I feel sort of glamorous." I giggle.

"You look glam. Now all you need to do is ditch all of the baggy clothes and you're set."

"Baggy? They're not baggy."

"Hell yes, they're baggy. You need clothes about two sizes

smaller than those."

"I guess that means you're going to help me find clothes that will attract a free-spirited guy. Whatever that looks like." Fashion is not my thing, but Peach knows clothes and makeup like the back of her hand.

"Ooh, yeah. I'm thinking tight, torn jeans and flowery, sexy Bohemian tops."

Not too tight. My ass and thighs aren't used to being constricted. "Let's hit the thrift store. They've always got some good stuff."

"Fine," Peach harumphs. She loves the mall.

We're able to find jeans Peach thinks will work along with some cutoff jean shorts and uber-short frayed skirts.

"These are too short, Peach," I whine.

"Your legs are your best feature. You need to accentuate those."

"My brain is my best feature," I mumble.

"You can wow them with your brain after you've attracted their attention. It's how it works, Virginia."

I toss the miniskirts into my basket. We find a few old concert tees that Peach says she can "make cute." She's an artist; I'm sure she'll be able to do something. Next, we head to the mall, to an extremely expensive store called Bohomoho. "It's an oxymoron that this," I say, holding up a sheer top, "is one hundred dollars."

"What do you mean?" she asks while searching through the racks.

"Because back in the day, it was meant for an artist or writer who was unconventional. Think starving artists and writers, Peach. They never would have spent this kind of money on clothes. It's too pretentious."

Ignoring my rant, she shouts, "Here!" and pulls an adorable eyelet top from the rack. "This is perfect. Go try it on."

"Ooh, it is perfect," I coo.

An hour and $360 later, I've got the wardrobe to catch me a

free-spirited skater boy. Now all I need is a few tips on makeup, and we're good.

"How do you know where to find this guy?" asks Peach as we sip a coffee at Starbucks in the North Grand Mall food court. I know, I'm a traitor, but The Coffee Bean is clear across town, close to campus. I give her a coy look and smile, saying, "I know where he works. I also know where most of his classes are located."

"Are you a stalker now?"

"No. They were questions on the interview questionnaire. He works at that funky record store called Spinners right down the street from the salon."

"So, you're just going to stroll into the record store and do what?"

"Flirt."

Peach spits out her coffee. "Flirt? You can't flirt. You're the worst flirter in the world."

"Gee, thanks."

"So, along with the clothes, makeup, and hair tutorials, you need one on flirting too. Well, lucky for you, your best friend is a master flirt."

Oh, I know that. "I've watched you in action. How hard can it be?"

"It's an art form. I'll teach you, my little grasshopper."

I scoff at her offer, then drink my coffee. The truth is, I could use her help.

"So, you spent a lot of money today. How much money did your dad loan you? If you don't mind me asking."

"A lot."

"A lot?"

"A lot, a lot."

"What? I thought he was a deadbeat dad."

"Turns out my mom is the deadbeat."

"Huh? I don't understand."

So, I tell her about the letters and my mom. I'm in tears by the time I finish. Saying it all out loud has made it real. The notion that my mom could be that vindictive and hate my dad so much that she'd keep him from me all these years is utterly heart-breaking.

"Why would she do that?" Peach asks.

"She hates him."

"But you could have had a relationship with him. That shouldn't have been about her."

"I know," I say, wiping the wetness from my face. "I know, but she loved being the hero. She used to say shit like 'At least you have me' whenever my dad disappointed me. You know, by not sending me anything for my birthday or showing up for important events like my graduation."

"She was behind all of that?"

"Apparently."

"What a bitch."

"Yeah." *What a bitch.* "She's called me several times, left me a few weepy voice messages asking me to let her explain."

"Have you called her back?"

"No. I've sent two texts, both asking for her to send me the letters."

"Do you think she's got them?"

I shrug. "Who knows?"

"I'm sorry, V."

"Me too. I guess the good part that came out of all of this is my dad is coming to visit. He's now going to be part of my life. I've missed him. We used to be so close."

Peach reaches over and squeezes my hand. "That is good. Plus, he gave you a bunch of money. That's nice too."

"It's not about the money." Although it helps a lot. I don't plan on it changing my life. I'm still going to work to help pay my expenses. I want to save it for my future. And hopefully, that includes graduate school.

CHAPTER 13

PEACH TOLD me my new hair would take extra time to style in the morning, and she wasn't lying. Since it's Thursday, I have to be at work at six thirty, so I wake up at five thirty, thinking that's enough time to wrangle the new hair. I was wrong. By the time I'm finished blow-drying it and attempting to flatiron the rat's nest, I give up and put it in a ponytail. It doesn't look terrible. Until I get used to it, I'm going to have to give myself an extra hour in the morning to make it look good.

When I walk in, Jackson is already refilling coffee beans and cups. The satellite music station is playing something mellow—perfect for this early in the morning.

"Hey, Jackson."

"Hey, girl. Clock in. I need help. This place is a disaster."

"Sure thing." I walk quickly to the back and toss my book bag and other stuff in the corner. I grab an apron from the stack of clean ones and punch in.

Tying my apron on as I head back to the front, I hear Jackson yell, "Get vanilla and mocha flavoring while you're back there."

I spin around and grab two large bottles of flavoring, then head to the front again. "Didn't they restock anything last night?"

"No. The little assholes."

"Wasn't Kip the closer last night?"

"Yes. He's worthless," grumbles Jackson.

"That he is. What else can I do?"

"Refill everything at the sugar station." That's what we call the area that has the extra sugar packets, stirrers, cream, and those things that you put around your to-go cup so you don't get burned. When I walk over, I see a literal disaster. "What were they doing last night? It looks like a murder scene over here."

"Back here too," mutters Jackson. "This is bullshit. Men suck."

"They do, but I can't believe you're saying that. Guys fall all over themselves when they see you."

"Except the one I want."

"Oh, wow. Is a boy playing hard to get? That's gotta sting."

"Shut up, bitch," he says, laughing. "I'll get it figured out."

"I know you will. Maybe he's just trying to get your attention."

"He's got it."

I wipe down the sugar station and run to the storage room at the back of the store to grab refills for everything. I also pull cream and milk jugs from the walk-in cooler so I can pour fresh carafes since I have no idea when anyone changed out the old ones. The cream could be curdled. I shiver at the thought.

The minute everything is restocked and wiped down, the front door opens to our first customer, and the stream of customers doesn't seem to stop for hours. I'm manning the machines while Jackson has the register. I'm the only one he trusts to do this job when he works, so I like to give him a break from making the drinks. As I'm concocting an iced caramel macchiato with extra pumps of vanilla and caramel, nonfat, and extra caramel drizzle, I hear a grunt above me.

"Hey," says Baker, the kissing bandit.

"Hey," I say as I continue making this ridiculous drink. Note to the person who ordered this? Leave out the nonfat. You're wasting your breath.

"What'd you do to your hair?"

"Nothing."

"Yeah you did."

"You did!" says Jackson way too loudly. "I didn't notice it before. What'd you do to it? Extensions?"

I squirt an extra ten pumps of vanilla and ten of caramel into the cup, muttering, "So! What's the big deal?"

Jackson is the first to speak. "Nothing. It's just—"

"Not you," mumbles Baker.

I slam the cup down on the counter and end up with half of it on my apron when it splashes out. "How would you know what's me and what isn't?" *I've met this guy once. Geesh.*

He shrugs. "It just isn't."

Ignoring him, I snap, "If you want coffee, you need to order it from him." I point him in Jackson's direction with a nod. "I have to start over with this drink."

Baker walks to Jackson but continues to look at me.

"Chicks, man," mutters Jackson.

"No shit, dude."

I watch them fist-bump and nearly gag. Men are idiots.

"Large black coffee, please."

Why does he come in here and just order plain coffee? He can get that anywhere. When I finally get the macchiato done, I reach for the next order.

"See you later, Virginia."

I mutter under my breath, "No you won't."

"Yeah I will," says Baker as he pushes the door open to leave. *How the hell did he hear that?*

"Someone has a crush," coos Jackson.

"I do not!" I retort.

"Not you. Obviously. He does," Jackson says, pointing at the door as it closes behind Baker. "He's got it bad for you."

"No way. He was just one of my participants for my survey. He's a hockey player." Besides, he's too much for me. Too much muscle, too much man, and too much experience. I bet he thinks I'm experienced in bed or something. I'd make a fool of myself with him. No. Thank. You.

Jackson looks at me, brows furrowed. "Well, sweet cheeks, he's hot for you." Then he adds with a mumble, "Lucky bitch. I'd give my left nut for a chance with that hot-as-fuck man."

"He's nothing special," I lie. His kiss says otherwise, but I'm not admitting that to anyone.

"Oh, my dear sweet Virginia. Someday you'll realize a guy like that"—he points out the door again—"is all you'll ever need."

That's not true. I need a man like Mr. Political Science. He's got goals. He's ambitious. He's sweet and thoughtful. But I'm saving him for last—the best for last, as they say. "Whatever, Jackson. He's very, uh, bossy."

"Oh fuck, you had to go and tell me that. I love domineering guys in the sack."

"Jackson. No. I'm not going there this morning." *Or ever.* I look up at the clock and see it's only ten. Two more hours here, and then I'm off to class. What a day!

CHAPTER 14

LOOKING at myself in the full-length mirror in Peach's bedroom, I chew my nails nervously. I can do this. It's time to snag myself a free-spirited man. The plan has been set. My outfit is on. My hair has been braided and coifed into a cute hippy-chick hairdo, and my makeup looks natural and fresh—Peach's words, not mine. Now all I have to do is walk into Spinners and talk to the guy.

I turn to my bestie, who's sprawled out on her bed. "I'm so nervous."

"No reason to be nervous. You look adorable, so hold your head up high and do exactly as I told you to do. And ask him to help you find a record."

I blink at her. "Right. I should go in asking for something."

Peach arches her brow.

"Not that. Some kind of music."

"Ooh, ask if they have any Tom Petty. I've been meaning to buy *Damn the Torpedoes*."

"Fine," I sigh, exasperated. "But do I *really* have to twist my hair around my finger while I ask him for help?"

"Yes. Definitely. It makes you look coy and a little dumb."

"Not all guys like dumb girls."

"They *say* they don't like dumb girls. Let's just test that hypothesis."

"Fine. Let's go, toots."

Since Peach has a car, she'll drive me down to Main Street. She'll park a block away and wait for me to do my thing at the record store.

"I feel like I'm robbing a bank and you're my getaway driver."

"It's sort of like that, but you're not stealing money. You're trying to... wait for it... *steal* his heart." Peach throws her head back in laughter. "I'm so punny."

"Oh, God. That was lame," I mumble and then laugh. It was pretty funny.

Peach laughs for a good five minutes over that one. "I'm *hilarious*."

Yeah. Hilarious. I'm so nervous on the drive over that I pull and twist the frayed ends of my jean shorts. My *short* jean shorts. I swear my ass is hanging out, but Peach assures me it's not. Yeah, like I believe her.

Peach pulls into a parking spot on Main Street as I turn to my friend and smile. "I can do this."

"Yes you can! He's just a guy. No need to get all worked up over him. You're sure he's working?"

"I called the store, and he answered. I told him I had the wrong number." I step out of the car onto the pavement and suck in a lungful of air. "Courage." I've got one block to get a grip. "He's just a guy," I repeat. "He's just a guy."

"Good luck!" Peach shouts through her open car window.

"Shh. Geesh, Peach," I hiss. She's going to make me even more nervous.

At the entrance to Spinners, I plaster a smile on my face and open the door. I'm almost knocked on my butt by the smell of incense. What are they hiding? I smell patchouli. I spot Mr. Free Spirit right away in the center of the store. His real name is Levi, but I'm not going to say it. Not yet anyway. If he recognizes me, then I'll say it. I make my way to the long aisle that holds bins of vinyl records, pretending to look at the list of artists next to each bin while really I'm watching him. He's talking to a girl. A cute girl. *Ugh. I knew this wouldn't work.* The urge to leave hits me, but I refuse to give up, so I start sifting through a bin just to have something to do.

"Can I help you?" says a voice to my left.

I turn to see Levi smiling at me. "Oh, um, yes." I giggle. That wasn't fake. I'm nervous as hell. I twist a strand of hair around my finger. "I'm looking for a Tom Petty album."

"Oh, man. That sucks that he died, doesn't it? That guy was amazing."

"I know. I cried."

"That's cool. So, which album?"

"Any of them."

"You don't have any of his music?"

"No. Is that terrible?" I say in a way too high-pitched voice.

"Nah. It's cool you want some now. Here, I'll show you where his stuff is. We moved it up front. There's not a lot left."

"Oh, I know! Do you have *Damn the Torpedoes*? My friend told me to get that one."

"That one is awesome, but we're sold out. We're supposed to get more in next week."

Stopping in my tracks, I say, "Oh, that's too bad."

"If you want, I could get your name and number and call you when the record comes in."

"You'd do that? That's so sweet of you," I say, touching his arm. Peach told me to try to touch his hand or arm during this whole flirting deal. It must work, because he looks down at my hand and then up at me with a huge smile on his face.

"It's no problem. Plus, if you give me your number, I can call you. We could hang out or something."

"Really?" I squeak, then quickly rebound. "That'd be cool. I'd like that." I look down at his nametag. "Bill."

"It's Levi. We all use fake nametags. The boss thinks it's hilarious," he says, rolling his eyes.

I giggle. "It is kind of funny." I step up to the counter and give him my name and digits. I decide to use a variation of my name so he won't make the connection between the survey and me. "It's Ginny, and my number is 515-202-4407."

"Ginny. That's a pretty name."

It seems to be working. I twist my hair again. "Thanks."

As I turn to leave, I hear him say, "I'll call you later, Ginny."

"Okay. Bye, Levi."

I pull open the door and step out into the sunshine. It's early October and has been unseasonably warm. My way back to the car takes much less time than the walk to the shop. I yank open the door and plop my butt in the car. "I did it!"

"What? You bought that album?" Peach smirks.

Opening the car door, I start the slide into the seat. "No. They're out of that." I laugh. "I snagged Mr. Free Spirit, though. He's going to call me."

"Yay! Congrats! I knew you could do it. So, about that album."

"Sold out. It'll be in next week."

"Cool. So, tell me everything."

I turn in my seat, bringing my leg under me until I'm facing her. I tell her everything, from the uncontrollable giggling to the hair twisting. "He says he wants to 'hang out.'"

"See! Guys never ask us out on dates anymore. 'Hang out' means just that. Ugh, it's so frustrating."

"Hanging out sounds fine to me. Baby steps."

"At least get him to take you out for food, even if it's at Torpedo Joe's Subs."

"Yes, ma'am. I'll do that."

"Good. Now, let's go shopping for a 'hanging out' outfit."

Ugh. "Not more shopping," I whine.
"Come on, *Ginny*. We'll just go to one store."
I groan.
Then I hear her whisper, "Or twenty."
Great!

CHAPTER 15

TRUE TO HIS WORD, Levi texted me that very night. He also sent a text the next morning, then that afternoon and evening. Actually, he's sent me several texts per day for the last four days. He seems sweet and funny, but that's through text messaging. I hope he's the same tonight. He's picking me up in a few minutes to hang out. I think the plan is "eating and then seeing where things go"—his words, not mine. Honestly, I'm more of a planner. I'd like to know his ideas for tonight, but since I'm supposed to be a free-spirited hippy chick, I need to go with the flow.

Standing in the living room, I'm nervously biting my nails. He'll be here any minute.

"You look beautiful, Virginia."

"Well, you constructed it, Peach. You know, like Dr. Frankenstein."

Peach has my hair in some intricate braided do that is supposed to look a little messy and tousled. It does. She did my makeup, and we found an adorable maxi dress at a discount store in the mall. I definitely look the part.

"What time is he picking you up?"

I peer down at my phone. "In three minutes." Twenty-five

minutes later, I'm about to give up when I hear a loud rumble from the street outside our apartment, then a honk. When I look out the window and down into the parking lot, I see a circa-1980s Honda that looks like it used to be blue but is now rust-colored.

"Please tell me he did not just honk at you."

"Okay, I won't tell you."

"Guys are such assholes," she grumbles. "He can get out of his car and—" Her words are interrupted by three more honks. "Tell him I'm going to nut him if he does that again."

"On that note, I'm out of here. See you later."

As I quickly make my way to the door, she adds, "I want a full report when I get home."

"You're going out?"

"I have a date with Ryan Reynolds. Well, not a date. I'm meeting him at Cy's."

"You're talking to that guy?"

"Maybe."

"Now *I* need a full report."

Three more honks sound, and I watch as Peach clenches her fists. "Swear to God, Virginia."

"I'm going. See you later. Have fun with Ryan," I singsong.

Jogging to Levi's car, I attempt to open the passenger door, but it won't budge. I lean down and say through the window, "It won't open."

"Oh, shit, dude. I forgot. You have to come in this way."

Dude? I have to climb in through the driver door? Great. I walk to his side of the car and wait for him to step out. "Uh, you need to get out."

"Oh, right," he says, smirking.

Outside the car, I glance at his outfit—old jeans and an even older concert tee. Gee, it was nice of him to dress up. I slide in headfirst and ass up over the gear shifter thingy. In the process, I hit my head on the rearview mirror, then again on the dashboard.

Ouch. When I'm finally in place, Levi hops in and starts up the engine. It pops and wheezes to life.

I look around and wonder how the car has made it this long. "Nice wheels."

"I know, right?" He pats the dashboard, smiling. "Good ole Civvy."

Civvy? It's a Honda Civic, so I guess it makes sense. We decide on a restaurant that's known for its burgers. When we reach the booth, I slide into my side and he slips in right next to me when there's a perfectly good spot on the other side of the table. Why do couples do that? It's awkward. I keep my mouth shut, though.

A waiter approaches the table to get our order, and Levi orders the Triple Bacon-Bacon Burger with a chocolate shake, fries, and onion rings. I order a single burger with a side of fries and a glass of water. While we wait for our food, our conversation revolves around music and extreme sports. Levi loves to watch skateboarding competitions and those bike races they do on the sides of mountains. Since I have no idea what that is, I just nod and listen. At some point in the conversation, I feel his hand on my thigh. Okay, *now* I know why people sit on the same side of the booth. He doesn't try anything but just sort of moves his palm up and down my leg. It's not unpleasant.

As soon as the food is in front of him, Levi scarfs down his burger like he hasn't eaten for days, maybe weeks.

"Hungry?"

"Starving," he says with a mouth full of, well, everything.

It's a little disgusting, to be honest. He doesn't speak another word until his food is gone and he's eying mine.

"Do you want to share some of your fries with me?" he asks with a sugary sweet smile.

I bet that smile works for him all the time. "Sure."

Okay, by "share," he means eat them all. The guy is a garbage disposal. I don't mind. I'm not super comfortable eating all of this food in front of him anyway.

"So, I thought we'd go hang out with some of my buddies after this. Thought you might want to watch me do some tricks with my board, man."

Man? First of all, I'm not a man. I hate that. I also hate being called dude. Second of all, the last thing I want to do is watch Levi and his buddies do skateboarding stuff. "Sure. Sounds good."

When the bill arrives, Levi does nothing. I expect him to reach into his wallet and pull some money out, but he just looks at his nails and then up at the ceiling.

"Uh, should we split it?"

"Uh, I think I forgot my wallet. Can you get it?"

I feel the heat rise from my chest up to my neck and to my cheeks. It's not like I expected him to pay the entire bill like this was a date or something, but I'm paying for all of it? I think Mr. Free Meal fits him better than Mr. Free Spirit. "Sure. I'll get it."

I reach into my little purse and grab my debit card. Setting it on the small tray, we wait for the waiter to pick it up.

"Cool." He leans back in his seat. Sounding disappointed, he says, "Dang, we should have ordered dessert."

"Oh well... too late now." Once the bill is paid, I crawl into his car and off we go. He drives us a few miles away to a more indus-trial area. As he pulls into an abandoned parking lot, I see a group of people with skateboards. "You skate here?"

"Until the cops come, yeah." He smirks. "Let me grab my board out of the trunk."

When we reach his friends, I count six guys and three girls. I call them girls because none of them look much older than middle school. I smile and am about to introduce myself to all three girls when they glare at me. "I guess not," I whisper to myself.

Finding a spot on a nearby concrete step far away from the prepubescent girls, I wait for Levi to introduce me to his peeps, but that never happens. Instead, I spend the next forty-five minutes watching them attempt and fail to skateboard. Levi has fallen or nearly fallen at least ten times. I'm surprised he's not bleeding. An hour after arriving, I'm ready to go. It's dark, and there's only one light on in this parking lot, and it's not enough to illuminate their skateboarding tricks. It's pointless to continue.

Walking over to him, I say, "Uh, Levi? You ready to go?"

"Huh?" he says, looking shocked. "No. We're just getting warmed up."

Okaaayyy. "I'm tired. I'm ready to go." I decide just to be honest.

"Okay. I'll see ya around, maybe."

He'll see me around? I don't have a car. "I don't have a car." *Like, duh, Levi. You drove me.*

"You can walk. It's not far."

I hear a bitchy female voice add, "Walking's good exercise. You could use it."

The other girls snicker, and I'm dumbstruck. Opening and closing my mouth like a fish, I wait for Levi to jump in to defend me. I look at him, and he shrugs. "It *is* good exercise."

Without another word, I start the long trek back toward campus. "Okay, what are my options?" I sigh. "One of them is never going out with Levi again. What a jerk!" Luckily, I'm wearing flat sandals, because if I had to estimate the walk from this spot on the east edge of Ames to my place, I'd say it was about five miles. I can't call Peach since she's on a date with Ryan Reynolds. She'd probably pick me up, but I don't want to interrupt her fun. I could jump on a CyRide bus, but I'll need to get closer to Duff Avenue to catch one of those.

Checking my phone, I note that I've been walking about half an hour and have made it to Duff and Lincoln Way, the main roads that run through Ames. I should be able to catch a bus, but I forgot my bus pass. "Great."

Periodically checking behind me to see if a bus is coming,

I make it another mile when I spot a bus stop with a bench and a streetlight above it. I'm so tired I decide I'll risk a shot at the bus. Maybe I can sweet-talk the driver into letting me ride for free. When I spot a car doing a U-turn in the middle of the busy road, I don't think anything of it. When it pulls into the area designated for CyRide, I look up and watch the passenger window of a shiny new Nissan roll down.

Great. Just great. "Hey, Baker."

"What are you doing sitting at a bus stop on Lincoln Way at this time of night?"

"It's not even midnight yet." I look down at my phone. *Okay, it's twelve thirty. Time flies.*

He's leaning over the passenger seat to talk to me through the window. "It's late. Too late for a beautiful girl to be out here alone."

Beautiful girl? "I'm fine. Thanks for stopping." I stand up and start to walk again. No need for me to sit there and listen as Baker chastises me.

"Virginia," he says with a deep, demanding voice. "Get in the car."

"No. I'm fine. See you later." Or not.

"Please?" he says sweetly. "Please get in the damn car, Virginia," he adds not quite as sweetly.

"Fine!" I say as I stomp over to the passenger side. I yank the door open and slide into the black leather seat, enjoying the new car smell plus something else. It's manly and something all Baker. "Nice wheels."

"Thanks. Gift from my grandmother."

"Wow, she must *really* like you."

With a chuckle, he says, "She loves me. I'm her only grandchild."

"Spoiled?" I mutter.

"Nah, I'm not spoiled. I help her out a lot. This is how she paid me back. Not like she needed to; I had a perfectly good pickup truck."

"Good to know," I mutter.

"Where do you live?"

"West Ames."

He puts the car into Drive and maneuvers it until we're back on the main road. "Why were you walking?"

Okay, there's no way I'm telling him about the date from hell. "Just felt like taking a stroll."

"A stroll? All the way out here?"

"Why are *you* out here?" I say, crossing my arms over my chest. *Yeah, take that, Mr. Bossy Pants!*

"I live about a block away."

"Oh. How did you know it was me sitting there?"

"I wasn't sure it was you. I circled the block a few times to be sure before I stopped. So, why were you walking this far away from home?"

Jeez, the guy should be a cop or in jail. Stalker. "Bad date," I mumble.

"You were on a date? Did you have an argument or something? Why would your date let you walk home?"

"Good question."

"You're not going to see him again, are you?"

"Nope."

"Who is this guy?"

"You don't know him."

"Try me."

Why does he care? "His name is Levi, and he works at a record store."

"Spinners?"

Oh shit. "I, uh, I'm not sure."

"You're a terrible liar, Virginia."

"It's fine. I was ready to go; he wasn't. I chose to walk."

"Liar."

"Fine! He's a tool. He was skateboarding with his buddies and —" I feel a hot tear roll down my cheeks. "It doesn't matter. It was just a crappy date. End of story."

Baker must be able to take a hint, because he keeps his mouth shut the rest of the way. Pulling into the lot outside my apartment, he puts the car into Park and jumps out. I watch him make his way around to my side of the car, open my door, and hold his hand out to me.

I take it. "Thanks." Once I'm out of the car, I find myself standing very close to Baker.

"You gonna be okay?" he asks softly.

"Of course. I'm fine."

"That guy your boyfriend?"

"No. First and last date." I scoff.

"Good to know."

I'm not sure how he accomplished it, but he's got my back pressed against the side of his car and my front pressed against him. It's the same move from the library study room.

"What are you doing?" I whisper. I'm not going to scare him away. This feels good. Wrong, but good.

"I haven't been able to stop thinking about that kiss, Virginia."

"Oh yeah?" I joke. "I was that good?"

"Fuck yeah. You were that good. But was it a fluke?"

"A fluke?"

"Yeah, babe. Was it a fluke? I need to know." His arms wrap around my lower back, pressing even closer.

"Okay," I say as his mouth finds mine.

It's tentative at first, but it doesn't take him long to get his groove back. When his tongue sweeps in to meet mine, I moan. I slide my hands up until they're around his neck and up into his hair. It's like we're starting right where we left off before. This time, my body wants to climb his body. I want to be higher and closer to him. He must read my mind, because his big hands slide down until they're cupping my bottom, lifting me until we're at eye level. Not sure what to do with my legs, I wrap one of them around his hip and press it into his firm ass. When Baker moans, I feel my panties melt. He presses his erection into me, then pulls away slightly. I want to feel him again, so I whimper just a little bit. I use my leg to press again. That's when I get a real taste of Baker's dirty talk.

"You like that, Virginia? You like the feel of my big, hard cock rubbing against your sweet pussy?"

I know I blush about fifty shades of pink, but I nod anyway. "Yeah," I croak. "I like it."

He takes my mouth so hard and so fast that I'm not sure what to do, so I push my fingers into his thick hair and pull.

"Goddamn, Virginia. I want to fuck you so bad, but...."

I release his hair and pull my face away from his. I look away, feeling humiliated. I can only guess what he was going to say. Something along the lines of me not being his type or being too chubby. I've heard it before.

I wiggle my leg loose from his hip, but he's still got his hands on my ass. I wiggle a little more to give him the hint that I want down. "Let me go, Baker."

"Virginia—"

"No! Don't say any more. I need to go!"

He slowly pulls back so I can slide down his body.

I can feel how hard he is with each inch I'm lowered. On solid ground, I bend down to pick up my purse that I dropped at some point. Still not able to look at him, I turn and walk away. "Thanks for the ride." I practically run to the front entrance of my building. I don't look back. When I reach the security door on the main level, I have my key out, ready to unlock it, but some jackhole has it propped open with a brick. They do it all the time. "That's so unsafe," I mutter, kicking the brick out of the way. I hear the door click shut behind me as I jog up the stairs to my apartment.

All I want to do now is take a hot bath and cry myself to

sleep. Opening my door, I hear nothing. Silence. Peach must still be out. I pull off the maxi dress and throw it on the sofa. I unhook my bra while kicking off my shoes, then pick those up and toss them unceremoniously in my bedroom. Nearly naked, I reach the bathroom and turn on the water in the tub. "A bath will cure everything." When the tub is full, I drizzle in some lavender oil, then slip out of my panties and into the warm water. "Finally." Laying my head back, I breathe in the lavender scent and do my best to let it wash away the memories.

I'm awoken by the chime of my phone. Texts. I guess I dozed off. I don't know how long I've been soaking, but the water is cold and my fingers are pruney. I climb out of the water and reach for my towel. Making my way back into the living room, I pull my phone from my purse and see a text from an unknown number.

Unknown Number: *You looked beautiful tonight, Virginia. That guy is an idiot.*

Baker.

Me: *How'd you get my number?*

Stalker.

Unknown Number: *You sent me a text to set up my interview for your "research."*

Duh, Virginia. Of course.

Me: *It is research.*
Unknown Number: *Sure.*
Me: *It is!*
Unknown Number: *Virginia?*
Me: *What?*

Unknown Number: *It wasn't a fluke.*

Crap! He's talking about the kiss. I don't think it was a fluke either. The kiss tonight was even better than the first one, but I decide not to reply. It does no good to respond, because nothing good can come of this. Hunky athletic guys like Baker Stark don't have relationships with nerdy girls like me. It goes against the laws of nature.

CHAPTER 16

"So, how'd it go?" Peach asks me as I pull on my work pants.

"Don't ask."

"Why not? What happened?"

"Long story. I'm late, so I'll have to tell you later." I zip up my pants and look at her. "How was *your* date?"

"Ah-maze-ing!" she squeaks. "I think I'm in love."

"Huh? Seriously?"

"Yeah," she says, coming down from her love balloon. Frowning, she asks, "Why?"

"It's just really soon. You've only been out with him once." I see her blink at me. "Right?"

"There may have been a couple of other times."

"A couple?"

"Or ten."

Ten? "You're dating someone, and you didn't tell me?"

"Well, I thought you'd be angry because he was a surveyor."

"A. Participant!" I yell. "God, I can't believe you. I tell you everything!" Well, she doesn't know about Baker and his lips, but that's nothing.

"I'm sorry, Virginia. I thought you'd be angry."

"Forget about it. I've gotta go. See you." Why did that whole conversation hurt so much?

As I walk to the bus stop, I do my best to fight the tears. One or two slip out, but I'm able to get it under control. At least that's one thing in my life I can control. Everything else is one big clusterfuck.

When I get to work, I see that trend is still going strong.

"Hey, Kip." *God, I hate working with Kip.*

"Hey, Virginia. Hurry up and clock in. There's a lot to do this morning."

"Why? Didn't the closers do their job again last night?"

When I see his face, I know I said the wrong thing. "We were busy!"

"Oh, right. Sure. Sorry." *Not sorry.* They weren't busy. I've worked that shift many times, and it's always dead after seven. We close at ten, so that gave him three hours to get stuff done. But he knew I'd be here in the morning. He knew I'd get it taken care of, even though all I want to do is throw a ceramic mug at his head. Jerk!

Working at Mach speed, I restock everything behind the counter and attempt to clean up the sugar station. Halfway through that job, the door opens and the first customers of the day walk in. I look around for Kip and see he's missing—again. I've had it. I really have. If I lose my job over this, who cares?

I march back to his office. The door is closed, of course, so I knock loudly and wait. When he says nothing, I knock again. Still nothing. I jiggle the knob and notice it's unlocked. I turn it and push the door open. What I see will be forever burned in my brain. I'll never be able to unsee it. Hell, I'd rather see dead people than that!

"Virginia! What the fuck? Get out of my office," he says, scrambling to zip up his pants. "I said get the fuck out!"

"No. I won't get out. I need help out here. I'm not doing this alone again."

"Do not tell me—"

"And if you don't start pulling your weight around here, I'm calling Don about that!" I say, pointing to his crotch. Don is the actual owner of the store. He's never around. He spends his time and money in sunny, warm locales.

"He'll never believe you."

I cross my arms over my chest. "Try me."

"I could just fire you."

I raise one eyebrow and throw my hip out to the side. "I'll sue."

"On what grounds?"

"I saw your dick. An employee should never see her manager's dick. It's technically sexual harassment. You made me feel uncomfortable." I could keep going, but he's squirming in his seat.

"You just barged into my office."

"I needed help. You didn't answer. The door was unlocked." I don't need more than that, but I say one more thing. "Maybe I should call the police before I call Don."

"Jesus. Fine," he mutters. As I turn to leave, I hear "Bitch."

I whip back around and glare. "What did you just call me?"

"Huh?" he asks, clearly surprised I heard him. "Nothing."

"That's it! I'm out of here. I'm calling Don on my way home. You'd better hope he's having a good time in Puerto wherever he is so he cuts you some slack." *Asshole.*

"No! Stop. I'm sorry."

"Too late. No one calls me that and gets away with it." I look out to the front and see a long line. "You'd better get out there. The line is getting longer."

I pull off my apron, clock out, and grab my bag. I'm out of here.

CHAPTER 17

I wasn't kidding; I called Don on my way home from the coffee shop. I'd like to tell you he was shocked and mortified, but he wasn't. When I told Don that Kip was rubbing one out in the office at six thirty in the morning, he just sighed. I'm not sure what to make of it, and honestly, I'm not sure where I stand at The Coffee Bean. He said he'd take care of it, so I guess I've got to let him do what he needs to do and see how it all plays out. After that, I'll decide on my next step.

As soon as I make it back to the apartment after my work drama, I change out of my standard uniform of black pants and a white button-down shirt and into sweats and an old tee. With my body in my cozy clothes, I make my way to the kitchen to pour myself some coffee. When I step into the kitchen, I see Peach.

"Oh, hey," I say as I pretend to search for my favorite coffee mug in the cupboard. It's a plain blue-gray color on the outside and white on the inside. What makes it funny is the bottom of the inside, which says, "You've been poisoned." It makes me giggle every time I finish a cup of coffee.

"Virginia?"

"Yeah?" I say, digging my dirty cup out of the sink. I quickly put a drop of soap into the mug and wash, then rinse it.

"I'm sorry."

Turning to face her, I say, "I know. I'm sorry too. I overreacted. I'm happy for you, Peach. I hope he's nice to you."

"He is. You'll like him. He's hilarious and *so* good in bed. He's huge and—"

"Not another word, Peach. I don't want to know about his body parts and his prowess in the sack." Maybe someday when I know what the hell the big deal is. Maybe.

"Fine. But let me just tell you, he's a stallion."

I nearly spit out my coffee. "A stallion?"

"Definitely. He's a stud muffin."

I crack up laughing again. "Peach, you're such a dork."

"I know. So, spill. Why are you home already?"

"Oh, jeez. One word: Kip."

Peach groans as she sips her coffee. "What'd he do now?"

"The usual. He wouldn't help me get the place restocked, and when I went in to get him to help with customers, I opened the door and he had his penis in his hand."

"*Penis?* Who says penis? Oh, and ew, gross."

I nod. "Well, if you'd seen it, you'd call it that too. It was, or I think it was, small. I mean, I've seen two penises in person, and I've touched one. Both of those were penises. I've never met a C-O-C-K. I consider those adult sized."

I look over and see Peach bent over at the waist, hand on the kitchen counter.

"Oh my God. You're so hilarious, Virginia."

"I wasn't kidding."

"I know! That's why it was so funny." She walks over and wraps her arms around me. "Don't worry. It won't be long until you're introduced to the wonderful world of C-O-C-K."

"I hope so!" I shout.

"So, did you quit or what?"

"Not yet. I called Don. He said he'd take care of it. I'm just going to wait and see."

"Good plan. Now, go put on shopping clothes. We've got a few hours. We need to find you something to wear for your next date. It's the musician, right?"

"You remembered?" I'm not surprised she remembered. I think she's almost as invested in this thing as I am.

"Of course. I also remembered you promised to tell me how the date with Mr. Free Spirit crashed and burned."

I moan into my coffee. "Don't remind me. It was the worst."

"Go get dressed. You can tell me on the way to the mall."

"Fine." I need to let Peach work her magic on me, and it is magic. "Let's get me ready for Kelvin Lewis." Better known as Mr. Punk Rocker. To get his attention, I'll need to make a few changes to my hair and wardrobe. Phase one is to make an appointment at the hairdresser to have a dark temporary dye put in my hair and to add some color. I think those changes will make me look a little more progressive.

With Peach's help, I'll shop for some darker clothing too, perhaps something that's ripped and torn. I don't know much about the punk rock scene, but I googled it and made a note of the clothing. When Mr. Punk Rocker came to the interview, he was wearing torn black jeans, combat boots, and a super-old Ramones concert tee. There were tears and rips all over the thing. So much so that I got a glimpse of his chest beneath.

Kelvin is tall and thin. Not super skinny, but he's no Baker Stark. He's over six feet tall with dark eyes and shaggy jet-black hair. Parts of his hair hit his collar, and other parts stick straight up. At the time of our one-on-one interview, he looked like he'd just gotten out of bed and run his hand through his hair, which was sort of adorable. He had a piercing in his lip and a gauge in his ear that was probably a half-inch wide. I don't get those things. What's the point in stretching your ear out until it's so big you could put your fist through it? I guess it's just a popular thing right now, like tattoos. I don't know if Kelvin has any tattoos. I couldn't see any, but he may be hiding some.

No matter. I liked Kelvin. He was very blunt during the interview, but not rude. He just leaned back with his arm thrown over the back of the chair and told me all about his sex life. He's had numerous sexual partners, has tried all kinds of positions, and likes a little bit of BDSM but not to the point of weird. I wasn't sure what he meant by any of that, so I nodded and pretended to agree with him. He didn't intimidate me or make me nervous like some people. I think this one is going to work out. I've got a good feeling.

CHAPTER 18

"SO, WHAT'S *YOUR* NAME?"

"Gin."

"Gin? Like the drink?"

It's taken several days, but I've finally got the clothes and the hair that is appealing to my second participant. "Uh, sure."

"That's cool," Mr. Punk Rocker—I guess I should call him Kelvin—says, standing next to a display of guitars. "So, what can I help you with today?"

"I'm thinking about learning to play an instrument. I've always wanted to play something."

"You wanna play something?" he says as he leans in close to my ear.

Damn, the guy doesn't waste any time. Peach told me to prepare myself, that this guy was going to be much more aggressive than Levi could ever be. I know she's right. I interviewed him, so I know he's super experienced. It's just... no matter how prepared I think I am, I'm not sure I'm ready for the Kelvins of the world.

Courage, damn it! I suck in a lungful of air, push my shoulders

99

back, look directly into his deep blue eyes, and say, "Yeah. I wanna play something." *I did it! Yay me!*

Chuckling in a deep rumble, Kelvin walks me over to the ukuleles. "This would be a good instrument for a beginner. You can pretty much learn how to play it by watching YouTube videos."

I place my hand on my torn black jeans-covered hip and shift it dramatically. "Well, what if I want personal lessons?"

He steps closer to me, right into my personal space. "You want personal lessons?"

Having no idea where this confidence is coming from, I step toward him and rest my hand on his chest. "Yeah," I whisper. "I want *very* personal lessons."

"Nice." He nods as he raises a hand to stroke a purple strand of hair that's resting on my shoulder. "Bring Out Your Dead is playing at Smith's tonight."

"Oh yeah?" Smith's is a local bar known for its eclectic live music. They'll play anything from country to whatever the hell Bring Out Your Dead plays.

"Yeah." He nods. "Be there. Ten thirty."

Ten thirty? That's bedtime on a school night, and he's just going out? I'll need a nap today to make that happen. "Maybe."

Chuckling again, Kelvin steps back. "Cool. Maybe I'll see you there."

"Cool. Now, can I buy one of those ukuleles?"

"Sure. What color?"

They come in a range of colors. I want the pink one, but I'm supposed to be punk. *Boo.* "The black one."

"Great choice. Be right back. It'll be fifty bucks plus tax."

"Cool." I nod as I start to grab my debit card. I think better of it and grab cash since my actual name is imprinted on the debit card. I'm sort of excited about the ukulele. The truth is, I've always wanted to learn how to play an instrument. I might as well start here.

Kelvin rings me up, and as I'm walking out the door, he yells, "See you tonight, Gin."

"Sure. Maybe." I look back, giving him a small smile. I don't want to sound too excited about my date tonight. I'm supposed to be cool.

Walking quickly down the block to Peach's car, I slide into the passenger seat clutching the ukulele box.

"Wait. You bought an instrument?"

"Sure. Why not? I've always wanted to learn."

"So, you're going to learn now? While we're living together? In the same apartment?"

I giggle. "Yeah. I'll be quiet. It's just a tiny guitar." I wait for a response, but all I get is a dirty look and a growl. "He wants me to meet him at Smith's tonight."

Her mood suddenly lifts, and she squeals with delight. "Sweet! You're getting so good at this flirting shit, Virginia."

"It's Gin."

"Oh, right, *Gin*. You've landed two out of two."

"I attribute it to the new look."

"That's true. Your makeup looks amazing, if I do say so myself."

She's got me looking very goth with an extra-light shade of foundation and powder, a dramatic cat eye with liquid eyeliner, and some mascara called Better Than Sex. I'll have to take their word for that. I've got on a dark purple lipstick that looks surprisingly perfect with the purple strands of hair my hairdresser gave me. She used temporary dye to make my hair a shade darker than my mousy brown, then added purple to several sections. It looks pretty cool.

"Guess what that means?"

"I know. Shopping," I deadpan.

"Exactly!"

AT PRECISELY ELEVEN O'CLOCK, I pull open the door to Smith's and nearly fall on my ass from the sheer volume of the music. This isn't my cup of tea. Give me some Meghan Trainor or some Charlie Puth any day. *Ooh*, or some Shawn Mendes. He's adorable. This loud, banging, screaming stuff hurts my brain.

I make my way through the sea of people all dressed exactly alike. I shouldn't judge since I'm dressed like everyone else too. Peach talked me into wearing a torn white T-shirt, a leatherlike miniskirt, fishnet tights, and some old Doc Martens she had in her closet. My makeup is the same as earlier today, only more dramatic. I fit in. *Yay?*

I stop at the bar first.

The bartender looks a little intimidating with his neck tattoos, bald head, and scowl. "What do you want?" he asks angrily.

"Uh, um, can I have a margarita?" I love me some margaritas. Strawberry and peach are my favorites. Instead of answering me, he just stares. I take that as a no. "So, what about wine?" More stares. "Fine. I'll have a beer."

He doesn't ask me what kind of beer, just pours me whatever he's got coming out of the tap and slams it on the bar top. "Seven bucks," he growls.

"Seven bucks?" *That's outrageous!* But instead of arguing, I pull out a ten and lay it on the counter. He grabs the bill and stuffs it into his pocket, then moves on to the next customer. I guess they don't give change.

"You overpaid, Virginia," says a deep voice next to me. "Beer is only a buck tonight."

I turn until I'm face-to-abdomen with *him*. "Baker? What are you doing here?" How did he recognize me? I look completely different.

Moving in a little closer, Baker has me blocked between the bar and his big body. "I'm here with some of the guys from the team," he says as he checks me out from head to toe. "What's with this look? Is it Halloween or something?"

"Ha-ha! *Very funny.* As a matter of fact, I'm meeting a date here."

"A date? You're on another date? Not the same guy...."

"Yeah, no. Not the same guy. Not that it's any of your business," I say defiantly, putting a fist on my hip. "Can you please move out of my way? I need to find Mr. P—I mean Kelvin."

"Kelvin? Kelvin Lewis?"

Great. He knows Kelvin. "How do you know Kelvin?"

"Everybody knows Kelvin. He's a douche and a player."

"He's nice." I haven't seen him be the least bit douchey. "Please step aside, Baker."

He slowly shifts his body just enough to allow me to escape his cocoon. Weaving in and out of the crowd, I'm bumped and jostled so much that by the time I spot Kelvin, my beer has spilled all over my white tee. "Great." You can see the lace of my white bra now.

I step up to Kelvin, who's bouncing up and down to the beat of the music in the middle of a group doing the same thing.

When he sees me, he smiles. "Gin!" he yells. "You made it!"

I nod as I pretend to drink from my empty cup. He weaves away from his little dance party and makes it to me. Leaning down, he kisses me on the mouth. It wasn't a quick peck either. Nope, it was tongue and everything. I wasn't ready for that or the slobbery wetness he left behind.

Discreetly wiping my mouth, I yell, "Great show!"

"It's fuckin' awesome!" He throws his arms into the air as he bounces back out to his circle, waving for me to follow.

I do so reluctantly. I'm not a good dancer, and I don't see myself being any better at bouncing. When I get close, he grabs my hand, spins me, and pulls me close, wrapping his long arms around me to rest on my stomach. I don't like it. My stomach is not my best feature. It's my worst feature, I feel. It's soft and round and... I can't think about what else it is because Kelvin's hand just slid into the waistband of my pleather skirt. Seriously? I just got here, and he's already got his hand down my pants, er, skirt?

I freeze where I am and place my hand over his.

"No?" he asks, confused.

I shake my head. "Not here."

"Whatever," he spits, pulling away from me. "I'm gettin' a beer."

I watch him stomp off toward the bar. "Sure, I'll take another one," I mutter to myself as I step off the dance floor. God, what is it with guys? Chivalry is most definitely D-E-A-D.

I wait for almost ten minutes before I give up and go in search of Kelvin. When I find him, he's making out with another girl. "She's not punk," I mutter. She's the opposite of punk. I'd say she's way more Malibu Barbie with her long blonde hair, pink miniskirt, and lace top. "She's got on four-inch bejeweled stilettos, for God's sake," I mutter.

"Another one bites the dust, eh?" Baker says smugly.

"Shut up, Baker." I throw my hands in the air in the universal 'I give up' motion. "Men suck," I growl.

"We don't all suck."

I spin around so fast I make myself dizzy. "You're the worst of all, Baker Stark."

"Me?" he says, looking hurt. "I'm one of the good guys."

Scoffing, I turn and make my way toward the door. There's no reason to stay in this godforsaken place any longer. I need quiet. I push my way through the throng and out the front door into the chilly autumn night. Stomping down the sidewalk, I realize my feet hurt. The damn Doc Martens I'm wearing are a size too small. "The things I do for research."

As I stroll, I hear a car behind me but ignore it. When it doesn't pass and seems to stay right behind me, I turn and find a black Nissan. "Great! That's all I need. The kissing bandit."

Rolling down the passenger window, Baker leans over. "Get in, Virginia."

"No. I'm fine. I can walk."

"Get in the damn car, Virginia." I look over at him just as he adds, "Please?"

I stomp one foot down hard like a spoiled child. "Fine!" Sliding into the passenger seat, I make myself look at anything and everything except Baker. It's bad enough I can smell him. He smells good. Besides, I know what he looks like, and he looks outstanding in his low-slung jeans and snug gray ISU Hockey tee. Because I'm angry and being a bitch, I snap, "Don't you ever wear anything other than ISU Hockey clothes?"

"Sure."

Sure? That's it? "Whatever," I mutter.

"What'd I do?"

I turn to look at him. "What do you mean?"

He hasn't pulled away from the curb yet, so his body is turned to face me. "What'd I do to make you so angry with me?"

"Nothing!" I spit. Taking a deep breath, I say calmly, "Nothing. You didn't do anything, Baker."

I feel his hand on my neck, and as soon as I turn to look at him, his lips are on mine. I moan into his mouth as I reach for him, scraping my fingers into his hair as he leans down until his upper body is on my side of the car.

"You drive me fucking crazy, Virginia."

I'm not sure what he means but I'm not going to overanalyze it right now. No, right now I need to kiss Baker Stark. Badly. So I ignore him and kiss him hard and fast. I'm in control of this kiss, and it feels amazing. I feel his big, warm palm slide up my leg and beneath my skirt. His lips leave mine, but they don't stop kissing me across my cheek and down the side of my neck. I shiver when he kisses the spot where my neck meets my shoulder.

Whispering as his lips touch my body, he says, "I don't like that you keep changing yourself, but I'm not gonna lie, this outfit is fucking hot, Virginia."

I gently pull his head up so our mouths are millimeters apart. I know I should say something, but I don't want to talk. I just want to kiss him, and I want him to kiss me back. I lean in and slide my tongue over his lips until he opens his mouth. I turn my head to the right just enough. I feel his hands moving again. I feel him touch me front and center. He's tentative, but when his finger presses down and circles me, I squeak. Jerking back, I place my hand on his wrist.

He quickly moves his hand out from beneath my skirt. Running his big hands through his hair and over his face, he says, "I'm sorry. I didn't mean to pressure you, Virginia. I just got carried away."

"It's okay. I did too."

Forcing out a big breath, he puts the car in gear and says, "Let me take you home."

"Okay."

We drive in silence to my apartment. When we arrive, Baker opens his door to step out.

"No," I say, touching his forearm. It's then I notice his nice, thick forearm. *Crap. Peach was right about those.* "Don't get out." I open my door and step out, then lean back into his car. "Thanks for the ride, Baker."

"No problem."

I'm about to say something more when he puts his car into gear. I shut the door quickly and watch him speed away. I think I made him angry. No, he's not angry. Is he disappointed? He seemed to want me sexually. What would have happened if I hadn't stopped him? Would I be in the back seat of his car losing my maidenhood?

I stop walking when the thought occurs to me: does Baker Stark want me? "Nah!" But he seems to be everywhere I am. He's always approaching me, talking to me, kissing me. Can it be? It doesn't seem possible, but there are just too many coincidences. Before my survey, I'd never laid eyes on Baker. Maybe it's true. It must be.

"Oh my God. Baker Stark wants me!" I shout as I enter my apartment.

CHAPTER 19

"WHO'S BAKER STARK?" asks my roommate from the lap of one Ryan Reynolds. I recognize him from the day of the survey, plus he's wearing those stupid striped overalls again.

"Baker Stark? He's the goalie for the ISU Hockey team. He's good. Could go pro. At least that's the word on the street," says Ryan Reynolds in the stupid striped overalls. "I've met him a few times. Nice guy." He looks up at Peach, then at me, asking, "You doing him?"

"Uh...."

"Ryan!" Peach squeaks as she slaps him on his chest. "Don't be crass."

"Well, I was just going to say that's a surprise. He's usually with chicks that are...." He looks at Peach, then at me. I can tell he's afraid to say the next word, but he does it anyway. "Different?"

"Different how?" asks Peach.

Damn it, Peach. Shut the hell up. That's what I want to say, but I don't.

"Uh, well, they're usually blonde and just a bit smaller."

"Smaller?"

Peach, jeez. This is getting painful.

"Yeah, smaller. Not fat."

"What!" Peach says, jumping off his lap. "Virginia is beautiful."

"Babe. Don't get upset. She's not that ugly or anything—"

"Get out, Ryan!" she says, pointing to the door. "If you're going to be so judgmental about a woman who is so obviously beautiful and sweet and kind, then you should go. I hate guys like you."

"Peach?" Ryan whines. "Babe, I didn't mean it like that."

Peach stands her ground, still pointing at the door. "Just go."

He walks slowly to the door with his head hanging low and shoulders slumped.

"Peach, he didn't mean it."

Ryan turns, hoping my words are enough, but they aren't.

"Out!" she shouts.

Like Eeyore, Ryan Reynolds lumbers out the door as Peach slams it shut behind him. "Men!" she shouts. Flopping back onto the couch, she says, "Okay. Spill. Who's Becker Sparks, and why do you think he wants to do you?"

"Uh, it's Baker Stark, and you just kicked out your boyfriend."

"Meh. It's good for him. He was getting a little complacent, and we've just started dating. Gotta keep 'em on their toes, grasshopper. Now start talking."

"Good to know." I sit down on the sofa and kick off the terrible shoes Peach loaned me, bring my legs up under my butt, and lean back on the pillow. "I need to start at the beginning."

"Hang on. Let me get a glass of wine. You want one?"

"Yes, please. I need a drink!" As soon as we're on the couch sipping our wine, I begin the story with the interview (and the kiss) in the library study room. I also mention his two visits to the coffee shop, the text messages, as well as the two times he gave me a ride home after my disastrous dates (and more kisses).

"Wow! You've been a busy girl," Peach says, sipping her wine.

"It's nothing."

"I don't think so. I think it's something. What's he look like?"

"I don't have any pictures."

"He's probably on the ISU Hockey team website. Bring that up on your phone."

I pull the phone out of my back pocket. "It's dead." I hop up and run to my room to grab my charging cord. Plugging it into the wall socket closest to the couch, I wait for it to come back to life.

"Oh, good Lord, girl. You've landed yourself a hottie," Peach says, staring at her phone. "Is this *him*?" She turns the phone to face me. On her screen is a picture of Baker Stark in his hockey outfit.

"Yep, that's him."

"*Mommy*," she whimpers. "He's the hottest thing I've ever seen in my life. You've kissed him? Three times?"

"Yes." I look down at my phone.

"Dayum," she mutters. While she does that, my phone comes to life and chimes several times, notifying me I've got some new text messages. There are three from my mom that I want to delete but won't and one from an unknown number.

Unknown Number: *I'm sorry about tonight. I let it get out of hand. You aren't the kind of girl I usually go for, Virginia. You're a good girl— the girl next door—the kind you take home to Mom. The problem is, I'm the kind of guy who doesn't take girls home to Mom. I'm sorry if I've confused you, but you and me? It's not gonna happen.*

As soon as I see the first four words in the text, I know it's Baker. I should probably add his name to my contents, but why bother after what he just wrote? How can a text be both thoughtful and gut-wrenchingly painful at the same time? I can only concentrate on the bad part, because the thoughtful part of it is already forgotten. The only thing that remains is the part where he said I wasn't good enough for him.

"What's wrong, Virginia? Your face lost all of its color."

Instead of speaking, I hand over my phone so she can read the text.

"Did Blake send this?"

"Baker. Yeah."

"What an asshole."

"Uh-huh. I think he was trying to be sort of nice."

"Sort of nice? Are you kidding me? This is ridiculous." Peach reads the text one more time. "Okay, you've got some options here."

"Options."

"One, you could ignore the text."

"Uh-huh."

"Two, you could send him an equally scathing rebuttal."

"Okay."

"Three, you could just reply with a simple F-U."

"Good. Yeah."

"Number four, and my personal favorite... you could reply with three words."

"Three words?"

"Yep. Just type 'Who is this?'"

"Who is this? But I know who it is."

"Trust me. It'll drive him bonkers."

"How? He won't care what I write."

"He will." Peach starts to giggle.

"Fine." I grab the phone out of her hand and type.

Me: *Who is this?*

"Believe me. I give him less than five minutes before he responds."

In two minutes and twenty-three seconds, we hear a ding.

Unknown Number: *Who is this? Virginia, you know who the fuck this is!*

I start to respond, but Peach touches my hand. "Wait. Don't reply. There'll be more."

How does she know this stuff?

Unknown Number: *This is Baker. BAKER. Jesus. I just had my tongue down your throat and my hand on your pussy. Remember me now?*

Peach turns to me with a little pink blush. Nothing compared to mine, though. "He had his hand on your lady-land?"

It's my turn to laugh now. "Lady-land?" I titter. "That's a new one. And not really. He touched me over the panties. He didn't actually touch *me*." I reread our texts and laugh again. "Now what?"

"Wait about an hour before you send a response."

"An hour?"

"Yeah, it'll make him crazy that you haven't written. He'll see that you read his text too. Hell, I wouldn't put it past him to write you back in the next thirty minutes."

"You've been right so far, Peach. I'm not going to bet against you."

"Wise, young grasshopper. Very wise."

❧

JUST AS PEACH PROGNOSTICATED, Baker wrote me again. I had to wait closer to forty-five minutes for it, but it came nonetheless.

Unknown Number: *Virginia? This isn't funny. I meant what I said in my first text. I'm sorry if it hurts you.*

Per Peach's instructions, my next response was simple and immediate.

Me: *Whatevs.*
Unknown Number: *Whatevs? WTF? I didn't think a girl like you would do this to someone like me.*

The next text is all me. The nerve!

Me: *Well, I have no idea what to say to that. A girl like me? Someone like you? You've piqued my curiosity. You mean a smart woman and a jock? Or do you mean a fat woman and a stud muffin like you? Either way, you can now move on with your life. I'm good.*
Unknown Number: *Jesus. You make me crazy. And you're not fat.*
Me: *Alrighty then. Good talk. See ya.*
Me: *Oops. Guess not.*
Unknown Number: *Jesus.*

There were no more texts that night, or for three nights after. On the fifth night, however, I get a little surprise at three in the morning.

Unknown Number: *Virgeninia?*
Me: *?*
Unknown Number: *It's me. What r u doing?*

Is Baker intoxicated?

Me: *Sleeping.*
Unknown Number: *You want company? I'd love to sleep with you. I miss you.*

I'm getting my first drunken booty call from a guy who doesn't even want to see me again. Wonderful.

Me: *No.*
Unknown Number: *Virginzia, you make me crazy.*
Me: *So you keep saying. Sorry.*

Not sorry.

Unknown Number: *Please? Let me come over. I make you feezl so goods, babe.*
Me: *I have company.*

I'm not making that up. My dad is here this weekend for homecoming. He got in late tonight. We've been up talking for hours, which is why I'm awake to respond to these texts at three in the morning.

Unknown Number: *Who? Who's there? I'm gonns kicks his ass. You r mine.*

Okayyyy. That's weird. I wish Peach were up so I could talk to her about this, but maybe I can channel her right now. She'd either ignore his texts or just shut him down.

Me: *It's none of your business. Go to bed and sleep it off.*

I opt for the shutdown. It's for the best. He'll regret this tomorrow. No reason to make it worse for him, because he's obviously a lot drunk and a little deranged. When he doesn't respond again, I sigh with relief. I pull my blanket up to my chest as I lie down on my couch. I gave the bed to my dad. He had a long drive, and he's no spring chicken. He deserves a good night's sleep.

I'm not sure what wakes me, but I'm startled out of sleep. When I hear knocking on my front door, I throw my blanket off and race to stop the noise. "Shhh, who is it?" I hiss.

"Bakerz."

"Shit. Go home!" I hiss.

"No. Open the door, beautiful. Let me see you. Then... then I'll go."

I pull the door open, but it only opens a couple of inches thanks to the security chain. "Baker. Go home. It's late. How did you get up here?"

He leans over, giving me a whiff of his breath. "The door was op-open."

No doubt some idiot in the building stuck the brick there again. Tomorrow I'm going to throw that brick into Lake Laverne.

"S-sorry. I went out with the guys. We, uh, I drank. A lot."

"No. Really?"

He smiles and points at me. "You're bein' s-sarcastic." He smiles with pride. "See? I'm not that drunk."

"Good for you," I deadpan. "You didn't drive, did you?"

"Nah. Tigger dropped me off."

Tigger? Wow, he's really out of it. Well, thank goodness for small favors. "Go home, Baker."

"Just let me come in. I'll just crash on your couch and leave first thing in the morning."

I'm torn. While I don't want him here, I certainly don't want him out on the mean streets of Ames, Iowa, either. Who knows what kind of mischief he could get into? "Fine. But be quiet. People are asleep."

I push the door closed and remove the chain. Opening it wide, I step aside to let Baker in. As he passes, he looks at me from head to toe.

"You're so fucking beautiful, Virginia." He touches my stomach, then slides his hand around my waist to my lower back.

My skin tingles from his touch. Damn it. "Yeah. Right," I mutter under my breath. I'm wearing a pair of old jogging shorts and a soft old T-shirt. Nothing fancy.

Leaning in to me, he presses a soft kiss on my lips, then whispers, "You make me crazy, Virginia." He starts to walk away but adds, "And hard. You make me rock hard, babe." We both look down at his jeans and see they're noticeably tented.

"Good to know." I'm trying to be cool. I really am. Seeing him aroused like that does things to me. I push those feelings down. Wayyyyy down.

When he spots the couch, he makes a beeline for it, kicking off his shoes. He pulls his sweatshirt and the tee he wore beneath over his head and drops them on the floor.

I see the bare-chested version of Baker Stark. Ladies, no lie, the guy is ripped. His muscles have muscles. "Wow," I whisper just loud enough for me to hear. Or so I thought.

"You like what you see?" he says, turning around to face me.

"No."

Baker chuckles. "Right. Chicks like all of thisss," he slurs as he runs his hands down his stomach to his crotch. He gives himself a little squeeze before he reaches out to pull his jeans down to midthigh.

"What are you doing?" I squeak.

"Getting ready for bed. I sleep nude, but I'm just gonna wear my boxers. S'okay?"

"Fine," I say resignedly. When he kicks his jeans off, I can't help myself. I stare. He's built like a Greek god, like Zeus. Yeah, definitely like Zeus.

Flopping onto the couch on his side, he twists and turns until he's on his back. In mere seconds he's snoring, and I'm just standing next to him, staring down at this man. I'm startled when he rearranges himself again, then smile when I hear him mumbling. I'd like to tell you I heard my name, but it's impossible to say.

Sighing, I grab my pillow from below his feet and head into Peach's room. She's only got a full-sized bed, so it's going to be a tight squeeze. I gently nudge her body, but she doesn't move. "Peach," I whisper-hiss. "Move over."

"Go away," she grumbles.

"Slide over. I need to sleep in here."

"No. Why?"

"Baker's on the couch."

That woke her up damn fast. "What? Why?"

"He drunk dialed me. I think he wanted a booty call."

"No way!"

"Way."

She slides out of bed and moves out to the living room to get a look for herself. "Holy hell. He's even better in person."

"I know. It's too bad he's such an asshat."

"Yeah, that's a shame."

"Come on. I'm going to need to be up with Dad in like two hours. I need a little sleep."

"You should slide in there next to him. Freak him out in the morning."

I look at her and blink. "You think?"

"Pretend you did it on the couch without a condom and that you want to name the baby after your father, who happens to be in the next room."

"Seriously?"

"No, dork!" She giggles. "Come on. Let's get some sleep. You've still got so much to learn, young grasshopper."

"Yeah." *Don't I know it?*

CHAPTER 20

Baker

POUNDING. That's what it feels like someone's doing to my head right now. When I blink awake, I see an unfamiliar light fixture on the ceiling. "Where am I?"

"You're at my daughter's apartment. Who are you?" asks an older dude standing over me.

"Your daughter? Who's that?"

"Virginia. I repeat. Who. Are. You?"

"Baker. Baker Stark." What the hell happened last night? I remember doing some shots with the guys from the team. *Shit! Shots. I can't handle shots.* I run my fingers through the hair that probably looks like it's been through a blender. Looking up, I see the older man, Virginia's father, and attempt a smile.

Surprising me, Mr. Virginia asks, "Coffee?"

"Oh, yeah. Thanks." Now if he just had some greasy bacon and eggs, I'd be set. There's nothing like a greasy breakfast to help with a hangover. And I've got one hell of one.

"Come on. It's in the kitchen."

I sit up and realize I'm only in my boxers. Great. Looking around, I spot my T-shirt and jeans. Slipping on the shirt first, I stand to hook my legs into my jeans, then quickly zip and buckle my belt. I grab my phone from the back pocket and make my way into the kitchen. Kitchen? I wouldn't call it a kitchen. A kitchenette is more like it. The thing is barely big enough for one person. I take the coffee that's offered and sit at the tiny breakfast bar.

"Sugar? Milk?" Virginia's dad seems nice.

"Neither. Black is good."

"Me too. You know, it's interesting. Most of you kids these days are so into the mocha-cheenos and the lah-tee-dahs. It's hard to keep up with all that fancy shit."

I chuckle and regret it. My head hurts like someone smashed a brick over it.

"So, are you Virginia's boyfriend?"

"Uh, no."

"No?"

"No. We're, uh, just friends."

"Friends?"

"Uh-huh." Well, we're sort of friends. I peer down at my phone to check for messages. I don't have any new ones, just the old ones from last night. Okay, maybe we *aren't* friends. Not after last night. She's gonna hate me now. Shit! Could I have been a bigger douche? *"Let me come over. I make you feezl so goods, babe"*? Jesus. I'm a tool.

"So, Baker, what do you do?"

Okay, here we go. The parental questions begin. I can't deal. Especially not questions from a dad who I'll never see again in my lifetime. "I'm a student."

"You're a pretty big guy. Do you play sports?"

"Hockey. Goalie."

"Nice. I love the Red Wings."

Ugh, *everybody* loves the Red Wings. I prefer the Sharks, though I'd play for any of them and be happy as a clam. Yeah, like I'm going to make the pros. By the time I pay my dues through the ranks of all the minor leagues, I'll be eighty before anyone even wants to call me up. Nope, I need to focus on graduate school and a degree in physical therapy.

I look up and remember I'm supposed to respond or something. "Red Wings are cool. I follow the San Jose Sharks."

"Brent Burns?"

"Yeah," I say, surprised. "He's awesome."

"He is." I watch the man sip his coffee. If I only knew his name....

"So, what are your intentions with my daughter?"

And boom, there it is. "No intentions. We're just friends."

"Hm," he says, sipping again. "She's a pretty special young woman."

"She is. She's a nice friend."

"She's got dreams. Goals."

"Cool." What the ever-loving...?

"She deserves to have the world handed to her."

"Okay. I'm sure she'll find someone—"

"But she's also vulnerable."

Vulnerable? "Okay. I'll keep that in mind."

"Good."

We sip our coffee, trying not to make eye contact with the each other. The awkward silence is cut short when a tall blonde woman walks into the kitchen. *Damn, she's smokin' hot.*

"Well, hello, gentlemen," she coos.

Fuck. I'd love to—

"Hey, Dad," says a much smaller woman with purple hair.

What is it about Virginia that makes me so nuts? Her hair is all wrong for her, and this morning it's a little bit all over the place, which is kind of cute. Her face is so damn pretty. It doesn't matter what color her hair is. She's got these little freckles on her turned-up nose, and the most beautiful blue eyes. Or are they gray? They sparkle, and they're just a tad too large for her small face.

But, hands down, her best feature is her lips. All I have to do is look at her lips and feel myself get hard. I can't help it. I know what she can do with those little babies. And they are little. Their shape is like a pink rosebud. It's why I kissed her that first day in the library. Those fucking lips were taunting me. She kept licking them nervously, then biting them with irritation when I wouldn't answer her questions with more than yes-or-no answers. It was fucking adorable. Yeah, her lips are stellar. They fucking haunt me.

"Good morning, peanut. Sleep well?"

"Um, sure."

Why do I get the feeling she's lying?

"Peach and I shared a bed." She looks over at me but doesn't smile or scowl. We just make eye contact for a second. "She's a bed hog."

"I am not!" snaps the stone-cold foxy blonde. "You're the bed hog. I woke up with no pillow or blanket. You stole them all."

Damn, I'd let her steal my blanket. *What? No. Stop imagining Virginia naked in your bed, Baker.*

"Sorry, Peach. I was cold," says Virginia quietly, almost shyly.

"Is your name Peach?" I ask.

"Nope. Penny. But everyone calls me Peach. And you're Brock?"

"Baker."

"You play soccer?"

"Hockey."

"Right. Damn, Virginia. You got all that wrong?"

"I couldn't remember. Sorry."

Okay, now she's fucking with me. Pretending she didn't

remember my name? I'll accept the confusion about my sport, but not my name. "Welp, on that note, I think I'll head out. Virginia?"

"Yeah?"

"May I speak to you out in the hallway for a moment?"

"Uh, I guess." She shrugs.

I look around to make sure I didn't forget anything. I don't want to have to come back here. I turn to the other two people, "Mr. uh...."

"Murray. Bill Murray."

No way! Bill Murray? I wish I'd known that before. We could have talked about his namesake instead of his "vulnerable" daughter, but I say nothing. I don't want to start up a new conversation. Nope, I want to get the hell out of here. "Mr. Murray and Peach. It was nice meeting you both."

"You too, son. Good luck with hockey."

"Thanks." I grab the doorknob and pull open the door, holding it wide for her to walk through first.

I can't help myself. I look down and see her plump, round ass in some of those skintight yoga pants chicks like to wear. Jesus. Her ass is perfection. I should know; I've had my hands on it several times. I practically have to will my dick to stay down.

When she gets out into the hallway, she turns around and crosses her arms under her breasts, forcing them upward.

Groaning at the sight, I force my eyes up. "I'm sorry about last night."

She shrugs. "It's no biggie."

"I shouldn't have gotten your hopes up like that."

She stares at me and blinks.

I can see all of her emotions as they pass through her eyes and over her face. She went from surprised to disappointed and has now landed squarely on anger. "Who in the hell do you think you are, Brock?"

"My name is Baker, and you know it," I say, pointing at her.

"You're really full of yourself, aren't you?"

"Sure. Why wouldn't I be?"

"You texted *me*, correct?"

"Yeah."

"You showed up at *my* door," she says, pointing at herself.

"Yep."

Turning her finger around to direct it at me, she says, "Then I think it's you who shouldn't get their hopes up."

"Why would I?"

"Exactly."

I have no idea where this conversation is going, or hell, what it even means. She starts to make her way past me and back to her door when I stop her with my palm on her stomach. I slide it around to her waist and pull her in to me. Leaning down, I get within about an inch of her lips. Her breath catches, and I can see her pulse beating in her neck. I've got her. Fuck. I was going to tease her, but it's impossible. I move to kiss her, but she pulls back.

"These lips"—she points at her mouth—"are off-limits to you. No more kisses!" She stomps past me and back into her apartment, slamming the door shut as she goes.

What the fuck just happened? "Jesus. That girl drives me crazy."

Before I walk away, I adjust myself in my pants, willing my dick to go back down. Pulling my phone from my back pocket, I call my buddy for a lift. I need to get the hell out of here.

"Tig?" I hear him drop the phone and curse in the background.

"What the hell time is it, Bake?"

"Early. Come pick me up."

"Walk, asshole."

"Please pick me up. I'll buy breakfast," I say sugar-sweetly so he'll do me this solid.

He shouts, "Fuck," in the background. "Fine. Are you at the same place I dropped you off?"

"Yeah. I'll be waiting outside. Hurry up."

"Fuck you. I'll get there when I get there."

Tig, also known on the team as Tigger due to his bright red hair and constant need to be moving, only lives a few blocks away. I lean against the brick wall and rest my head on the rough surface. I'm so tired I don't notice the tall blonde standing next to me in some tight-ass running gear.

"Blake?"

"It's Baker and you know it," I reply without opening my eyes.

"Whatever. Listen, I know all about this thing you've got for Virginia."

"And?" She wants in. I know chicks like her. They'll fuck over their friends to get to me. I've seen it. Friendships lost over it. It sucks, but whatever.

"And... I want to give you a little piece of advice."

"Advice?" Okay. Not what I was expecting. "What advice?"

"If you don't stop dicking around, you're going to lose her."

"Lose her? I don't want her."

"Sure you don't. You—"

This is pointless. "I don't."

She pushes a short strand of hair away from her stunning face. She's pretty. Gorgeous, really, but for some reason, I'm not interested.

"Can I finish?"

I nod.

"You do want her. Who wouldn't? She's beautiful, kind, sweet, honest, smart as hell, loyal, and, dare I say, sexy."

"You gay?"

She throws her head back to laugh, exposing her long neck. "No, asshat. I'm not gay. Not that there's anything wrong with that. I just think the guy that gets with Virginia is going to be one lucky guy. You'd better not sit on your ass too long, Blake. She's got lots of offers."

"Offers? What off—"

Tig pulls up in his piece-of-shit Chevy Cobalt and honks, then yells out his open window, "Let's go! I've got shit to do."

"You'd better go. Your, uh, chariot awaits."

I watch her set off on a run down the street. She's down the block and around the corner before I even get to Tig's car.

"That her?" Tig says with awe. "She's hot as fuck, dude."

"That's the roommate."

"Holy hell, is your girl as hot as that?"

I squeeze my eyes shut and think of Virginia. "Hotter."

"Fuck! You lucky sum-bitch."

"It's not serious. Just a hookup."

"Well, then. I can't wait to meet her," he says, winking. "Fair game."

I turn and slap Tig on the chest. "Don't even think about it," I growl. "Don't even think about it."

"Jeez, dude, get a grip."

We drive in silence to IHOP. I promised him breakfast, and he picked this place? It's surprisingly expensive for a pancake house. I know I won't get out of here without spending thirty bucks on him. But Tig's a good guy. He's the only friend I've got here at Iowa State. I get along with the other guys on the team, but none of them get me like he does.

As soon as we've placed our orders, Tig starts. "So, tell me what's going on with your girl."

See? He knows me. "She's not 'my' girl," I say with air quotes. "Her name is Virginia, and I can't seem to shake her."

"Shake her? She a stalker, dude?"

"No," I say as I reach out to punch him on the arm. "I can't stop thinking about her. Everything she does surprises me. She's different."

"The keepers usually are," he says with a sigh.

"I'm not 'keeping' her. I'm throwing her back. I don't have time for a girlfriend."

Tig tilts his head back and laughs. "Too busy? What do you do besides go to class and play hockey? You don't have to work. *Ever.*"

I nod. "I know." Another thing Tig knows is my net worth. I confided in him one drunken night over a bottle of Jack. I made him swear secrecy—practically a blood oath. I don't want anyone to know I've got money. The team thinks the house belongs to my grandmother and that it's off-limits for parties and shit. I run my hands over my tired face. Hangovers suck. "I just need to shake her. Trust me. She's not for me."

"Bro, I wish you'd let someone in. You deserve to be happy. You deserve a good woman in your life."

I scoff. "Yeah, right."

"You do."

When our breakfast lands in front of us, neither of us speaks until it's all devoured, so about ten minutes. What can I say? We were hungry.

"All right, I'm gonna drop you off at home, and then I'm due for a workout. What about you?"

"Later. I need some sleep." Now that I've eaten enough for three men, I need to pass out.

"Call me. Maybe I'll go in for a second one later."

"You're a machine. Thanks for the ride, man. See you later." Stepping out of his car, I make my way up the brick sidewalk to my house. It's a nice four-bedroom, four-bath house on the east side of Ames. I wasn't lying to Virginia the night I saw her on the street. I live a couple of blocks from there, in a newer housing development. According to my grandmother, this neighborhood has large lots and plenty of curb-appeal.

Flopping onto my king-size bed, I grab my phone to see the text messages from last night.

Me: *Virginia? This isn't funny. I meant what I said in my first text. I'm sorry if it hurts you.*
V: *Whatevs.*

Me: *Whatevs? WTF? I didn't think a girl like you would do this to someone like me.*
V: *Well, I have no idea what to say to that. A girl like me? Someone like you? You've piqued my curiosity. You mean a smart woman and a jock? Or do you mean a fat woman and a stud muffin like you? Either way, you can now move on with your life. I'm good.*
Me: *Jesus. You make me crazy. And you're not fat.*
V: *Alrighty then. Good talk. See ya.*
V: *Oops. Guess not.*
Me: *Jesus.*

Then the drunken texts begin. I'm not sure I can bring myself to read them, but I do.

Me: *Virginia*
V: *?*
Me: *It's me. What r u doinz?*

Doinz?

V: *Sleeping.*
Me: *You want company? I'd love to sleep with you. I miss you.*
V: *No.*
Me: *Virginzia, you make me crazy.*
V: *So you keep saying. Sorry.*
Me: *Please? Let me come over. I make you feezl so goods, babe.*
V: *I have company.*
Me: *Who? Who's there? I'm gonns kicks his ass. You r mine.*
V: *It's none of your business. Go to bed and sleep it off.*

I cringe as I read through everything. Maybe Penelope or Peach or whatever her name was is right. Virginia doesn't seem to play games or mince words. At least now I know that when she told me she had company, she *actually* had company, her dad. It's not something I'm used to—a truthful girl. I'm used to women who pout and whine until they get their way. I could barely get this one to let me crash on her couch. After reading my text messages, I'd say the roles are now reversed. I was the one whining and pouting.

As I'm about to fall asleep, I murmur, "Damn, Virginia Murray, you make me crazy."

CHAPTER 21

"Dad?"

"Yeah, honey?"

"Thanks for coming. I've had such a great time with you." We did have a fantastic time. We went to the football game and then out to eat. I gave him a campus tour, showing him where all of my classes are held. At the university bookstore, he bought himself a new T-shirt and bought me a new sweatshirt.

We stopped into The Coffee Bean to say hello, but things there are still a little weird. Jackson has been blowing up my phone since the 'incident' with updates and information and messages begging me to come back to work. Evidently, Kip resigned. I think it was his only way to save face and be able to find work in Ames. Word travels fast in this town about stuff like that. Don really wants me back too. He offered me a raise and weekends off. Then he offered the manager job to Jackson, but he turned it down because he wants to concentrate on school and not on running "The dysfunctional-as-fuck Coffee Bean." Maybe they'll hire a new manager who doesn't suck. That'd be awesome.

The one thing Dad and I didn't do was talk about Mom or anything related to the past. We focused on the time we had together and on the future—our future. It was wonderful. But I'm so sad he's going home already. It's Sunday afternoon, and as he's packing his car for the six-hour drive home, he turns to me and wraps his big arms around me. I hear him sniffle just a bit, which causes me to finally lose it.

He rubs comforting circles on my shoulder, saying, "I want to talk to you at least once a week, and I want to see you every month, peanut. We'll talk and figure things out. Come to our house for the holidays. I'll cover your gas and—"

I look up at him. "You know I don't have a car."

"I know, but why don't you?"

"It's a hassle. Peach gets three tickets a week here."

"Well, I'll rent you a car. Or I'll come get you and bring you back. I don't care what it takes, honey."

"Okay, Dad. I'll come visit you for the holidays." Why not? I'm not going to see my mom. She hasn't sent me the letters or even told me if she still has them. All she's done is text me nonstop and leave me super-whiny voice mail messages. Every once in a while, I respond to a text she sends that makes me feel guilty. I get over that quickly, though, the second she starts saying mean things about Dad.

"That's wonderful! I can't wait to tell Tina. She's going to go nuts with the food and the gifts." Dad is smiling from ear to ear.

I don't think I've ever felt this loved, honestly. He sincerely wants me to be part of his family. His wife wants me to be there. I smile up at him and squeeze him tightly. "I can't wait, Dad."

Wiping away a tear, he slides into his compact SUV. "Call me," he says before he shuts the door and quickly rolls the window down.

"You call me when you get home so I know you got home safely."

"Yes, ma'am." He chuckles. "Oh, and good luck fending off Baker."

Huh? "Dad! What do you mean?"

"The guy has it bad for you."

"Trust me. No, he doesn't."

"No, trust me. I'm a guy. He's got it bad for you."

I shake my head and laugh. "Love you, Dad." My dad's wrong, but he's sweet to think someone like Baker could want me.

"Love you more, peanut."

I watch him pull out of my parking lot, waving like an idiot even after he's out of sight. I suck in a deep breath to fend off more tears. They're happy tears. Trust me. They're very happy tears.

Walking back into our apartment, I see Peach stretched out on the couch and Ryan Reynolds sitting on the end of said couch, rubbing her feet.

"Ryan. You're back?" I look at Peach as she winks at me.

He nods smiling brightly. "Thankfully, she forgave me. I'm sorry I said those things the other day. I didn't mean them. I think you're very pretty. Baker would be an idiot to pass up someone as perfect as you."

"Okay, that's enough," Peach mutters. "She gets it. You're sorry."

"I am. Very sorry, Virginia," he says, nodding frantically.

I can't help giggling. My beautiful friend has this guy wrapped around her little finger. I wonder if that will bore her eventually. In the four years we've been friends, she's never had a boyfriend for longer than a month or two. But maybe this will be different. Who knows?

Clapping my hands together, I give myself an excuse to give them privacy. "Okay, well, I've got a paper to write. I'll be in my bedroom."

"Great!" Ryan squeaks.

I can hear them as I walk back to my room. I don't mean to listen, but it's fascinating.

"Down boy," Peach mutters. "You're still on probation."

"Oh, okay. Sure. I agree. I was thoughtless and—"

"Shh, rub my feet and let's watch some porn."

"Oh, God," he moans. "Not porn. Now you're just being cruel."

As my door clicks shut, I hear Peach coo, "Oh, poor Ryan. Come 'ere, babe."

CHAPTER 22

Baker

IT'S SUNDAY NIGHT, and I'm wiped out. I worked out late Saturday afternoon with Tig and again before practice today. Thankfully, I've sweated out all the toxins in my system from my Friday night binge. Now I'm just exhausted.

I plop my ass on my leather sectional and contemplate my next move. It's only nine thirty. I could watch some television; I'm sure there's a game on some cable channel. I could do some homework, but I'm caught up with everything. I slide down onto my couch until my head hits the throw pillow my grandmother insisted I buy. She was right, by the way. It ties the room together. Bringing my arms back behind my head, I stare up at the ceiling. A cobweb has made a home in the corner near the fireplace. I need to make a note of that for the cleaning service. I hate spiders. I shiver just imagining one crawling around my place. They're so fucking *sneaky*.

I'm not sure how it happens, but my mind turns to Virginia.

No, I don't associate her with spiders. I've known some girls that could be, though. You know, spiders in a former life. Not my Virginia. She's the opposite of a spider. *My Virginia?* What the hell?

Sure, I hate the idea that she could be right this minute hanging out with another guy. Maybe hate is the wrong word. Fucking despise is more like it. Imagining her using those luscious lips of hers on some other guy makes me want to punch something. I feel my fists clench.

Rather than drive myself crazy wondering what she's doing, I decide to ask her.

Me: *What are you doing?*
V: …

I watch those three little dots repeatedly move across my screen. It means she's there and thinking about what to say. Or maybe she's trying to decide if she wants to reply. So, I wait. And wait.

Jesus.

Me: *I know you're there. I see the little dots moving.*
V: ***groan** I thought you were through with this little thing with us.*
Me: *There is no 'thing.' I'm just checking on a friend.*
V: …
Me: …
V: *We aren't friends.*
Me: *Sure we are.*
V: *I've got friends. I know how the friend thing works, and you're not my friend.*
Me: *I haven't treated you badly.*
V: …
Me: *I haven't!*

Goddamn it! I haven't!

When she doesn't reply again, I toss my phone on the coffee table. It's my turn to groan. I've got myself turned on again, and she did nothing but piss me off. *I wonder what she's wearing.* Being the glutton for punishment that I am, I ask.

Me: *What are you wearing?*
V: *Nothing*
Me: *Jesus.*
Me: *You drive me crazy, Virginia.*
V: *So you keep saying. Maybe we need to stop texting so you can get over me.*
Me: ***chortle** Yeah, right.*

Yeah, right.

Me: *What are you doing for Halloween?*
V: *Going to a party.*
Me: *Dressing up?*
V: *Of course.*
Me: *I'm going as Jon Snow from Game of Thrones.*
V: *My favorite is Khal Drogo.*
Me: *What about you? What's your costume?*
V: *I'm going as a student.*
Me: *A student? You mean like a nerd?*
V: *Something like that.*
Me: *Sounds, uh, cool. Not. LOL*
V: *...*
Me: *What party are you going to?*
V: *A fraternity party.*
Me: *Which one?*
V: *Baker. Why do you care?*
Me: *Just curious. I'm invited to a few parties. Maybe we'll run into each other.*

When she doesn't respond, I know I went too far. If I find out which party she's going to, I'll look for her, and she knows it. But it occurs to me....

Me: *Wait. Do you have a date?*
V: *Do you care?*

She does. She has a fucking date.

Me: *Who is it?*
V: *No one you know.*
Me: *Try me.*
V: *Goodbye, Blake. Have a good life. Er, I mean week. Have a good week.*
Me: *It's Baker, and you know it!*

Jesus, I hate when she does that. I'm tempted to throw my phone across the room to keep me from texting her again because I'm getting nowhere this way. Now I have to find out which fraternities are having costume parties so I can crash every fucking one of them. I need to find out who she's with so I can beat the asshole to a pulp. I hop up from the couch to grab my phone. Time to get organized.

Me: *You and I are going to some Halloween frat parties next weekend. Get a costume.*
Tig: *Which frat?*
Me: *All of them.*
Tig: *?*
Me: *I'm going as Khal Drogo, so don't pick that one.*

Fuck. I already have a Jon Snow costume from last year. Now I've got a week to get a new one together. Don't say a word, people. The fact that I feel the need to change my costume isn't something I'm ready to talk about, maybe ever.

Tig: *I'll think of something.*
Me: *Cool. See you at practice in the morning. Nite.*
Tig: *Yep. See ya.*

CHAPTER 23

As I stare at myself in the mirror at the salon, I'm nearly speechless. "Wow, I look so different."

"You do! You look gorgeous as a blonde."

"It's not too blonde, is it?" I ask, turning to face Peach.

"No. She just added lots of highlights to your natural color. It looks terrific. You may want to keep this up after all of this, uh, research is finished."

"Maybe." I turn back to look at myself again. The process to get my hair from purple to blonde took over three hours. She had to remove the purple and dark brown dye, then highlight my hair and extensions with blonde. "Do you think Mr. Political Science will notice me?"

"After I get done dressing you up in your costume, you'll have to beat away the admirers."

I know what she's got planned for my costume, and I'm nervous. I'm not one to dress in a sexy or even provocative way, but Peach guaranteed I'll love my outfit. She hasn't told me which costume she decided on for herself either, so I ask, "What costume did you finally choose?"

"Wonder Woman. Ryan's dressing up as Captain America."

"Oh, how sweet," I say a little sarcastically. "A couple's costume?"

"Shut it. It was his idea," says Peach with a laugh. "So, the plan tonight is we're going to meet up at the fraternity, right?"

"Yep, Beta Theta Pi at nine thirty."

"All right. Let's go home and get ready. I've got to meet Ryan at his place at seven."

"Sounds good."

At home, I shower, shave, exfoliate, give myself a manicure and a pedicure, and even throw in an itsy-bitsy nap. Sometimes fifteen minutes is all you need to rejuvenate. At nine o'clock, I stand in front of Peach's full-length mirror and stare. I seem to be doing that a lot lately. I don't recognize myself. I look good. *Really* good. Honest to goodness, I sort of look like Britney Spears in her "Baby One More Time" video. Don't get me wrong; I'm not nearly as pretty as Britney, or as thin, but I've got the loose sort of messy braids and a white button-down shirt that's not buttoned but tied at the waist just like the video. I'm also wearing a plaid skirt that's so short if I even reach for anything, my ass hangs out the back. Peach told me to wear a lacy black bra underneath the white shirt along with black cotton boy short panties. That way if I do bend over, it's opaque. Once I stop staring at myself, I reach for the knee-high socks we bought and a pair of platform heels that aren't *that* uncomfortable.

When I've got everything on, I smile into the mirror. "Yeah. I look good."

CHAPTER 24

Baker

"Dude. What's the deal? We've been to three parties already, but we've barely spent any time at any of them. I was hitting it off with that sexy witch back there," grumbles Tig.

"Sorry. I just haven't felt that thing."

"What thing?"

"You know, that thing that tells you it's a good party."

"I have no idea what you're talking about. Are you drunk?"

"Nah, I'm not drinking."

"Why the hell not?"

"Tell you what, uh...." Glancing over to Tig, I can't help but look him up and down. "Wait, what are you supposed to be again?"

Sighing in frustration, Tig responds, "I'm Jamie from that show *Outlander*."

"Isn't that a chick show?"

"Uh, yeah!" he says like I'm an idiot. "Chicks love that guy, as evidenced by the amount of attention I've been getting. Haven't you noticed?"

I had noticed. My friend doesn't usually draw a lot of attention when we go out, but maybe it's the fact that he's shirtless and wearing a kilt. "I've noticed. Good for you, Tig. Choose wisely."

"Oh, I will."

As we approach the Beta Theta Pi house, I check my watch—11:20 p.m. "This is the last one. If she's, uh, if I don't feel the vibe here, we can go back to your sexy witch."

"She?"

"Huh?" I say, playing dumb.

"This is about a girl? Seriously? The one from the apartment?"

"Maybe." I sigh. "Yeah. Don't give me shit. I'm having a hard time figuring out why I give two fucks about her." Besides the fact that she kisses like a porn star and feels amazing when she's pressed against my body. *So soft*—

"Alrighty then. Let's check this party out and see if she's here. What's her costume?"

"She said she's going as a student."

"A student? Damn, that's boring."

"I know." Entering the front door of the Beta house, all I see are sweaty drunk people. "Fuck. This is gonna suck."

"This party is off the hook!" shouts Tig.

Off the hook? Nobody says that anymore. "Let's find the beer."

"I thought you'd never ask."

Weaving in and out of the throng, all I feel are hands on me as I pass. A few women stop me to ask about my costume. "Yo!" shouts one such female who's so drunk she can barely stand. "You suppoz'd t' be Khan Drapo?"

"Khal Drogo."

"Yeah, that guy," she says, pointing at my face. "You look *hot*. Wanna do me?"

"Nah. I'm here with my girl."

I walk around her, scanning the room for my lost Tig and a beer when I hear her scream, "Wait! Khan Drapo! I love you."

Ugh.

When I see Tig, I notice he's encountering the same attention as at the last three parties. A sea of lovely ladies are feeling up his chest. Assuming he's going to be busy for a while, I move through the crowd, keeping my eyes peeled for a purple-haired girl dressed as a student. As I circle the room, I find the keg and opt for one beer. The heat in this place is stifling. So many drunk, sweaty bodies in one space can do that. When I can't find her in the main room, I start moving into other parts of the house. I've been in this frat before. They've got several party rooms on this main level, a family room in the basement, and there's a lounge area upstairs on the third floor. It's a big house. When I make it to the game room on the main level, I lean against the wall. This room is packed with people playing cards; it looks to be poker in the far corner. There's a pool table in the center of the room with one guy shooting while a girl lies on top of the felt. Interesting.

Sipping my beer, I scan the room and spot someone I know. It's Apple. Or was it Pear? No, Peach!

I suspect wherever she is, my girl is close. *I need to stop referring to her as mine. Jesus.* As I start to move, I feel a hand on my shoulder.

"You deserted me, dude. Those girls are *cray cray*."

"God, get with the times, Tig. Cray cray? Off the hook?"

Chuckling, Tig slaps my back again. "It's funny. Retro."

"Come on. I see her roommate over there."

Tig looks from me to the crowd. "Oh, holy fuck. Wonder Woman?"

"Yeah."

"She looks like a wet dream."

"Down, boy." I point to the guy next to her. "I think she's with Captain America."

"I'm Jamie fucking Fraser, Scottish warrior," he says with an authentic Scottish accent.

"You're good at that."

"I'm Scottish. My grandparents are one hundred percent Scot. I've heard it all my life."

"Huh. I had no idea."

"Now you do."

I watch as Tig makes his way toward Peach, stopping to let some ladies touch his chest along the way. Yeah, he's a gentleman like that. I follow Tig's lead. I don't want it to seem like I'm here to find her or anything. I told her I was going to a few parties, right?

When we get close, I casually look at the people in Peach's circle. There's a woman dressed as a sexy cat, and another one has her face painted like a sugar skull. It's kind of cool. Several guys are there too. One's dressed up as a football player, another a basketball player, and one idiot is wearing a T-shirt that says "Yes, this is my Halloween costume." Clever. *Not.*

When I make eye contact with Peach, she quickly turns to look at a blonde in a sexy schoolgirl outfit. I can't see her face, but if her ass and legs are anything to go by, she's hot. When the blonde turns around, our eyes meet. *Oh hell no! It can't be.*

I move forward in double time. She's turned completely around now, and I see her entire outfit—what there is of it. She's barely wearing a shirt, and that tiny fucking skirt? If she so much as bends, the world is gonna see that sweet pussy of hers.

"No!" I bark.

"No what?" she says, putting her hands on her hips.

Sassy. "No! You're not wearing that"—I point at her tiny costume—"in public."

"Yeah, I am. What's it to you?"

"It's, uh... it's too provocative."

"It's supposed to be, asshat," says Peach as she moves up beside Virginia. "She's a sexy schoolgirl."

"I know what she is," I growl. "You said a student."

"And?"

"Not a *sexy* student."

"Again, Baker, why do you care?"

"I don't," I say, crossing my arms over my chest. But I do care. I care a lot. Virginia is a nice girl.

"Fine," she mutters as she stomps right past me, heading out of the room.

"Wait! Where are you going?" I say, following right behind her.

"I need a beer."

I turn back to Peach, who is mimicking my stance. Her arms are crossed angrily. As she gets closer, she mutters, "I told you not to wait. She's with someone else tonight."

"Who?"

Smirking, she looks from me to Tig but does a double take when she looks at him. "Hi!" she says with a gleaming white smile. She reaches her hand out toward Tig. When he takes her hand in his, she says, "I'm Penny, but my friends call me Peach."

"Ian, but my friends call me Tig." They continue to hold hands and stare at each other for an uncomfortable amount of time. "You're beautiful," Tig adds shyly.

"And you're smoking hot. Are you Jamie Fraser?"

"Aye, Sassenach," he says in a perfect brogue.

"Oh, holy hell. You can speak Scottish?"

"Aye. *Me seanair*, my grandfather, is pure Scot," he says in his fake accent.

"Wow, that's so cool," Peach coos. "Is that a wig or your natural hair? Because it looks like his on the show. You know, long auburn waves."

I watch as the idiot pushes his hair back behind his shoulder. It's not *that* long, though he has let it grow quite a bit. He told me he's working toward the man-bun look the ladies are into these days. "It's *all* natural, Sassenach."

"Wow, I love it," she says, running her fingers through his hair. "Do you play hockey too?"

"I do. I'm a forward."

She steps closer to him. "Well, now I think I need to *bone* up on my hockey."

That comment makes Tig choke on his drink. "You do. You *definitely* do."

I know I'm being an ass, but I feel like shit right now. "Where's Captain America?" *There, that'll make her feel stupid.*

"Last I saw he had his tongue down the throat of an Ewok."

Damn. That was a fail. "Bummer."

She shrugs. "No biggie." Turning back to Tig, she smiles at him.

Feeling like I may throw up from the lovefest, I decide to look for Virginia and don't bother telling the two of them I'm leaving. They won't notice anyway; they haven't even stopped shaking hands yet. It takes me several minutes to weave through a group playing beer pong and another one playing quarters until I reach the doorway. When I finally make it to the bar, there's no Virginia. I scan the room again. Thankfully, my height gives me an advantage. I can see over almost everyone. When I spot her, I want to punch something, anything. She's in a corner talking to a douche dressed up like fucking Jon Snow.

"She said she liked Khal Drogo," I growl.

"Who doesn't?" says a cute redhead. "Mm, you look good enough to eat."

Seriously, what is the deal with women these days? Don't get me wrong; I love a woman who takes what she needs or wants. And in the past, I've been happy to oblige, but not now. No, now I need to find out who the fuck Virginia's talking to in the damn corner. As I press through the crowd, I keep my eyes on the prize. The douche has her in the corner. I know him. It's Copeland Montgomery, a privileged little dickhead whose father is some sort of politician. I'm watching him move closer to Virginia, and all she does is smile up at him and giggle. I move behind a partition directly to her left. Once I'm closer, I can just barely hear her voice.

"Oh, Cope, you're so funny," she says in a strange voice. It's more high-pitched than her actual voice. It's sugary sweet and annoying as fuck.

"Well, Jennifer..."

Jennifer? WTF?

"...I'd love to get to know you better. Why don't I get you another drink, and we'll go downstairs to the family room? It'll be quieter there."

"Okay, Cope," she coos.

No. Fucking. Way. He's going to get her downstairs and do unspeakable things to her. My first instinct is to grab her and pull her away from him, but I'll wait. I'll just stay close, keep an eye on her. I don't want to force her to be with me instead of him. But if what I've heard about Cope is true, she'll be over this guy in no time.

I wait five minutes, then make my way to the basement. He was right; it is quieter. There are only a handful of people in the room, and most of them are couples using the space to play tonsil hockey. None of those couples are Virginia and Cope.

"Where the hell did they go?" On the left, I see a hallway with several doors. I walk down the corridor, hoping to either see or hear her. Creeping slowly, I place my ear on each door as I go. The house is vibrating from the music upstairs, so it's difficult to hear anything. "I know she's down here," I mutter to myself. "But where?"

"Wow, is this your bedroom?" I ask nervously. I can't believe I just followed him blindly down to one of these bedrooms. *Not smart, Virginia.*

"No, mine is upstairs, but this place is much quieter, don't you think? Now we can talk."

I nod and smile. "It is much quieter." I glance at Cope but keep looking around the room. There's not much in here, only a couple of pictures, an old rickety dresser, and some textbooks on the floor. In my peripheral vision, Cope now has his back against the headboard. I look over at him as he kicks off his boots. He also maneuvers himself out of the thick jacket he wore with his costume. Now all he's wearing is a white button-up shirt that looks like something Jon Snow would wear. "Your costume looks authentic."

"Thanks, our housekeeper made it for me."

"You have a housekeeper? Here?"

"Nah, at home." Patting the bed, he adds, "Come over here and sit by me, Jenny. Let's get to know each other."

It's unnatural, but I giggle. I can't help it. I'm nervous. Don't misunderstand; I have no intention of giving up the V-card tonight. I'm just nervous because I've dubbed Cope "the one."

I walk toward him and sit on the edge of the bed. Cope scoots over and pats the seat next to him again. "Hop up here."

Careful not to flash him, I scoot up onto the bed and sit with my back against the headboard just like him.

He slides down until he's on his back. "Come down here. It's more comfortable."

Holding my skirt in place, I wiggle until I'm on my back, head on a pillow, staring up at the ceiling. In the corner of my eye, I watch him roll to his side and face me. I feel his hand on my thigh, and I'm pretty sure that's the moment I realize I'm in over my head.

"Uh, Cope?"

"Yeah, baby."

Baby? "I, um, thought we were going to talk." I turn my head to look at him. He's good-looking with his dark hair and square jaw. This close up, though, I notice his thin lips. He's also got a pimple on his nose. The good news: he's got a scruff of a beard going just like Jon Snow.

"We are. I just want to hold you. You look so fucking sexy, I can't help myself," he says shyly.

"Okay," I whisper.

When he wraps his arms around me, it feels awkward and uncomfortable. His face is now pressed into my neck, and I feel his tongue. He's licking my neck.

"Mm, you taste so sweet, Jennifer."

"I-I do?"

"You do. Your skin is so soft." His palm has moved from the front of my thigh to the back and is making its way up to my ass. "You've got an amazing ass too. So big and plump."

I blush when he says it. Big and plump? I'm sure that's a compliment, but for me, it just reminds me that I'm fat. His palm squeezes my bottom just a little too hard, which makes me squeak. "Oh, you like that? You like it rough, Jennifer?"

"No, not really. It hurts."

"Whatever. Pain can be very erotic." He squeezes my ass again as he rolls on top of me. Pressing his torso up and away from me, he looks down at my shirt and says, "Show me those big titties."

Blinking frantically, I am struck dumb. "My what?"

"Your tits, woman. Show me those fucking tits."

"Uh, you want me t-to take off my top?"

"Well, yeah. Why else are we here?"

"T-to talk?" Yeah, I believed him. Why wouldn't I? When I interviewed him, he said he was practically a virgin, that he wanted to wait for marriage. He was looking for "the one." Was he lying? "But, I—"

"You what?" Without giving me a chance to answer, he reaches out, pulls one cup down, and stares. "Better than I imagined, Jen. Big and perky. I'm one lucky bastard." He moves fast, latching onto my nipple with his mouth and sucking hard. I'd like to say it felt good, but it didn't. It hurt. A lot. He sucks so hard that when he bites down, I scream. I attempt to pull away, but he's strong. "What are you doing? I thought you were a nice guy."

"Oh, I'm nice. I'm about to be *very* nice to you." He slides his palm up my thigh, toward the front of my panties. He kisses me, and it's wet and slobbery; his tongue is sliding inside my mouth like an angry eel.

Wiggling to get away, I mutter, "I don't understand. You were the one."

He stops. Lifting his head, he looks into my eyes. "The one what?"

"I, uh, thought you were looking for a serious relationship," I whisper. At least that's what he said he wanted. All lies.

"Are you talking marriage or something? We *just* met. I'm not looking to get married. Fuck that. I just want to fuck. I'm a young man. I've got my whole life ahead of me." He sits up, pulling himself off the bed. "Shit. Why do I always find the ones like you?"

"Like me?"

"Yeah. The fucking crazy bitches."

"Bitches?" I hate that word. I'm not a bitch. At least I try not to be.

I feel a tear start to fall. Why? Why had I placed all of my hopes in *this* guy? I only met him once. He just seemed so perfect.

"Yeah. You're a Fucking. Crazy. Bitch. Now get out."

Rather than let this jerk see me cry, I pull my white shirt over my exposed breast, grab my shoes, and yank the door open. Pulling the door shut behind me, I let the tears fall as I start to run down the hallway and right into Baker.

"Virginia?"

I nearly fall back, but Baker places his big hands on my shoulders, holding me steady. His hands feel good, but I need to get out of here. Pulling away, I mutter, "Leave me alone, Baker."

"What's going on? What happened?"

"Uh, nothing. He tried, but—"

"He tried what?" He snarls. His face is turning red and his fists are clenched.

I blink up at him.

"What. Did. He. Try?"

Afraid he's going to do something violent, I place my hand on his chest. "Nothing. He didn't do anything."

Looking down at my tears, then farther to see my shirt is askew and half my boob is out of place, he reaches down and pulls my shirt closed, buttoning it all the way up.

"Well, well, it sure didn't take you long to find someone else to leave with blue balls. Slut," Cope mutters as he tries to pass us.

I'm nudged aside, and in a flash, Baker's fist makes contact with Cope's smug face.

He falls to the ground with a loud thump, grabbing his face as he goes. "Fuck, you broke my nose, you motherfucker."

"Good. You touch her again, dickhead, and I'll break a lot more than that. You get me?"

"I'll sue!" he screeches.

"Go ahead. I'll go to the papers and tell them how Copeland Montgomery assaulted my girlfriend. Good luck getting elected then."

"Fucking asshole," he screams.

Girlfriend? Why out of everything that just happened is that the only thing I heard?

"Come on, Virginia, let's get out of here." Pulling me by the hand, Baker leads me up the stairs and through the sea of people. Once we're on the sidewalk, he pulls his phone out of a pouch and starts to text. "I just sent a text to my buddy Tig. He's with Peach. I told him I was taking you home."

"Okay." I'm still shell-shocked. Numb.

Baker sends another text, then says, "Let's walk up to Lincoln Way. I've got an Uber coming."

"Okay."

Taking my hand in his once again, he leads me down the street. When we get to the corner, he wraps his arm around me and pulls me into his warm body, whispering, "You're shivering."

"It's been a rough night."

"You'll be okay. I've got you," he says, kissing the top of my head.

I'm not sure what to say. I'm a little confused. When the Uber arrives, Baker opens the door for me and I slide in first. He moves in next and gets close enough to wrap me in his arms again as we ride. I lay my head on his shoulder, and before I know it, I feel myself being lifted up. "Baker?"

"Shh, you fell asleep. I've got you."

"I'm too heavy."

"Shh."

When I turn my head, I don't see my apartment. I see a huge brick house. "Where are we?"

"My house."

"Your house?" I look at it again. "This is *your* house?"

"Yeah."

"It's huge."

"I know," he grumbles.

Using a keypad to unlock the front door, Baker turns the knob and pushes the door open with his foot.

"You should put me down."

"I will in a minute."

Walking into the large foyer, past a formal dining room, and through a humongous kitchen, Baker takes the stairs to the second floor. Through a set of double doors, I see a massive bedroom with a bed big enough for an army. Setting me down on the bed, he turns to a dresser and slides open the second drawer.

"Here, take this," he says, handing me a white T-shirt. "There's a bathroom there," he says, pointing to an open doorway to my right. "Take a shower, whatever you need. Put this on. I'll be back in a few minutes."

"B-but—"

"Virginia, it's been a long night. Just do it. Just get ready for bed. Okay?"

"Okay." I walk into the bathroom, clutching the tee. When I step inside, a light turns on automatically to reveal a bathroom like one you'd see on HGTV. It's all done in a dark, sleek stone and marble. There's a huge bathtub with jets next to a giant shower with glass walls. I peek inside and count four—no, five showerheads. I shut the bathroom door and begin undressing.

Oh, what the hell. I can't pass up the chance to take a shower in that spa setup. I've never seen one like it and probably won't see one again in my lifetime, so I'd better take advantage. Besides, I want to wash Copeland Montgomery off my body. There's a control box on the outside of the shower that takes me a few minutes, but once I have it figured out, I step into a warm, exhilarating shower.

When I hear knocking at the door, I freeze in place.

"Virginia?"

"Um, yeah?"

"You okay in there?"

"Yeah, yes. Why?"

"You've been in there an hour."

Have I? "I have?"

I hear him chuckle. "Yes. Hurry up. I made us a frozen pizza. It's getting cold."

"Okay."

Hitting the End button makes me feel a little sad. Drying off with a huge plush towel, I brush my hair with Baker's brush and slip on his tee that falls to my knees. I grab my panties from earlier and cringe at the idea of putting them back on. *Ugh, Cope.* I take a risk and go commando. Baker won't know. I'm sure he'll sleep in another room.

Opening the door, I spy Baker in a pair of baggy sleep pants that hit him low on his hips. The fact that he's shirtless isn't lost on me. His body is out of this world. I follow his six-pack to the line of hair that slides down into his pants. He's got that Adonis belt—you know, the V guys get when they have zero body fat and nothing but time to work out.

Ignoring the tingle coursing through my body, I say, "That was hands down the best shower I've ever had."

A warm chuckle erupts from Baker. "I'm glad you liked it. Now, come downstairs. I've got some food."

My stomach growls as if on cue. "I could eat," I say, smiling.

"Good." Taking my hand in his, he leads me into a huge room with vaulted ceilings. There's a sectional so big I think it'd take up our entire apartment. Don't get me started on the television.

"That's got to be like seventy-five inches," I say, pointing at the TV.

"Nah, eighty-eight."

"No way."

"Way."

It makes me giggle. "Can we watch something?"

"Sure. What do you feel like?"

"Anything. I don't care."

"Hockey?"

"I don't know anything about hockey, but if you explain it to me, sure."

"Will do, princess." Handing me a plate with two slices of pizza, he asks, "What would you like to drink? I've got soda, Gatorade, beer, wine, milk, water, and juice."

"May I have a glass of milk?" I love pizza and milk. I know it's weird. Deal with it.

"Sure. Be right back."

I slide back onto the couch. It's so deep my feet barely hang off the edge. Biting into the pizza, I take a minute to scan the room. He lives here alone? I'd love to ask him questions, but I don't think tonight's the night. So, that means never, because I'm sure I won't ever be back. He just wanted to take me somewhere safe, that's all.

"Here you go."

"Thanks." I place the glass between my legs, and that's when I remember I'm going commando. The shirt is so long he can't tell, but *I* know. I feel the heat rise from my chest to my neck and onto my face.

"What's wrong? You're all red."

"I think I bit into something spicy."

"Oh, sorry. I added some of those dried pepper things. I should have asked."

"No. I like it." *Wow, how did I get away with that fib?*

Baker slides back into the seat, his knees fitting in exactly the right spot on the couch. I bet he had to shop around until he got one big enough to fit his frame. "Now. Here's your first lesson on the sport of hockey. One," he says, lifting a finger, "it's the best sport in the world."

I giggle.

"Two, it's the most challenging and difficult sport to master in the world."

I giggle again.

"Why are you laughing? Do you think basketball players could play if they were on ice skates?"

"No."

"*No*. They could not. What about football players?"

I shrug. "No."

"Rugby?"

"Nope."

"Well, hockey is all of those things but with a smaller ball called a puck, and on the ice with skates."

"Obviously. I see your point."

"Lesson three. I'm the best goalie in the world."

I throw my head back and laugh so hard I cry.

"You wound me, Virginia," he says, placing his palm over his chest.

Still laughing, I pat his thick thigh. "Sorry, babe. That was funny."

I smile over at him and see his expression change right before my eyes. He looks down at my hand still resting on his thigh, then back up to me. "You called me babe."

"Oh, sorry. It just slipped out."

"I liked it."

"You did?" I say so quietly I'm not sure he heard me.

"I did."

"Okay."

"I also like your hands on me, Virginia," he says, looking back down at my hand. "But do you know what I like more than that?"

I know what he's going to say, but I shake my head.

"Your lips on me."

That's what I thought he was going to say.

Baker takes my plate out of my hand and the milk from between my thighs. He does that slowly, watching himself do it. I know I should feel nervous, but I'm not. I'd say I was excited more than anything. He's right about anticipation.

"Kiss me, Virginia."

I move toward him as he lowers his head down to me, kiss his lips softly, and then pull away. "There. How's that?"

Growling, Baker slides both hands around my waist and lifts me up and over to his lap. Straddling him, I squeak as I feel my bare center hit his pajama pants. He uses his palms to slide my body until I fit perfectly against him.

"Now," he says with a husky voice, "kiss me again, Virginia."

"Bossy," I mutter. But I do it.

I run my fingers through his hair and lean down. When our lips meet, I feel his hands move from my back to beneath my breasts, and I arch my back when he touches the side of each one. I didn't realize I was doing it until I feel his fingers brush over my hard nipples and a groan escapes his mouth into mine. I feel myself breathing harder with each touch, so much so that I can't control it.

Pulling away from his lips, I moan, "Baker, don't stop."

Without a word, he slides his hands beneath my shirt. "Fuck. You're not wearing panties."

It wasn't a question. I squirm in his lap. I feel his erection beneath me, and these sensations are overwhelming. I'm not sure what I want more, his hand or his—

"Lift your arms."

I lift them and feel the huge shirt fly off.

"Holy hell," Baker groans. "You're fucking glorious, Virginia."

I look down and watch him use his hands to squeeze and manipulate my breasts. I arch my back farther. I can't help it. When I look down and see my complete nakedness against his clothed lower half, I start to slide off him to get to the shirt.

"No. Sit still."

"But I'm naked."

"I'm well aware, Virginia."

Using his hands, he brings me back to the spot where my center meets his. "Unless you want to stop. If you do, I'll stop. I don't want to pressure you into doing anything you don't want to do."

"I know. It's just...."

"What?"

"Nothing." I should tell him about my virginity problem, but I don't want to right now. I just want to feel him touching me. This is only for one night. I need to enjoy my time with him. At least that's what I tell myself.

"What is it? Tell me."

I don't know how to say it, so I'll just say it. "Am I your girlfriend?"

He blinks at me with surprise. "No. Why would you think that?"

I feel the heat of humiliation burning up my neck. "You told Cope I was your girlfriend."

"No I didn't."

Now, combine humiliation with anger and you've got "Yeah. You did. You said something like, 'I'm going to tell people you assaulted my girlfriend, blah, blah, blah.'"

"You must have misheard. You aren't my girlfriend. We're friends."

I nearly choke. "Do you usually have your friends over to sit on your lap naked?"

"Sometimes."

Oh. My. God. I'm such an idiot. "Close your eyes," I snap.

"Huh?"

"Close your eyes, Baker. I need to get up, and I don't want you to look at me. You've seen enough."

"Virginia."

"Shut them!" I shout.

"Fine."

I watch him close his eyes and flop his head back on the sofa. I slide off his lap and race to the shirt, sliding it over my head as I make my way back upstairs. As fast as I can, I find my clothes and slip on my bra under the T-shirt, turn the panties inside out and slide those on, and pull on the skirt. Forgetting about the socks, I put the shoes on with a wince. I was wrong; the shoes are a painful nightmare, just like tonight. I turn to make my way back downstairs, but the exit to the bathroom is blocked by a big dumb asshat.

"Please move."

"No."

"Baker," I say, looking up at him. His expression changes the minute he sees my face. "Please move."

Baker steps back, giving me the space to exit the bathroom. "Let me give you a ride home."

"No, thanks. I got an Uber."

Following me down the steps, he says, "You don't know my address."

"I'm meeting it. Just like we did earlier."

"Virginia, come on," he whines.

"Thanks for, uh, everything. See ya."

I make it to the front door, open it, step out onto a huge front porch, and march down the steps and long brick path to the street. Not knowing where I am, I've got two choices: right or left. I choose to turn left. I know he's watching me, so I make it look like I know what I'm doing even though I don't. I stomp down the block and come to a four-way intersection. I listen for traffic so I know which way to go. When I don't hear any, I take a right.

"My phone!" I grab my phone and bring up my map application. When I see where I am, I realize I've got to go back the way I came—past Baker's house. "Great," I grumble. With my head held high, I walk back. As I pass his house, I see he's sitting in his car at the end of his driveway.

Rolling down his window, he calls out, "I wondered when you'd figure it out."

I ignore him and walk around the back of his car and down the street. I don't need to look back to know he's following me, but this time I'm standing my ground. I will not get into the car with Baker Stark.

On Lincoln Way, I find a CyRide stop with a bench and sit down. It's Saturday night, so there will be a bus by soon enough, though it may not stop if Baker leaves his car parked in the designated bus spot. "Move your car, Baker. The bus needs the spot."

"Not until you get into the car."

Sighing, I look him in the eyes. "Baker, I need you to leave. I want to take the bus to conserve what little pride I have left."

"What are you talking about? We were just messing around. No big deal."

"To you, that's probably true. To me, it *was* a big deal. Now go. The bus is coming." *And I want to get home to lick my wounds.*

I see him peer into his rearview mirror. "Fine. I'll pull up to make sure you're safely on the bus."

I turn to watch CyRide get closer. When the doors open, I step up and realize I've got a problem. I don't have my wallet, which holds my money and bus pass.

"Shit," I say, looking at the bedraggled bus driver. "I forgot my pass, and I'm out of money."

The driver rolls her eyes. I'm sure she hears that story all day long. "You'll need to step off the bus."

"I will. Can you just pretend I'm getting on the bus, so that guy in the black car leaves?"

"He bothering you?" she says, picking up the walkie-talkie.

"No. It's my ex. He wants me back, and I'm not going back." Yeah, I lied.

She pulls the doors shut, and the lights in the front of the bus flicker off. We watch as Baker drives away and around the corner.

"Thanks."

"No problem. Have a good night."

"You too." I step off the bus and onto the sidewalk for the long trek home.

CHAPTER 26

Baker

"So, what happened with you and the sexy schoolmarm?"

"*Schoolmarm?*" I say, chuckling. "You say the weirdest shit, Tig."

Shrugging, he rotates to the next machine.

We're in the weight room at the hockey arena doing a circuit even though we're both wiped from practice. We've lost the last three games, so Coach made us skate laps until we practically crawled off the ice.

It's my turn on the Lat Pulldown machine, so as I get ready for another set of reps, I answer Tig's question. "Nothing happened. I took her home. End of story."

Tig looks at me from his spot on the Pec Deck equipment like he knows I'm full of shit. "You're full of shit. In your text, you said you were taking her to your place and that Peach didn't need to worry."

I let go of the bar above me and run my hands over my face. "I took her to my place. I made a pizza, things got heavy, and then she went home."

"You mean she *walked* home."

"No! I tried to give her a ride, but she insisted on taking the bus." *So stubborn.*

"Well, she didn't take the bus. She walked."

"The fuck she did. I watched her get on CyRide with my own eyes," I say, pointing at my eyes.

"Apparently she didn't have any money or her pass, so she walked."

Fuck! "How do you know any of this?"

"I was at their place when she got home."

I throw my head back and roar like a fucking lion. "Why? Why the fuck is she doing this to me?" Now I feel fucking guilty. A gentleman never lets a woman walk the fuck home. My grandmother would have my balls right about now.

I pick my phone up off the floor and whip out a text to Virginia.

Me: *You walked home?*
V: *...*
Me: *Virginia? I know you're there. You fucking walked home?*
V: *Maybe.*
Me: *I watched you get on the bus. I watched the bus door shut. What the fuck?*
V: *I didn't have my pass or any cash. The driver told me I needed to get off the bus.*
Me: *I can't believe you. Something bad could have happened to you. It was my responsibility to make sure you got home safely, and you didn't let me do that. Jesus, I'm pissed.*
V: *Sorry.*

I can't respond. All I'm going to do is say the wrong thing because when I'm angry, I tend to blurt shit.

Pulling me back to the conversation, Tig asks, "Doing *what* to you, exactly? Making you care about something other than yourself?"

I turn and stare at my so-called friend. "I care about other people," I say defensively. *I do!*

Counting on his fingers, he says, "You care about your grandmother." Then he stops. "Who am I missing?"

For some reason that makes me laugh. Tig has a fucked-up sense of humor. "I care about the guys, the team, school... you."

He stands up from his machine, walks over, and sits down on a bench nearby. "When are you going to forgive yourself?"

"Forgive myself? For what?"

"It's not your fault–, the shit with your parents."

"I know that, dickhead. I was just a kid."

"Just because their relationship was fucked up doesn't mean yours will be."

"I know." *Wait, do I know that?*

Sure, I suppose my view of love and relationships is a little skewed. My parents... their relationship was fucked up. All I remember of them before my dad joined the service was their constant fights—the yelling and screaming. Mom blamed Dad for getting her pregnant, for the crappy apartment we were living in, and for killing her dream of being a famous something or other. It was something different every week. She never stopped yelling, and he couldn't seem to give her the last word. It was pure hell. So, after 9/11, Dad took the opportunity to join the service. That act accomplished two things: one, he was serving his country; two, he was getting as far away from his wife as he could.

It's tragic that his plan to get away for a while ended up being forever. He was killed in Afghanistan by a roadside bomb. He was twenty-eight. I was six when he joined up and eight when he died. I only saw him a few times in those last two years, but the time we had was good. I know he loved me. I know his leaving had nothing to do with me, at least consciously. Consciously, I knew he just hated my mom with a passion. Subconsciously, I probably felt responsible. I probably still do.

After Dad died, Mom and I grew apart. Literally. She left me with my grandparents for weeks at a time while she went away with one rich asshole after another. She always wanted more—more money, a bigger house, shit like that. Each time she came back, she was a little different. She had a different hair color, a smaller nose, a bigger chest, and she also got progressively nastier to me with each passing year. It's the reason I haven't seen her for eighteen months. She's a bitch. I know what she wants because it's all she ever wants. Money.

It's okay, though. I've been lucky. My grandmother has always been sweet and kind, at least to me. I loved living with Grandma —or Granna. as I call her—because she gave me stability. Plus, she taught me a lot about manners, being a gentleman, and working hard to achieve my goals. She came to every hockey game I ever played in back home and to every important school event. She's amazing. I think she'd love to go to games here, but it's too far to drive, so she watches our games online.

On the other hand, my grandfather, who died three years ago, was stubborn as a mule and heartbroken when his son, my dad, joined the army, then devastated when he died. He blamed himself because he cut my dad off financially when he and Mom got pregnant and Dad decided to get married and work instead of going to college. Lack of money only added to the stress at our house, but I don't blame my grandfather. I guess he did it because he wanted the best for my dad.

"Bake?"

I shake my head as I step off the treadmill, realizing I ran five miles and don't remember any of it.

Tig asks, "Food?"

I look over at him. "Sure. I could eat."

"Good, because we need to talk about the new practice schedule."

"Don't remind me," I groan. We practice Monday through Thursday because most of our games are Friday and Saturday. Right now, we skate or practice as a team early on Tuesday and Thursday mornings and lift weights sometime in the afternoon. On Monday and Wednesday, we practice in the afternoon and lift whenever we have time in our schedule. All we have to do is check in with one of the managers so Coach doesn't kick our asses for not lifting weights.

"So, what's he doing now?"

"Apparently Dixon and MacKenzie haven't been lifting."

"Of course they haven't. Those guys are two of the laziest assholes in the world. All they want to do is drink and hunt for pussy, then rinse and repeat."

"Well, they sweet-talked one of the managers into forging their names on the check-in sheets."

"And?"

"So now, starting next week, Coach has specific times for us to use the weight room, and *he'll* be supervising."

"Awesome." I have a routine. I like how I've scheduled my weeks.

"Oh, and Sundays are now mandatory."

Sundays were usually free for us. There are times when we've played a shitty game the night before and Coach makes us skate, but for the most part, Sunday is our day. "I'm going to kill Dixon."

"And MacKenzie."

"Yeah, him too." *Fucking assholes.*

CHAPTER 27

"Come on, Virginia," Peach whines. "I'm not going to Tig's game alone. I have no idea what to expect at a hockey game."

"And I do?" I've never been to a hockey game in my life. Sure, Baker and I started to watch one last weekend, but I'm not going there.

"That's why. If we go together, we can just fake it. We don't have to watch the match or whatever it's called. Tig just asked me to come, and, well, I don't want to disappoint him."

She doesn't want to disappoint him? What is it with Tig and Peach? I've never seen her like this with a guy. It's only been a week, but she practically falls all over herself to dote on him. It's entirely out of character. She's *always* the dotee, not the doter.

"Wow, he must be something in bed."

"I wouldn't know," she says, lifting her head proudly.

"Huh? What? You haven't slept with him yet?" Peach is a firm believer that having sex with a potential partner needs to happen right away so she can weed out the duds.

"Nope. He wants to wait."

"Huh? And you're on board with that?"

Shrugging, she adds, "He wants it to be special. Ooh... he

wants to take me out. On a *real* date. I didn't even have to hint around about it." Peach walks to stand in front of me, then grasps my hands and sighs. "Virginia?"

"Yes?"

"I don't want to jinx it, but I think Ian Hetherington might be the one."

"*The* one?"

Nodding, she repeats, "The one."

No way. "Wow! That's, er, amazing."

"I know!" she practically squeals. "So, bestie, it's Saturday night, and I know for a fact you've got nothing better to do. Now get your ass ready to go. Bundle up. It's an ice rink. We're probably going to freeze our balls off in there."

"Fine. I'll go. But I'm not talking to what's his name."

"You don't have to. This is all about my man and me."

"Right. Got it."

At the arena or rink or whatever it's called, we find a place to park on a side street since the lot is full. After Peach pays our admission, she instructs me to find us a couple of seats while she grabs popcorn and something for us to drink. "Sit at the other end, close to the net thing," she says, pointing to the end farthest away.

"Fine." I know enough about sports with nets to know the goalie works there. "Fine. Great. Whatever," I mutter to myself as I walk the length of the rink. At the farthest end, I stomp up the steps to the top row of bleachers. If I have to be here, I might as well sit as far away from him as I can.

There are quite a few people at the game. So far, Peach and I have the row to ourselves in this section, but the spots below are filling up fast. As soon as I'm seated, I watch as a team in red starts to emerge from a room across the rink. The ISU team steps onto the ice, then speeds around and around the oval. I scan the names on the backs of their outfits as they warm up, but I am not looking for Baker Stark. I'm looking for Tig, for Peach.

Speaking of warm, it's not nearly as cold as Peach suggested. I'm currently wrapped up like a mummy in winter gear: a hat, a scarf, gloves, and my warmest winter parka. I may have overdone it. When I feel warm air on my only exposed skin, my face, I look up. A heater. I'm sitting directly below a heat vent. "Sweet," I say softly.

As I start to unwrap myself from my cocoon scarf first, I catch a glimpse of a man in red speeding to my end of the rink. He's so fast I think he's going to run right into the wall separating us from them. When he stops, he skids to a halt, ice chunks flying everywhere.

"No! No way! I don't want you here. Get the fuck out!"

I'm completely shocked and speechless. I didn't think he was angry with me. The last time I spoke to him was in a text earlier in the week. Well, okay, he was pretty upset with me when he found out I'd walked home from his place, but I brushed it off. Could that be it? What's the big deal? I walk everywhere. I don't think it warrants this reaction.

I blink furiously at him, then subtly look to my left and to my right and see people turning their heads to look at me. I look back at him as he continues his rant.

"You heard me! Get out!"

I feel my chin quiver. Jeez, I've been emotional lately. When my eyes start to burn, I know what's coming. But screw him. I'm not going to sit here and let him talk to me like that. I stand up abruptly, put my hands on my hips, and yell back, "Screw you, Baker Stark. It's a free country. I can watch a hockey match if I feel like it. And I don't feel like it anymore!"

I quickly run down the bleacher steps until I'm only a foot from the jackass. Without saying another word, I lift my head high and march past everyone, straight to the exit.

CHAPTER 28

Baker

"No! No way! I don't want you here. Get the fuck out!" I shout at my mom sitting near the top of the bleachers, probably in an attempt to watch the game without me noticing. Ha! Like that's possible.

I spotted her as soon as I skated onto the ice. She's hard to miss in her bright red outfit that shows way too much skin. Her lips are bright red, and her hair is big and poofy and extra, extra blonde now too. She's not dressed for a fucking sporting event. Her hair is so perfectly styled it's like she's going on the hunt for another rich asshole who will put up with her bullshit for a few months.

Well, she won't find that here. Oh, who the fuck am I kidding? I know why she's here. My birthday is tomorrow. She's here for money.

For a split second, I see the shock on her face. She didn't expect me to confront her in front of an audience.

She regains her composure quickly and smiles.

Fuck, I can't stand her. "You heard me! Get out!"

Glaring at her, I'm ready to spew a few more profanities but am distracted when a woman sitting behind Mom stands up and slams her fists on her hips angrily. I'm even more shocked when I hear the woman yell, "Screw you, Baker Stark..." I don't hear the rest of it because when I look at her pretty face, I see my girl. I see Virginia.

Virginia? She's here? At my game? She came to watch me play? Fuck.

I blink in confusion as she marches down the bleacher steps and stops momentarily. Glaring at me with those pretty eyes, she turns and walks quickly down the length of the ice. I can't help myself; I watch her go. I'm speechless.

Fuckety, fuck, fuck, fuck! I'll fix that later. I need to deal with the unwelcome visitor.

I turn to face the bleachers again and see my mom is standing in front of me, smirking. "Oh, cupcake...." She calls me cupcake thinking it's hilarious since my name is Baker. *Not funny.* "Don't get yourself all worked up. It's your birthday. Of course I came to see you."

Gritting my teeth, I repeat, "I don't want you here."

Sighing dramatically, she says, "Fine. I'll go." As she turns to leave, she looks back. "I'll see you at home."

At home? Fuck! "It's not your home!" I shout as she walks away.

Lifting her hand with her long red fingernails, she flutters her fingers at me.

I guess that means I'll fucking have to deal with her later. "Fuck!"

I'm about to skate back to the guys when an angry blonde stomps over to stand in front of me. "You asshole!"

"Peach, I—"

"Virginia left crying. You made her cry, *again*! You're a fucking dick!"

Again? "I thought—"

"No, you didn't. You never think. Oh, wait, yes you do. You think of yourself. God. I'm so pissed at you."

"Peach, I—" I don't get anything else out because she's turned around and is walking to the other end of the rink. "Great. Just fucking great. This night sucks already."

And the sucking continues. My head is not in the game. Surprisingly, my mind isn't on my mom but worrying about Virginia. *"You made her cry… again!"* keeps rolling around in my brain. That's all that's rolling around in there. It certainly isn't the puck as it flies past me six times in the first two periods. I'm not shocked when Coach pulls me and puts a freshman goalie in my place, muttering, "Jesus, Stark. Where's your fucking head? This loss is on you, asshole."

It is on me, and the rest of the guys know it. A few of them are glaring at me, one guy I hate smirks, and the others give me an expression that says "It's okay, Baker. You'll do better next time." The pity look. I hate it, but I'm going to accept it. I will do better next time. We've got another game next Friday, so I'll need to get rid of my mom and fix this shit with Virginia before then. The question is, how?

BY THE TIME I get back to my house, my mood is worse. All I see in my head is Virginia's pretty face, her little chin quivering as she walked past me. She was trying to be strong when she yelled back at me, but I know my words cut her deep.

"How am I ever going to make it up to her?" I say as I enter my house through the garage entrance.

"You can make it up to me by giving me a big ole hug, cupcake."

"How the hell did you get in here?" I growl.

"I let her in," says Granna.

I look up and see my favorite person sitting at the long table in the dining room to my right. "Granna?"

She stands up and walks toward me as I cut around Mom to get to her. Wrapping her up in my arms, I squeeze. "I've missed you," I whisper in her ear.

"I've missed you more, baby boy," she whispers right back.

Our reunion is interrupted when my mom clears her throat. "Well, isn't that precious."

Granna and I step back and stare at Dawn. From time to time, I call her by her first name rather than giving her the courtesy of the moniker Mother.

I speak first. "What are you doing here, Mom? I haven't seen you for almost two years."

"I know. I've neglected you so much, cupcake."

God, I hate that nickname. "It's okay." No, really it is. She's so dramatic and needy when she's around; it's exhausting.

"No it isn't, sweetums. I should have moved closer to you when you started school here. I know you've only got a year left, but I thought I could move in and—"

"No!" says Granna angrily. "This is my home. You will not live here."

"Well, after he inherits tomorrow—"

"No! That money is his, not yours."

"But I'm his *mother*. Now that he's going to be set for life, I'm sure he'd want to help his mom out. Right, cupcake?"

I stare at her, then turn to look at Granna. I want to ask her what to do but remain silent. The truth is, at midnight tonight, I *will* be set for life—sort of. My grandfather took the money intended for my father and put it into a trust for me. I'll get the first portion on my twenty-second birthday. That milestone happens at midnight tonight. It's why she's here. She wants part of it—hell, she probably wants all of it.

"You'll not take one cent of that money, Dawn."

"It'll be his money, Katherine," Mom says, pointing at me. "He can give it to whomever he wants. He's a good boy. He wouldn't want his mother homeless and destitute."

I watch her lips turn down into a fake pout. I'm not falling for it. "Mom, there are stipulations to the trust."

"What kind of stipulations?"

Granna takes over. "He can only use this initial disbursement of his trust for specific things. Handing it out to family isn't one of them."

"How would they know?" she squeaks.

"I'm not going to lie about how I use the money. The attorneys will—"

"It's *your* money," Mom shouts. "It should have been mine, but they kept it from me. It should have been mine!"

"It never belonged to you, Dawn." Granna sounds almost bored. "It was never Keith's."

"You are a fucking bitch," Mom says as she lunges for Granna.

I step in front of her to block her from Granna just in time. Her red-tipped claws lash out, catching on my forearms. Long red streaks start to appear on my arms as blood rises to the surface.

"Jesus, Mom. Get a grip."

"A grip? You want me to get a grip? If it wasn't for you"—she points at my face, her nail an inch from my eye—"I'd have been someone!"

"It's not my fault. I didn't get you pregnant. You did that."

Screaming at the top of her lungs, she lunges for me again. Before I can grab her wrists, her nails drag down my cheek, starting at my eye.

"Fuck!" I shout. "Motherfucker!" I yell again, pushing her back with one arm and grabbing my cheek with the other hand.

Dawn stumbles and falls on her ass.

I feel blood dripping onto my hand and down my wrist. It's coming out fast enough that drips are now appearing on the floor.

The sight of blood isn't my favorite thing. I, uh, um—

CHAPTER 29

Baker

I WAKE up to some dude leaning over me, and he's way too
fucking close.

"What the fuck?"

"Shh, I'm taking your vitals."

"My vitals? What for?"

"You passed out and hit your head on the floor."

"Huh? I did?"

"Yes. What's your name?"

"Um...." I have to think for a minute. "Baker."

"Good. What's the date today?"

Oh, shit. I have no idea. Doing my best to remember, I say,
"November?"

"Right. Do you know the date?"

Sighing with irritation, I say, "Mid-November?"

The paramedic looks up. "I think he's got a concussion. Plus, I
think these scratches need to be assessed. He may need stitches
for one of those on his face. It's deep. I'd like to transport him."

Scratches? I raise my hand to my face, but the dude stops me. "Please don't touch your face."

"Yes, that's good. Please, let's get him to the hospital."

I look over and see Granna standing next to a guy in a dark uniform. A cop? "Hey, Gran."

Turning to me, she smiles. "Hey there, baby boy. You're going to be all right. I'll be with you."

"Virginia?"

"Virginia? Who's Virginia?"

Who's Virginia? "Um, I'm not sure."

At the hospital, I'm sent directly to the emergency ward. There, I'm poked and prodded and stitched up like Frankenstein. They said they could suture two of the cuts on my face, but one, the deepest one, would require plastic surgery or I'll "end up looking like Scarface."

I stay the night at Mary Greeley Medical Center. Granna stays with me on the pullout sofa in my room. I told her to go home and get a good night's sleep, but she wouldn't hear any of it. She asks me several times who Virginia was, and by the time I remember, I just tell her, "Nobody." I know she doesn't believe me, but there is no Virginia. Not anymore.

In the morning, a doctor in a pair of khakis and a polo shirt stops in to check on my face. "Baker Stark?"

I nod.

"I'm Dr. Morris, a plastic surgeon here at MG." He's an older man, probably in his sixties I'd guess.

"Okay."

"What do you think, Doctor? Does he need plastic surgery?" asks Granna with concern written all over her face.

"If he were my son, I'd recommend it. It's jagged and deep. It won't heal the way we'd like if we don't do something now. He's too handsome to let this heal wrong." He winks, seeming relaxed but confident at the same time, which is helping me worry less.

Standing up, he looks at Granna. "I'd like to do it this week. Tomorrow, preferably. It'll be a relatively simple outpatient procedure. We'll even use local anesthetic, if that's all right with you, Mom."

Mom? I smirk, and ouch! It hurts. The fact is Granna isn't that old. She's in her sixties, but she looks younger. Her hair is always styled sort of simply. There's still a lot of blonde mixed in with the silver. She dresses in nice clothes she calls "classic" styles, plus she's really pretty. The fact that she's always got a smile on her face just makes her more so.

She chuckles. "I'm Baker's grandmother."

"No way," says Dr. Morris.

Granna giggles like a schoolgirl, her cheeks turning bright pink. "It's true."

"Well, you don't look a day over thirty."

I smile at the two of them. Is he flirting with Granna? Is she flirting back? Watching them is like watching a tennis match, and I can't look away. Back and forth they banter.

Granna giggles again. "I'm sixty-two."

Looking sincerely shocked, Dr. Morris blushes a little himself. "I'm sixty-three."

"You look good too," Granna says softly.

"Not as good as you."

Finally, I interrupt. "Hey, you two should go down and have a cup of coffee. I know Granna could use a cup, but she doesn't know where the cafeteria is located."

"Well, I could show her," he says to me. Turning to Granna, he asks, "May I escort you to the MG cafeteria? It's known for its stale coffee and even staler donuts."

Giggling, Granna walks toward him, lifts her hand, and says, "Katherine Stark, but please call me Kate. And I'd love an escort."

"Thomas Morris, but call me Tommy, please."

"Tommy. It suits you."

"Kate suits you too. Perfectly." The doctor turns back to me. "We'll be back soon."

"Take your time. I'm going to get some sleep." I'm exhausted from my night here. Someone woke me up every twenty minutes last night thanks to my concussion. I need sleep.

CHAPTER 30

THE WEEK after Hockeygate drags on and on. It doesn't help that I've got two papers to write, a major test in chemistry, and a scheduled meeting with my major professor to discuss my research. Ha! That's a joke! What research? The problem is, I have no idea what to write about. Both my research and survey are a bust. I ruined it myself when I decided to date my participants. In good conscience, I can't write out my findings with the knowledge that everything is slanted and tainted by my stupid, stupid actions. God, I'm stupid.

With my papers turned in and my chem test completed, I make my way to East Hall and the sociology department for my meeting with Dr. Kellogg. I've decided to be completely honest with him. I'll tell him about my initial reasons behind the survey and see what happens. Maybe he'll just go ahead and flunk me. I deserve it. It means I'd have to go to summer school, or maybe even the fall semester next year. I'll do what I need to do.

Knocking on his door, I wait for him to respond. When he does, I turn the knob and step in. "Hey, Dr. Kellogg."

"Miss Murray, how are you today?"

"Good. Fine."

"Have a seat. I'll be with you in a moment."

I sit, twiddling and twining my fingers nervously. In my mind, I'm chanting, *It'll be okay. It'll be okay.* I hope I'm right.

Setting aside a large stack of papers, Dr. Kellogg leans forward. "All right, Virginia, let's get started."

Instead of letting this drag on, I just start spewing truths right at him. "Dr. K, I screwed up everything. I thought I could kill two birds with one stone and still have a thoughtful and academic study, but I was wrong. I behaved inappropriately with several of my participants, which I think makes their feedback null and void. Besides, none of them represented themselves truthfully. They were nothing like they described in their surveys." Taking a deep breath, I prepare to continue.

Dr. Kellogg raises his hand in the air. "Please slow down, Virginia. Can you start again? At the beginning?"

I groan to myself because I really just wanted to say it all at once. But he's right. I need to start over. So, here goes. "I'm a virgin." I blush like crazy, so much so it feels like my face is on fire. "It's so embarrassing to admit that."

Dr. K arches an eyebrow, then nods.

"This whole idea for a research study on sex germinated from that and because I didn't want to graduate college in that, uh, state."

"As a virgin?"

"Uh-huh."

"Continue," he says, leaning back in his chair.

"So, my roommate and I talked about a way to combine my senior thesis project with my desire to change my status from, um, a virgin to not a virgin."

Dr. Kellogg stays quiet, my cue to continue.

"My plan was to do the survey, then have one-on-one interviews. From those, I'd pick three candidates."

"Candidates?"

"Yes. Candidates to help me with my, um, problem."

"Virginity is a problem?"

"Uh, yeah." *Duh.*

"You talk about it like it's a disease."

"It *is*, Dr. Kellogg! I'm almost twenty-two. How many twenty-two-year-old virgins do you think are left out there? I'll tell you: one. Well, two. I interviewed a woman who's in the same boat as me."

"So, after your survey and interviews, are you still...?"

"God, yes! Like I said before, the three finalists? None of them were as they seemed. I think they just told me things that sounded good. Heck, I even changed my appearance for those idiots: hair, clothes, makeup, et cetera, just to appeal to the types of women they liked."

"You changed your appearance for them?"

"Well, they each had a type of girl they liked. One of them liked a free-spirited person, the other one liked a more goth or punk type, and the third one—" I roll my eyes before mentioning Mr. Political Science. "—was the biggest liar of all. He liked blondes. I'll just leave it at that."

"Okay, so let me see if I understand. You're a virgin."

I nod.

"You created a survey and research study to find the perfect person to help you, um, alleviate that... issue."

I'd like to giggle at how uncomfortable Dr. Kellogg seems but remain quiet and just nod again.

He continues. "But what you found is that none of the men you interviewed and subsequently chose for your, um, challenge was truthful when responding to your questions about their preferences for a partner or about sex?"

I blink a few times. "Well, I found one person, a guy, who was truthful."

"But he wasn't one of the three final choices?"

"No."

"Why not?"

I look at Dr. Kellogg like he has three heads. "I'd rather not say."

"Did you find the other three more attractive physically?"

"No." None of the three finalists could hold a candle to Baker's looks.

"Then why?"

Why is he asking me that? It doesn't matter. It has nothing to do with my research. I blink a few times, trying to come up with a good response to his question. I feel a little cornered.

"Let me ask you this way. Do you think you liked the other three better because you knew they were full of shit?"

I choke out a laugh. I didn't expect my professor to say "shit." "Maybe."

"What happened during the interview with the honest guy that made you shy away from him?"

Sitting back in my chair, I close my eyes and think back to my interview with Baker. "Well, it didn't seem like he was interested in answering my questions until...."

"Until?"

"Until I asked him about kissing."

"Kissing?"

"Yeah, when I asked him why he listed kissing as the most important trait of a potential mate, he started to be more engaged."

"How so?"

"Oh, um, he just described how it felt to kiss someone for the first time and that, um, if the person couldn't kiss, he wasn't going to sleep with them. Stuff like that." I'm blushing so profusely now that I can tell Dr. Kellogg is on to me.

"Did he kiss you?"

I nod as the sweat takes a stand on my forehead. "Yeah, he kissed me." I quickly add, "For science."

Dr. Kellogg does his best to stifle a chuckle, but it doesn't work. Then he says, "And?"

"He was right."

"About what?"

"The kiss. You know. The physiology and psychology of the kiss."

"Aha!" he says with his hand raised, finger pointing upward. "Now that's a cool topic."

"A cool topic?"

"Yes! At first, I was pondering this notion about virginity and your feelings about it being like a disease, but that's prosaic. But kissing? That'd be fascinating to see how the kiss has evolved through time. From the sounds of your young man, he seems to have grasped the romance of the kiss—its secrets, if you will. The kiss is the beginning, the start of something special. Wouldn't you say?"

"Yes, but what about expressions like the 'kiss of death' and the 'goodbye kiss'?"

"What about 'kiss and make up,' 'kiss my ass,' 'kiss my grits,' 'kiss of life,' 'kiss up,' 'kiss and tell,' and 'sealed with a kiss'?"

"I think we're getting off track."

"Are we? Think about this. Kissing varies within cultures. Maybe it changes generationally too. Your young man seems like he's got an old soul. He thinks of the kiss like a man three times his age."

I look up at the ceiling, letting Dr. K's words roll around in my head. "This kiss...."

"I liked what you said earlier about the physiology and psychology of the kiss. I think if you speak specifically about millennials and their thoughts on kissing, you could compare and contrast your findings with research done on the kiss on previous studies from other decades, other generations."

"So you think I should change my topic to kissing?"

"Well, I think you're correct in assuming your first study is tainted and therefore not appropriate for your senior project. You've got plenty of time to start over. You aren't the only one who has started one study and finished with something that was a variation of the initial idea. It's just part of the process. I'm glad you're able to see the need for a shift. I think it'll make you a better researcher and a better sociologist, because you were able to recognize your failures and be open and flexible to turn them into successes."

"So, kissing?" I ask with a sigh.

"Kissing," Dr. Kellogg says, nodding. "Get to work, Miss Murray. I'd like to see your revised research proposal next week, shall we say same time?"

"Sure. Yes." I'm smiling as I leave his office. I'm relieved and excited about this idea. I can't wait to tell Baker.

I stop walking. "Oh, hell. Baker."

CHAPTER 31

Baker

AT WELCH AVENUE STATION, one of our favorite watering holes, Tig grabs a booth while I head to the bar to get us a pitcher of beer and two glasses.

"Grab two more glasses," yells Tig.

Two more glasses? "Who else is coming?"

Before he can respond, I see the door open from the corner of my eye. *Fuck! Goddamn Tig. I'm going to kick his ass.*

Making my way back to the table, I see there's only one seat open in the booth. I slide in next to Virginia and glare at Tig. "You didn't mention we'd have company," I say with a scowl. I don't like being duped by Virginia. I'm not prepared to see her. She's going to ask questions about my face and want an apology for the night at the game.

"Yeah, Peach," says Virginia with just as much vitriol. "Thanks for warning me."

Okay, so Virginia was taken unawares as well. At least that's the way it appears. Appearances can be deceiving. I tend to believe her, though, because she won't look at me. Her eyes are staring straight ahead until she's forced to turn to take the glass of beer from my hand. I know the moment she sees the scratches on my arm because her little fake smile turns into a frown. When she looks up at me, she gasps as soon as she sees the long lacerations and sutures on my face. "Baker! What happened to your face?"

I chuckle. "You should see the other guy?"

"You got into a fight?" she asks, perplexed. "With what? A bobcat?"

"Kind of." My mom has claws, for sure. And now she's got a record thanks to those claws. Granna and I pressed charges. I'm sure it'll end up being a misdemeanor or thrown out of court, but at least she got to experience the wonderful world of the Story County jail for a night. Damn, I'd have loved to see her as she walked out of jail. It would've been an Instagram hit.

"So that's it? You're not going to tell me what happened?"

I shrug. "Nah."

She's glaring at me now. Jesus. I can't win. Leaning toward her, I smell her sweet scent. I force my mind off my dick for just a second since this is serious. Speaking softly, I say, "I'm sorry about the game. I wasn't yelling at you."

"Yeah, that's what Peach said." She shrugs. "You were yelling at your mom?"

"Yeah."

I see her expression soften. She's no longer scowling. It's nice. "You don't like your mom?"

I sit up in my seat again, not willing, or maybe not ready, to tell Virginia about my personal life. "That's none of your business."

She looks at me for a few seconds. I know what she's doing. She's trying to hold back feelings. I watch it pass over her face—anger, then hurt—but she rebounds quickly and leans over to whisper in my ear. This time I feel her breath on my neck, and her scent wafts up into my nose again. My damn dick reacts. Bastard. What is it about this girl?

She whispers, "Excuse me. Can you please let me out?"

I don't want to let her out. I want to hold on to this moment for a little longer. I'm startled off my ass when she shouts in my ear, "Yo! Douche canoe. Let me out."

Douche canoe? I want to laugh, but that just pisses me off. "Douche canoe? That's rude."

"So is blocking my exit. Let. Me. Out. *Please.*" She says "please" so sarcastically I'd like to spank her bottom for it.

I move out and stand next to the table as she slides out. Without a word, she walks toward the restrooms. I can't help it; I watch her go. She looks hot again tonight in her tight jeans and a flowing top. I couldn't help noticing how low cut her top was in front. I got a glimpse of the edge of her bra and the soft round top of her breast. Since I've seen them up close, I happen to know they're fucking all-star tits. Her hair is different tonight. It looks a little blonder than before, and she's got it in this sort of Princess Leia pigtail bun things on each side of her head. They aren't braids, but they're twisted up like that. It's cute and hot at the same time. I can picture myself holding on to one or both of those from behind. *Ugh, stop it, Baker. It's never going to happen, and you're okay with that.*

"So," I say, turning to the lovebirds. "What's up?" Yeah, lame. I just don't know what to talk about. My mind is on Virginia. I look over at the bathroom door, but she must still be inside. I look at the clock on my phone, then at the bathroom again. "How long does it take to pee?"

"As long as it takes," Peach deadpans. "I warned you."

Ignoring her dig, I catch something from the corner of my eye, a glimpse of Virginia coming out of the bathroom. On her way back to the table, a tall hulking guy steps in front of her. She looks up and smiles. When I see her step closer to him and then nod, I nearly lose it. I watch her pull out a bar stool and sit next to the asshole.

"What the fuck is she doing?" I say with clenched teeth.

"Looks like she met a new *friend*." Is she trying to annoy me? I turn to Peach for a second, then look back at Virginia. It's working. "She doesn't need another friend."

Peach laughs. "I told you. You didn't listen. You snooze, you lose. It's as simple as that."

I turn back to Virginia and the fucker at the bar as she stands up and makes her way back to the table. Thank fuck.

"Hey, guys, I ran into a friend of mine. We're going to head down to Cy's."

When the big guy moves in behind her and slides a palm onto her hip, I want to murder everyone. "Who's your friend?" I ask, attempting to be calm. It's not working.

Scowling at me, she says, "His name is Taylor. We had philosophy together last year, didn't we?"

The dumbass simply smiles and nods.

"He also plays football here. Right, Taylor?"

Nodding again, the Neanderthal actually speaks. "Linebacker." His voice is so deep it rumbles.

"Cool." I nod. "Cool."

"Okay. See you at home," Peach singsongs.

"Yep. Bye." Virginia waves as she leaves.

The big guy places his paw on her lower back, escorting her out the door.

I turn to Peach, then point to the door. "You're okay with her leaving with that guy? You don't even know him."

She shrugs. "Virginia is a grown-up. She won't do anything stupid. I'll head down to Cy's in a bit to check on her. No worries."

Peach sips her beer, then turns to Tig. I don't hear a word either of them is saying. All I see is Virginia and Taylor in my head. What if she lets him touch her? What if she kisses him?

"Fuck!" I growl as I slide out of the booth.

"You ready to make it official?"

I look at Peach. "What are you talking about?"

"With Virginia. Are you ready to make it official?"

"Official?"

Sighing like she's frustrated with me, she says, "Ready. You know? To make her your girlfriend, dingus."

"No!" *Am I? No! No way!*

"Then leave her alone, Baker. She deserves to be happy."

Leave her alone? With *that* guy? No fucking way. "Whatever," I say as I slam back the rest of my beer. "I'm out of here." I march to the door and yank it open.

"Leave her alone, Baker," Peach repeats.

Ignoring her, I step out into the cool air of November and head north. I'm hungry, and wouldn't you know it? Cy's has food. Good plan.

CHAPTER 32

I COULD *LITERALLY* KILL PEACH. The last person I wanted to see was Baker Stark, and she knew that because I told her those exact words, and she still set me up. "Witch," I mutter.

"Who's a witch?" asks the ginormous guy beside me.

Giggling, I put my hand on his thick, furry forearm. "No one. I was just, uh, thinking about the Halloween party I went to a couple weeks ago. Next year I'm going as a witch."

Nodding, Taylor just says, "Cool."

"Did you go to any Halloween parties?"

"Yeah."

"Did you dress up?"

"Yeah."

Okay, this is sort of like the first time I had to talk to Baker. "What was your costume?"

"Costume? I didn't wear a costume. I just dressed up. Coach's orders. We always have to dress up when we go to parties and shit."

"Oh, right." I take a sip of my beer and look around Cy's, then back at Taylor and smile. He's good-looking, that's for sure, with his shoulder-length blond hair and light blue eyes. I could get used to seeing his face. When he smiles back, I notice he's got a crooked smile and a chipped tooth. It's adorable. It's too bad he's got no personality.

Trying again, I say, "Did you have a game this weekend?"

He blinks at me and scowls. "Of course. You didn't watch it?"

"Um, no, I—" *Quick, Virginia, make something up.*"—had a hair appointment."

"Chicks," he grumbles.

"Yeah, chicks," I say with a laugh.

"You look pretty, so the hair thing was probably a good call."

I blush a little and smile. "Thank you."

"You're welcome."

Okay, maybe I could get used to Taylor. "Did you play a good game?"

He gives me that look again, the scowly one. "I'm an All-American."

I shrug. I know I should be honest here, but he looks hurt, offended. "I don't get sports. Maybe you could teach me about football."

His frown turns upside down, and I get another glimpse at his wonky but adorable smile. "Okay. I can teach you."

A dark shadow crosses over our table. My first thought is that it's the server, but the shadow is too big. When he grumbles, "I thought you wanted to learn about hockey?" I feel my eyes roll involuntarily.

"Baker? Leave. Me. Alone."

"Nah, I think you and Taylor should invite me to sit at your table. There're no seats left in this place except these two," he says, pointing to the two empty chairs at our table. "And since we're *friends*, I thought you wouldn't mind sharing."

"I—"

"Sure thing, dude. Any friend of... uh... hers is a friend of mine," Taylor says.

Great! Taylor doesn't remember my name. Ugh. Will the humiliation ever end?

"Her name is Virginia," Baker deadpans.

Taylor nods. "Oh, right. Virginia. Sort of an old-fashioned name, right?"

"Right. It was my grandmother's name," I explain.

"That's cool." Taylor nods again as he sips his beer.

"Wow, riveting conversation," mocks Baker.

Okay, I'm not sure how or why this happens, but it just hits me like a shit storm. The tears just start falling out of my eyes. Maybe it's because my mom is the queen of guilt trips and she's sent me on a big one after she found out I wasn't spending any time at home over the holidays. Or maybe it's because Baker Stark is fucking with my head. Either way, the frustration and stress hit me like a Mack truck.

"Whoa, what's wrong, Virginia?" Taylor uses his massive hand to pat me on the back so hard I lurch forward.

At least he remembered my name. I hiccup then say, "I'm on my period. It happens." Okay, why did I just admit that? Could I be any more embarrassed tonight? I look over at Baker, who seems sincerely worried about me.

"You weren't on your period last night."

And boom. There it is. The answer to my earlier question—yes, things can get more embarrassing. *So much more embarrassing.* "Baker!" I hiss. "Shut the hell up."

I turn to Taylor. "He's kidding. We weren't together last night."

"I thought you guys were just friends," asks a confused Taylor.

"We are!" we both shout in unison.

Baker winks, saying, "With benefits."

"No, that's not true. There are definitely no benefits to being friends with you, *Blake*." I stand up from the table and look at Taylor. "Taylor, it was nice seeing you again. I don't feel well. I'm going home."

I stomp away from the table just as Baker shouts, "It's Baker, and you know it!"

Turning, I shout right back, "Yeah, I know it. I just don't fucking care!"

CHAPTER 33

Baker

I WATCH her walk away and wince when she says, "Yeah, I know it. I just don't fucking care!"

"What's the deal with you two?" asks Taylor as he finishes off his glass of beer and refills it with more.

"We're friends."

"She didn't seem too friendly when you sat down."

"It's a long story."

Taylor leans back in his seat. "Spill."

So I spill. I tell him every single thing about my life, and I'm not sure why. Maybe it's because he's a good listener. He sits there, nodding and looking contemplative as I ramble on and on. When I finish, he rubs his chin.

"Well, did you just want me to hear that story, or do you want my advice?"

"What's your advice?"

"Well, first of all, I'd like to thank your dad for his sacrifice. Guys like him will always be heroes in my eyes."

I nod and smile. "Thanks."

"As for the rest of it, I think you need to fucking get over it. You've led a charmed life, it seems. None of the shit with your parents was your fault. I think you're just using it as an excuse."

"An excuse? No, I'm—"

"You are. For some reason, the thought of being in a relationship scares the shit out of you, and I'm not just talking about women. You said you have what? One friend?"

"Two if you count Virginia."

"If I were you, I wouldn't count Virginia. She doesn't want to be your 'friend,'" he says, using air quotes.

"No?"

"No. And you damn well know it."

"But my parents...."

Taylor rolls his eyes. "It's not your parents' fault you can't commit. Sure, your mom sounds like a real piece of work, but that's on her. I don't know Virginia well, but I know she's cool, and sweet, and pretty damn hot now, so I think you've got two choices."

"Two choices."

"Yep. One, let her go."

I nod, scowling. I don't think I can let her go.

"Or two, go get her and do your best to keep her."

Go get her? Keep her? "Why the fuck does that terrify me?"

"Which option, one or two?"

"Both of them."

He shrugs. "Shit or get off the pot, dude."

I know he's right. "That's not bad advice for a jock."

He chuckles. "The only reason I play football is for the scholarship. Unlike you, I wasn't born with money, so football has given me a chance at an education."

"What's your major?"

I'm expecting him to say something like exercise science.

When he says, "Physics," I nearly spit out my beer. "I'm an academic All-American and All-American linebacker."

"Congrats, man. You going pro?"

"Nope. I'm hoping for NASA, not the NFL."

I stand up, holding my hand out. "Good luck to you, Taylor. I'll be sure to catch your games. Maybe I'll see you around."

"Let's work out sometime. You need to work on your deltoids," he says, smirking.

I chuckle. "Fuck you, man." I shake my head. "Fine, whatever. Catch you later."

"Later," he says, sipping his beer.

He's pretty cool. Virginia could do worse than that guy. "Yeah, she could have me."

I need to think about Taylor's two choices. The thought of walking away and never seeing her, talking to her, or kissing her makes me feel sick. I guess I know my answer, but am I ready for that? If I let her in, she'll be in for good.

Fuck, I don't want it any other way.

CHAPTER 34

Jeez, I wish I'd worn a jacket. It's been unseasonably warm for autumn in Iowa, so I've gone without a coat or even a sweater for most of October and the first week of November. Now, Mother Nature has decided to do her job; the temperature has dropped twenty degrees since yesterday.

Shivering, I bring my arms up and cross them in front of my chest, hoping I can use my body heat to warm up. I walk at a brisk pace down Lincoln Way, the six blocks to my street. I've stopped crying, thankfully. I know I blabbed that I was on my period, and I do think it's about to start. I always get a little weepy around that time, so it makes sense. Taking a deep breath, I make myself think about other things—anything but Baker Stark.

"Work! I can think about work," I shout.

I start back tomorrow. I've had a few weeks off, and it's been pretty great, honestly. I know Dad gave me money to help with expenses, but I don't want to use that savings account unless it's absolutely necessary. Since my checking account is dwindling, I need to get back to earning some cash, and Jackson promised me that everything at The Coffee Bean is better than ever. Even the new manager is a hit—at least that's Jackson's story. I'll find out more tomorrow when I work with both of them.

When I get close to my turn, I see a familiar black Nissan parked on the street corner. There's a large hockey player leaning against it. Groaning, I let my shoulders slump and my head hang low as I step in front of him. "What do you want now, Baker?"

"Wow, you're happy to see me. *Not.*"

"I'm exhausted from you. I'm tired of fighting with you. I'm tired of thinking about you. I—"

"You think about me?"

The involuntary eye roll happens again. I can't control it. "Seriously? You're asking me that?"

He steps toward me, taking off his jacket as he walks, and throws it over my shoulders. "I'm seriously asking."

I look up at him, sliding my arms into the warmth of his coat, and his sincere expression surprises me. "I think about you all the time."

"I think about you too."

"I know. I'm your *friend*," I say, defeated.

"No. When I think of you, we're definitely not just friends."

I blink up at him again. "What do you mean?"

"I think about having you in my bed and about me sinking into you. I think about what it'd be like to wake up with you, your hair all messy from sleep and hot sex."

I feel my face turn pink. No, I bet it's magenta.

"You're blushing."

"Of course I'm blushing. Jeez, Baker. You've got such a smut mouth."

"Sometimes you act so virginal. I...." He looks into my eyes. His next four words are painful and embarrassing. "No. No fucking way."

I pull off his jacket and hand it to him, then run toward my apartment. I can see it from the corner, so it only takes me a few minutes to make it to the door. "Oh, of course," I hiss. The one time I need the door propped open with that brick, it's not. I dig through my purse, frantically searching for my keys.

"Virginia?"

Frick! He's so close to me now; I feel his breath on my neck. "What!" I shout, turning to face him. "I'm a virgin, okay? Now you know." I turn to unlock the door but can't seem to get the key in the freaking lock. "Damn it." A hot tear strikes my cheek, then another one and another. My eyes are wet and blurry. I can't see what I'm doing.

He puts his hands on my shoulders and turns me around. "Babe, stop."

Stop what? Stop crying? Stop trying to unlock the door? Stop trying with him? What! "I need to go, Baker. I've got stuff to do." I wipe away the tears from my cheek. "I want to be alone."

"I know the feeling."

"Wow, you know how to make a girl feel special." I try to turn around again, but he keeps me in place by holding on to my upper arms.

"I didn't mean it like that. I've always liked my solitude, liked being alone. Until I met you. You're on my mind 24-7. Even when I'm at home, I want to text you or talk to you. You invade my space even when you're not there."

"Gee, I'm so sorry I—"

"You're getting peeved at me when what I'm trying to tell you is I *like* you there–, in my space."

Sniffling, I say, "You do?"

"I do. The thought of you invading someone *else's* space, however.... When I saw you with Taylor tonight, I nearly came unglued. After you left, he and I talked. He gave me some great advice."

"He did? What advice?"

"He told me I either needed to let you go—"

"Uh-huh." I know he's going to pick that one.

"—or go get you and fight like hell to keep you."

I blink up at him, waiting for him to tell me which way he's leaning. When he says nothing more, I bend at the knees to get away from his hold on me. "I guess I know which one you chose." I finally get the key in the lock and turn.

"You do?"

"Of course." I push the door open and step inside. I attempt to move fast enough to lock him out, but he's wily. His body is through the door before I've even turned around.

He moves toward me slowly as I back up, our steps in sync. "So, which one did I choose?"

In no time my back is against the wall of mailboxes and Baker is pressed against me. "What is it with you cornering me against walls and shit?"

"I like it. I get your undivided attention this way."

Eye roll. "Whatever."

"Since I can't seem to get you to answer, I'm just going to tell you which one I picked."

"Uh-huh."

"I picked the second one."

I look up at him, startled. "You did? Why?"

"Why?"

"Yeah. You've made it clear from the beginning that this thing"—I point back and forth between us—"isn't going anywhere."

"I was wrong, or at least I hope I was wrong. Do *you* see us going somewhere?" he asks as he moves a strand of hair out of my face.

"How should I know? The longest relationship I've ever had was two months. That was in high school, so that doesn't count."

"Well, you know about my high school girlfriend."

I do. I remember the story from our one-on-one interview.

"Here's what I know," Baker says with a sigh. "I know you're smart, beautiful, caring, and sexy as fuck. I also know that no one can kiss like you." He's staring at my mouth as he says the last part.

"You think I'm sexy?"

"Holy hell, yes. I spend my days and nights rock hard thinking about you, especially after that night on my couch. Goddamn, your body's made for sin."

"I wouldn't know," I deadpan.

Sliding his finger down my cheek to my lips, he mutters, "You will. When you're ready. Until then, we'll go at your pace. I'll wait."

"Y-you'll wait?"

"I will."

"Why?"

"Because, babe, when you and I finally connect, it's going to be out of this world."

"How do you know that?" I'm confident I'm going to be terrible in bed.

"The kiss. I can tell by the way you kiss me that it's going to be better than anything I've ever had before."

Shit, now he's got me intrigued. "Well, hell. Now I want to go do it just to see if you're right."

Baker throws his head back and laughs loudly. "If that's what you want," he says, bending down to get closer. "Let's start with a kiss and see where it leads."

Straight to bed, that's where. "Wait! What happened to your face?"

"My mom scratched me. Had to have surgery to repair this big cut on Monday."

I blink at him, waiting for the rest of the story. "That's it? You're not going to tell me the rest?" I try to pull away from him, but that's not happening.

He lets out a deep and frustrated breath. "I will. Let's pack you a bag so you can come to my place. Stay with me. I'll tell you everything. Okay?"

I push myself up onto my tiptoes. "Okay." Just before our lips meet, I ask, "So, you're my boyfriend now?"

"Babe. Do we have to label it?"

"Yes. Absolutely. I'm not moving forward without labels."

Running his hand through his hair, he sighs. "Then yes, I'm your boyfriend."

"And I'm your girlfriend."

That makes him smile. "Okay. I like the sound of that. Virginia Murray is my girl."

"Girl*friend*."

"*Girlfriend*. Now kiss me, girlfriend, before I die of need."

I giggle as our lips meet. In no time he's got me lifted up and I've got my legs around him. The wall behind me is keeping me up. When he grinds his hardness against me, I moan. Kissing my way to his ear, I whisper, "I don't think it'll be long before we test that hypothesis of yours."

"No?"

"No. I'm so wet for you, Baker."

"Fuck, you drive me crazy, Virginia."

"I know."

CHAPTER 35

Baker

UP IN HER BEDROOM, I watch as she packs an overnight bag. My hands twitch with the need to touch her. She's bending over in front of me, picking up something off the floor. Next, she's stretching up into her closet until her shirt slides up her side, showing me her soft little belly. Jesus, she has no idea what she does to me. Okay, maybe she has some idea, since I keep telling her she drives me crazy, but now that I know she's inexperienced, maybe she doesn't know what I mean. I'm about to show her, though.

"Fuck!" I growl. I move up behind her, wrap my arms around her middle, and pull her back so tightly against me that no light can shine through. If I could get closer, I would. I let my hands slide up beneath her flowing top until I reach wonderland. Using both hands, I cup her breasts and squeeze.

"Baker." My name escapes her lips like a breeze.

I tweak her nipples and quickly pull the cups of her bra down and away from her. "I'm not going to do anything you don't want to do, Virginia. I promise. I just need—"

"Touch me, Baker," she says, arching into my palms. "Please?"

I move my hands down to the edge of her top. "Lift your arms."

She follows orders and hurriedly lifts them above her head. Reaching back, she unhooks her bra. As I slide the straps down her arms, I kiss her shoulder and neck. "You're beautiful."

Turning in my arms, she reaches up and puts hers around my neck. Without a word, I palm her ass, squeezing her round bottom. We kiss slowly with our tongues swirling and twining against each other. It's a fucking hot kiss. The only thing missing is her skin touching mine. I walk her over to the bed and urge her to sit down. Reaching back behind my neck, I pull my shirt off.

"Wow." She says it so quietly I could have missed it if I hadn't been staring at her lips.

"No. You're the *wow* in this room, Virginia." And that's no lie. Sitting on her bed in nothing but her tight jeans is fucking sexy as hell.

I look down at her jeans. I've seen her nude before. I'm not sure she's ready for it again, but when she stands to unbutton and unzip her jeans, I get my answer. She shimmies out of them with the cutest little wiggle. Once they're down at her feet, she steps out and tosses them away so she's standing in only a tiny pair of baby blue panties. My first instinct is to dive in, but this is Virginia. My girlfriend. My *virgin* girlfriend.

I stare at her panties, then let my eyes move slowly upward. Her tits are fucking perfect. They're full and round with nipples pink like her lips. I lean down and kiss those little rosebuds softly, then move down her neck until I reach them. Swiping my tongue over one tip, I watch it pebble and peak. Virginia's breathing is labored and erratic. I look up and ask, "Is this okay?" When she nods furiously, I chuckle. "You like it?"

"Y-yes. Don't stop."

I use the flat of my tongue to swipe the nipple over and over. Moving to her other breast, I do the same. I feel her fingers slide into my hair to hold me in place. When I suck the hard nub into my mouth, Virginia releases a moan so fucking sexy I want to sink into her this second. I move to the other breast and give it the same attention. Slowly, I slide my palm into the top of her blue panties and cup her. She doesn't shave, but her hair is soft down there. I need to know. Sweeping my finger into her, I moan. "You're dripping."

"I know," she says in a husky voice.

"I love that you're wet for me, babe."

"Me too. Don't stop."

"Don't stop what? What do you want me to do?" I'm not asking to be difficult. I really want to know. I'm not going to do anything she's not one hundred percent sure of, no way.

"Everything, Baker. God, *everything.*"

Growling once more, I stand up and unzip my pants, pushing them along with my boxers down to my feet. Kicking them off, I lean down and place one hand on either side of her. I move in closer until skin touches skin. Virginia slowly lies back on the bed, and I move with her until we're not only chest to chest but center to center. With my body pressed between her legs, I kiss her so hard and so deep, I imagine what it's going to feel like when my cock makes it home.

She's frantically touching my hair, arms, and back. When her hands find my ass, she squeezes it so hard I wince. She must not have noticed, because she uses her hands to pull me into her.

"Baker. I-I need you."

Latching on to her breast again, I lick and suck and nibble on and around the nipple.

Squirming against me, she starts to get frustrated. "Baker! Do something. I-I need to...."

"You need to come?"

"Yes, damn it. Stop toying with me."

Chuckling, I move down her body until I've pushed myself to standing. I watch her legs close. Bending again, I slide my fingers into the top edges of her baby blue panties and pull them down her legs. "Open your legs for me."

"Huh?"

"You want to come?"

She nods hurriedly.

"Then open those legs. Let me see that sweet pussy of yours."

"Oh, God. You talk so dirty, Baker."

"I know. Now do it." I watch as she opens her legs slowly. It's like she's opening up one millimeter at a time. Like a flower. The wait is killing me, so I help her; placing my hands on her knees, I gently pull them open until I get a glimpse of her. "Fuck, sweetheart."

"What's wrong? Is it ugly?"

I can't help it, I laugh. She thinks I'm laughing at her because she tries to pull away. "Shh, Virginia. Trust me when I tell you you've got the prettiest pussy I've ever seen. It's pink, and you're so wet you're practically weeping for me."

"Are you being honest with me?" she asks softly.

"I'd never lie to you about something as important as your pussy, babe."

She starts to laugh, slapping my arm at the same time. "You're such an ass."

An ass about to make her come so hard she'll launch off the bed. I lean down, using one arm to brace myself above her, and kiss her lips as I run my fingers through her wetness. I use my middle finger to circle her clit, varying the pressure. As she squirms, I sink my tongue into her mouth while sliding a finger inside her. Her moans reverberate in my chest. I insert my finger but not far, just enough to rub the inner wall as I play with her hard little clit. As I work her, I feel her touch me. My dick jerks in her hand. He's very sensitive right now. I use my hand to show her how I like to be handled. Before she can protest, I'm back to touching her and moving my finger back and forth over her slit.

"Oh, Baker."

"Good?"

"Oh, oh, that's definitely good, Baker. S-so good. Don't stop, please."

I know she likes it because she's wrapped her little hand around my cock, and she's pumping me like a damn pro. "Fuck, don't stop, Virginia." When I moan out my pleasure, she seems to get a little braver. Increasing her speed, she repeats the move. "Twist your palm a little as you move up and down. Oh, fuck, yeah. Like that. Oh, shit. You're good. Yeah. Oh, fucking hell, Virginia. Don't. Ever. Stop."

Working like a madman to get her to come before I do, I press my finger farther inside and use my thumb on her clit. "Oh, oh, I-I'm almost, *ahhhhh*. Oh, my, yes, Baker."

She keeps her hand moving up and down my shaft, twisting her palm around me as she goes. Hearing her release is all I need to come like a fucking rocket. Her moans and whimpers are enough to make me go goddamn crazy. "Virginia. That's it. Stop. I'm gonna come."

But she moves faster.

One, two, three more pumps and "Oh, fucking motherfucking Jesus, hell *yessssss!*" I come so hard and so fast I'm dizzy. Panting, I look down at her pretty flushed face and see a bright smile.

"That was good, right?"

"Babe, that was fucking perfect." I peer down at the mess between us. Pulling away from her and off the bed, I grab my shirt and wipe off her stomach and chest. Then I wipe myself off and smile down at her. "You good?"

"So, so, so good, babe."

Ah, there it is. I love that. "I like when you call me babe."

"You do?"

Nodding, I stand up. Her eyes lock onto my dick as soon as I'm at full height. "What about me? Do you like what you see?"

"Well, I can tell you this. That"—she points at little Baker—"is not a penis."

I peer down. "Huh? Yeah, it's a penis."

"No, that's a *C-O-C-K*."

"It's both, V." *What the hell is she talking about?*

"No. A penis is little. A cock is B-I-G."

"Whatever you say, Virginia." I can't help but chuckle. "We're going to have a lot of fun together, V."

"We are?"

"We are." Placing my knee back on the bed, I move to slide up close to her. Wrapping my arms around her, I pull her in to me and kiss her nose, then her mouth. "You're amazing, Virginia."

"I am?"

"You are. I can't believe how lucky I am."

"You can't?"

Chuckling again, I kiss her deeply. "No, I can't. Thankfully, I finally got smart."

"That's true," she deadpans.

Smiling, I reach to the end of the bed and pull a quilt up and over us. When her breathing evens out, I know she's asleep. Peeking down at her naked body, I smile. For the first time in my life, I feel like I'm right where I'm supposed to be. This has been hands down the Best. Night. Ever.

CHAPTER 36

I'M LATE. My first day back to work and I'm frigging late. Hopping off the bus, I sprint down Lincoln Way, turn right up Welch Avenue, pass two shops, and I'm there. I yank the door open and step inside.

Between gulps of air, I say, "I'm sorry I'm late. I overslept."

Bending at the waist, I work to catch my breath. When I look up, I see Jackson and some hot-as-shit man next to him. He's got short blond hair and he looks sort of like Chris Pine. Yum.

"Well, hello!" the new guy coos. "You must be Virginia!" Sauntering over to me, he bends down so we're face-to-face. "I'm Johnathan, but you can call me John John."

"John John?"

"Yes, *indeedee*. It's what my friends call me, and from what my new man tells me, you and I are going to be *besteeees*."

Wow, he's so perky this early in the morning. Not necessarily a good thing.

He claps his hands rapidly in front of his chest. "I can't wait 'til we have a sleepover. I've heard so many cool things about you."

A sleepover? I've just ignored half of the stuff he said. "A new man?"

As I stand, he stands. He's not much taller than I am, so he didn't have to go far.

"Yep." He cups his hand over his mouth like he's going to whisper, but he says it at full volume. "It's Jackson."

Giggling at John John, I peek over at Jackson. He's got the sweetest pink blush on his high cheekbones. "It's true. We're dating."

"Well, congratulations, you guys. Jackson's pretty awesome, isn't he?" I ask John John. Geesh, I wish he'd go by JJ instead. It'd be so much easier at 6:40 a.m.

"Girl," he says, slapping my arm. "Jackson is f-i-n-e, fine. Now go get clocked in so we can chat and get paid."

I smile, looking back and forth at both guys as I walk back to the break room. I take off my coat, clock in, and grab a green apron. Stepping out into the shop, I look around. "What do you want me to do first?"

"Oh, it's all done. JJ came in early."

Yay! I can call him JJ.

Jackson chuckles as he wipes off the counter nearest the register. "He wanted to focus all of his attention on you this morning."

I turn to see JJ leaning on the counter with his chin on his hand. "It's true. When Jackson told me about you and the deal with—" He does that thing with his hand again. Not whispering, he finishes his sentence with "K-I-P, Kip."

I see a T-R-E-N-D, trend. Not wanting to answer questions about K-I-P, Kip, I ask, "So, what are your thoughts about kissing?"

"Kissing?" asks Jackson.

Before I can respond, JJ says, "Oh, girl. Kissing is everything."

"It is?"

"It is. If you can't kiss, why bother?"

"I can kiss," Jackson says defensively.

"Honey, you're the best kisser I've ever had. Trust me. You can K-I-S-S, kiss."

Relieved, Jackson goes back to wiping shit down. When we both hear a harrumph, I look at Jackson. "Oh, um, you're a good kisser too, JJ," he says.

"Oh, honey. I *know* I can kiss."

Before I can ask another question, our first customers step into the shop. According to JJ, thanks to the cold, our business has picked up. It could be the cold, or it could be that JJ is a natural customer service schmoozer. K-I-P, Kip would never have had people laughing while he's upselling more expensive drinks like lattes and frappuccinies (our version of our competitor's drink). Nope. JJ's good. *Really* good.

By eight o'clock, I'm beat. I haven't worked in almost a month, so I need to get back into barista shape. Not to mention the fact that Baker woke me up several times in the night for some lovely kissing and touching and amazing orgasms. I wanted to do, you know, *it*, but Baker wants to wait. He wants it to be special.

As I'm cleaning out the espresso machine, I hear someone clear their throat. I look up and see Baker wearing one of my old T-shirts that's got to be three sizes too small for him. I want to ask him about it, but when I look at his face, he looks downright grumpy. How could that be after last night?

"Virginia? Can we talk?"

Oh, shit. "What? Why?" I look around. There's no one around. JJ and Jackson are in the back doing "inventory." Yeah, right. There's a young couple sitting at the table near the front window. "I can't leave the counter."

"It's okay. We can talk right here."

Wow, he looks angry. Hesitantly, I say, "Okay."

"If this thing between us is going to work—if we're going to be a couple—we need to get some things straight."

"Okay, I—"

"One. You will not leave me in bed alone without waking me

up before you leave. When I woke up alone, I felt, well, a little used, to be honest."

I start to giggle, but when I look at Baker, he looks hurt. "Oh, Baker. I'm sorry. I woke up late, and I didn't want to wake you. You needed your rest," I say shyly.

"I appreciate that. It's why I'm mentioning this now, but I didn't get to kiss you goodbye."

And there it is. I'm blushing again. "Okay."

"Two. You will stop walking everywhere alone."

"But I don't have a car and—"

Holding his hand up, he says, "Please let me finish."

Nodding, I remain silent.

"If my granna knew my girlfriend was walking around this city unaccompanied, she'd whip my ass."

"But, Baker, I'm used to walking and taking the bus. It's no big deal."

"It is to me. So, I'd like to propose a compromise."

"A compromise."

"You will stop walking everywhere, especially when it's dark outside. That means early mornings and evenings. If you need a ride, I'll take you. I will pick you up from work and class whenever I can. The only exceptions would be if I were in class, at practice, or at an away game. When I'm at away games, you'll drive my car and I'll—"

"No! That's too much."

"It's too much?" His lips go thin as he arches his brow.

He's mad again. I nod, afraid to say more.

"Fine. I'll buy you a car."

"No! If I wanted a car, I'd buy one. They're a hassle."

"And now we're back to number two. You will not walk unaccompanied in this city when darkness is imminent. I'll drive you."

Imminent? "Geez, Baker. What're you gonna do, spank me if I don't obey?" When he doesn't respond, I know I just stepped into a brand-new world. "You wouldn't!" I whisper-hiss.

"Try me."

We're in a stare down, and I'm losing. "Fine. We'll play it by ear. But you can't just say I'm not allowed to walk places. I like to walk."

Smiling from ear to ear, no doubt because he believes he's won, Baker nods. "I'll pick you up after work and take you home or wherever you need to go. I have to be at the gym later this afternoon. What time do you get off here?"

"One."

"I'll be here. As for the rest of the details, we can work those out tonight."

"Tonight?"

"I was hoping you were free. I want you to meet someone. Someone very important to me."

"Oh, sure. Of course. When? Where are we going?"

"My house. Dress casual. I'll cook." He leans over the counter until we're inches apart. "I'll pick you up at six." He moves the rest of the way and lays a soft, slow kiss on me.

My knees almost buckle, and my panties? Well, they melt.

"Bye, babe," Baker says as he walks toward the door.

"Bye." I wave and keep waving until he's out the door and halfway to his car.

"OMG," squeaks the man to my left. "You're with him?" JJ says, pointing to the door. "He's your boyfriend?" He's cupping his mouth like it's a secret. Well, not anymore. I watch JJ jump up and down, clapping his hands like an overly peppy cheerleader. "You. Are. Da. Bomb. Girl. We are so having a slumber party tomorrow night."

"Uh, I—"

"Just go with it," says Jackson with a smirk. "It'll just be easier."

"Oh, shush, you bad boy, or Virginia won't be the only one to get a spanking."

I feel my eyes double in size with shock. Jackson is blushing like a virgin on her wedding night. Okay, that made me giggle. The virgin joke, not Jackson's spankings. Although....

"Tomorrow night. Your place. I'll bring the wine. You bring the deets about that hot man of yours." JJ bounces his eyebrows.

"Fine." I'll have to be sure Peach is there. I don't think I can handle JJ alone.

"Hurray!" he shouts as he hops and dances into the back room.

I turn to Jackson. "Seriously? You and JJ?" He doesn't seem like Jackson's type at all.

Shrugging, he responds, "We can't help who we love."

I nod because truer words were never spoken.

CHAPTER 37

Baker

PROMPTLY AT SIX, I knock on Virginia's apartment door and then look down at myself to make sure everything is zipped and buttoned. Running my fingers through my damp hair, I relax my shoulders. I had to run around like crazy to be ready in time for tonight. I had my workout, then had to stop for a few groceries on the way back to my place. At home, I started the meal, showered, and shaved. All in order to get here on time. I made it.

When her door opens, my heart nearly stops. She's fucking stunning. It was well worth all of the running around to see her like this.

"Babe. You look beautiful." I know I probably sound surprised, but I've never seen her like this. She's got on a black dress that's not too short and definitely not too long. It hits her in the middle of her gorgeous thighs. Her legs are covered in black hose or tights or whatever they're called. I pan down her legs to see she's wearing heels. They aren't stilettos, but they're a few inches high.

"Nice shoes." I wink.

She doesn't have a lot of makeup on, but her lips are pink and glossy, which makes me want to kiss them. Better not. Chicks get all weird about ruined lipstick. Later.

I can tell she's changed something. "Your hair. It's shorter than it was this morning." It's still sort of blonde, but her hair is flowing just past her shoulders. It's wavy and shiny. I want to touch it, so I step closer and reach my hand out. "It's so soft."

"Oh, yeah, I had it done this afternoon. And don't worry, Peach drove me."

"Good to know. You ready to go? You'll want a jacket. The temp has dropped."

"Got it," she says, holding up a jacket. Sliding it on over the dress, she steps toward the door.

I wait until she starts out the door and put my hand on her lower back.

She looks up at me with a pretty little smile. "So, are you going to tell me who I'm meeting tonight?"

"My granna. She's in town meeting up with her new boyfriend."

She giggles. "Your grandmother has a new boyfriend?"

"Yeah. My plastic surgeon. They hit it off when I was in the hospital."

"Are you ever going to tell me about what happened, Baker?"

I pull her to me to give her a small kiss. "Yeah. I'll tell you about it. But not tonight. Tonight is about my girl meeting the most important person in my life."

"Okay."

At the car, I hit the unlock button on my key fob and open the door for her. As I watch her slide into the seat, my eye is drawn to her legs. The little dress has ridden up, revealing some of those sexy-as-fuck thigh-high hose. "Jesus, Virginia. What are those?" I ask, pointing to her legs.

She nervously attempts to adjust her dress to cover her legs. "No. Don't you dare. Pull your dress up a little. Let me see them."

"Baker."

"Do it." Okay, I'm bossy, but I'm not angry. I'm fucking hard as a rock. Not a good look when visiting your grandmother.

Shyly, she pulls the skirt up another few inches.

"No way, woman." Her brows are drawn together like I've confused her. "They're fucking hot." I step around the door and lean into the car. Sliding my palm up her thigh, I whisper close to her lips, "You're a very naughty girl, Miss Murray."

She's blushing profusely. "I am?"

I let my palm climb higher. "You are. You knew what those little stockings would do to me, didn't you?" I look down at my crotch. Her eyes follow. My dress slacks are tented as far as they'll go.

"Maybe?"

"So, you did know. *Tsk, tsk, tsk.* What am I going to do now? I can't very well see my grandmother like this. Besides, I'll spend the entire evening thinking about those." Looking down again, I say, "Show me your panties." My voice is husky now. I'm so turned on I'm about to unravel.

Slowly—too slowly—she pulls her skirt up to reveal a dark pair of panties with symbols all over them. I lean in closer. When I can't see, I ask, "What are those all over your undies, babe?"

"Uh, they're insignias."

"Insignias? Of what?"

She giggles. "They're the insignias from all of the houses from Hogwarts."

I look up at her face. "From Harry Potter?"

"Yeah."

Holy hell. The perfect cocktail of nerdy and sexy is sitting in my car. If that doesn't make me want to fuck her right here and right now, I don't know what will. "Naughty girl, Virginia."

Squeaking nervously, she attempts to defend herself. "I'm not naughty."

"Do you know what happens to naughty girls?" I run my finger up the front of her panties.

Her breathing has become labored. She's flushed with arousal. "What?"

"They get a red little bottom."

"Huh?" she squeaks again.

"That's right," I say as I dip my finger underneath the elastic of her Harry Potter panties. "You're fucking drenched," I growl. "I've got a mind to take you right back upstairs and—"

"But we need to go... your grandmother."

Sighing, I pull my finger out of her center. We're so close that I can feel her breath on my face. I bring my wet finger to my mouth and suck. "Mm, sweet."

"Oh, God. Baker," she moans.

"Later. I'll deal with you later." I lean down and kiss her shocked little lips.

Adjusting my rock-hard dick as I walk around the car, I hop in and start it up. I look over at her and smirk. "Later."

CHAPTER 38

I KNEW I was playing with fire. I had planned to wear some Spanx and black hose, but Peach talked me into the thigh-high stockings. I'd bought them to go with my sexy schoolgirl costume but ended up going with knee-highs. Honestly, I thought my dress was long enough to cover them; I just didn't consider what would happen when I sat down. I'm not disappointed in his reaction, but spanking? I'm not sure how I feel about that.

As we drive, Baker is moving his palm slowly up and down my upper thigh. It's driving me crazy. I'm on edge as it is with what happened earlier. Squirming in my seat as inconspicuously as possible, I keep my eyes forward. But Baker knows.

Winking, he says, "You keep wiggling around in your seat like that, I'm going to have to pull over and help you out."

Yep, he knows. "I can't help it. You make me crazy, Baker."

Throwing his head back, he laughs. "Now you know how I feel about you 99 percent of the time."

When his finger slides up and into my panties, I open my legs a little bit to give him easier access and moan, "Baker, don't tease me."

"If we had more time," he mutters. He pulls his hand away from my center and puts it back on the wheel.

I close my legs and scoot closer to the door. I'm not sure how long this dinner is going to last, but I hope it's not long. I need him. Baker pulls into the two-car attached garage. Placing the car in Park, he presses the garage remote to shut the door behind us.

I start to open my door. "Ah, ah, ah. Wait for me, please."

I wait and watch as he comes around the car. It gives me a moment to glimpse him in his suit. He's so handsome in his dark gray duds. He's paired the jacket and slacks with a light blue shirt. He's tie-less, only having one button undone on his dress shirt. It doesn't detract from the overall look. The suit fits him perfectly across his shoulders and chest. The slacks are snug on his thick thighs, and I can only imagine how they'd hug his ass. Maybe he'll model for me later. A shiver runs through me at thinking about later. He made quite a few suggestions. The question is, am I ready for them?

Baker steps to my side and pulls the door open the rest of the way, holding his hand out for me to take. "We have arrived, milady."

I giggle at his attempt at an English accent.

Taking my hand, he leads me into the house through a side door that opens into the kitchen. It smells like there is something Italian cooking. Yum.

Once inside, he announces, "Granna? We're here."

Oh. My. Gosh. I'm so nervous. All of my focus is now on the beautiful woman walking toward me. *She's* his grandmother? She can't be older than forty-five. I raise my hand to shake hers, but she waves me off. "Oh no, sweetheart. Give Granna a hug."

Before I know it, I'm wrapped up in her arms. She's about my height, maybe slightly taller. She smells like expensive perfume, but it's not too strong; it's subtle and sweet. When she pulls away, she holds my arms out in front of me. "You're beautiful, Virginia."

"Thank you, ma'am."

"Granna. Please call me Granna."

"Granna."

"Now, come with me. I'd like you to meet my hot man."

I let out a startled giggle. *Hot man?* She leads me into the formal sitting room, stopping in front of a handsome older man. "Virginia, this is Tommy. Tommy, this is Baker's girlfriend. She's a senior studying sociology with the hopes of going to graduate school." She looks over at me. "Am I right?"

"Right." Wow, I feel I'm at a disadvantage. I know nothing about her.

"Virginia, Tommy is a plastic surgeon." I start to speak, but she has more to say. "And before you ask, no, I haven't had a boob job."

I start to giggle and can't stop. She's funny. "Noted," I say through fits of laughter. I look behind me to see Baker leaning against the doorframe. He's smiling from ear to ear at his granna.

"Virginia, can I get you something to drink? I've got wine, water, soda, beer, and milk."

I look to see what Granna's drinking. "May I have a glass of wine, please?"

"Red or white?"

"White. Thanks, Baker."

He winks at me, then makes his way back into the kitchen. I turn back to the remaining guests and smile. What should I do? Should I say something like "nice weather"? I'm saved when Baker's granna says, "Let's sit, shall we."

I take a seat on the sofa, leaving a spot open for Baker to sit on my right. When he returns, he hands me my glass of wine as he sits beside me. Sipping his own beer, he slides his hand over mine until our fingers are intertwined. He squeezes my hand gently, and it's all the reassurance I need that everything will be okay.

"So," says Granna after sipping her drink. "When's the wedding?"

I spit out the sip of wine.

"Jesus, Granna. Give her a heart attack, why don't you? She hasn't been warned about your wicked sense of humor. Baby steps," Baker says with a chuckle.

Granna winks at me as she says, "Well, shoot. Why didn't you tell her?"

"Actually, Granna, he didn't tell me anything," I admit. "He just invited me to meet his 'favorite person' without any information."

Her face softens at those words. "He's my favorite person too, honey." She turns to Tommy. "No offense."

Tommy releases a soft laugh. "None taken, my dear. I'm partial to my children too."

"How many children do you have Dr.—er, Tommy?"

"Four. Sam is thirty-five, Becky's thirty-four, Elizabeth is thirty-two, and Shanna is twenty-eight."

"Wow! One boy and three girls?"

"All girls. Sam is short for Samantha."

"Wow, I bet that was something having all those girls growing up in the same house."

"It was a nightmare. I almost built myself a clubhouse just to have somewhere to hide when the fights over clothes and makeup got going. But I adore them, and I couldn't imagine my life without them, so it was all worth it."

A ding from the kitchen alerts us that something is done.

"Food!" says Baker excitedly. "I hope you're all hungry. I made lasagna. Granna's recipe."

"It smells amazing, Baker," I tell him. "You cooked it all?"

"He's a wonderful cook, Virginia. I told him every man needs to know how to cook." Granna shrugs, then chuckles. "I didn't want him to starve to death when he was on his own."

"Never, Granna," Baker says softly. "You've taught me a lot of important things. I'd be lost without you."

"Oh, now would you listen to that? Isn't he the sweetest?" she says, pinching his cheek.

"Come on, let's eat," he grumbles, embarrassed.

Dinner's amazing. The best lasagna I've ever eaten. I compliment the chef over and over again. Everything I put into my mouth is perfect. I am in awe of him. After dinner, he serves us warm apple pie with vanilla ice cream in the living room.

"Before you think I've somehow developed superpowers, I did not bake the pie. I bought it at a bakery on Main Street."

I'm so stuffed with pasta that I only nibble on my slice of pie. I don't want to be rude.

After Baker and Tommy finish off their pie, Granna clears her throat. "The girls are going to clean up."

"No. I'll do it later, Granna."

"Nonsense. You cooked. Right, Virginia?"

Okay. I know what this is. This is Granna's attempt to get me alone. I'm going to play along, because I want to hear what she has to say. I'm nervous, though. What if she doesn't like me and wants to use this time to tell me so.

Oh hell. I hope she likes me. I nod at Granna. "Of course. That's the rule."

Making our way into the kitchen, we both take dishes from the dining table, returning several times to get the rest. I hear the guys talking in the living room. Tommy wanted to check out Baker's face to see how he's healing, so this is a good time for that.

Granna stops rinsing dishes and turns to face me. "Now, I know you figured out my little ruse—I wanted to talk to you alone."

I nod.

"How much has Baker told you about his mom and dad?"

"Nothing. Well, he mentioned something about not liking his mom very much, but that's it. He's promised to talk to me about her later."

"Good. Give him time. He's pretty closed off normally, but I can tell it's different with you, Virginia."

"It is?"

"Definitely." She smiles at me warmly. "I like you very much, sweetheart. I liked you before you even walked in the door."

"How?"

"Because I could see a change in Baker since the last time I was here. He's smiling. I heard him whistling as he cooked tonight. And seeing the two of you together, I know why."

"Why?"

"You two fit."

"We fit?"

"He's more relaxed when you're with him than when it's just the two of us. To use a movie cliché, I think you complete him."

"Oh, that's nice." I feel the same about him. "But we just started dating. It's too soon to—"

"Nonsense. I bet you knew the first time you two kissed."

I feel the heat of the blush as it moves to my cheeks.

"Oh, goodness. You're adorable. You're blushing."

"I do it a lot."

Without warning, Granna wraps her arms tightly around me. "I'm so fucking happy you two found each other," she whispers. "Don't you dare tell Baker I just dropped the F-bomb. He doesn't know I cuss."

Giggling, I promise her, "Your secret is safe with me."

"Wonderful. I don't want you to keep things from Baker, but sometimes you need to have a secret or two with your granna, am I right?"

I nod. "You're right."

"Okay, let's get these dishes done. Tommy and I have a movie date after this."

"Tommy's great." I doubt Granna is worried about my opinion of her new boyfriend, but I feel like I need to say something. Awkward silence is, well, it's awkward.

"He is, isn't he?" It's her turn to blush now. "I'm pretty smitten."

As we work side by side, we chitchat about everything from clothes to politics. We finish the dishes in record time and make our way out to the guys.

"We'd better get going, Tommy," Granna says. "The late show is going to start soon, and I'd hate to miss the previews."

"Right. Well, thank you for dinner, Baker." He turns to me. "It was nice meeting you, Virginia. I suspect I'll be seeing more of you two." He looks at Granna. "If Kate doesn't get sick of me, that is."

She blushes again. "Oh, Tommy. I'm not planning on it."

"Good." He holds his hand out, and Granna takes it.

Granna reaches out and takes Baker's hand in her free one. "I'll call you tomorrow, Baker."

"Sounds good. Love you, Gran."

"Love you more, baby boy."

We watch the older couple walk down the front steps and out to the driveway. We're like an old married couple waving to them as they drive off.

"Wow, that was—" I squeak in shock because before I know what's happening, Baker has me over his shoulder in a fireman's hold, kicking the door shut as he passes.

"What the hell, Baker!" I screech. "What are you doing?"

"Taking you to bed. Fuck, I thought they'd never leave. I adore my granna. I can't imagine my life without her, but tonight was excruciating. My dick has been hard since we left your place. I need you, babe."

"I, uh, need you too." I'm being jostled around over his shoulder, but we're almost there. He sets me down next to his bed, and I watch him step back, yank off his suit jacket, and toss it on the floor. He starts working the buttons on his shirt frantically.

"Dress off. Leave those fucking stockings and panties on. That's an order."

Damn, he's so bossy. I know my eyes are as big as saucers, but I do as he asks. I'm as turned on as he is, so I'm playing along. Pulling the dress up until it's over my head, I toss it on the floor next to his shirt and jacket.

"Bra off."

"You're very bossy, Baker."

"Can't help it right now."

"Fine." I unhook the bra from the front, watching him as I do it.

His eyes dilate as he stares at my breasts. "Fuck. You're the hottest, sexiest woman I've ever seen in person or anywhere, V."

"Thank you," I say shyly.

"Don't you dare get shy on me now."

He unbuckles and unzips his dress pants, letting them fall to the ground along with his boxers. He kicks them, then grasps his cock and pumps up and down slowly.

Distracted, I flinch when he asks, "What do you want, babe? I don't want you to feel pressured. Tell me what you want to do next."

"Kiss me?"

"*Abso-fucking-lutely*." He reaches me in two long strides and slides his hands into my hair as soon as he's close enough. When our mouths meet, we're immediately all tongues and teeth. I nip at his lip while he sucks on mine. It's hot as hell.

"Lie down on your back, V."

I sit, then scoot to the center of the bed and lie back on my elbows, keeping my eyes on him. He's been stroking himself leisurely as I moved to my spot.

"Open your legs for me."

Slowly, I open my thighs. I'm a little nervous about it. I know we did things before, but this is much more intense. My feelings are so much stronger. It feels like there's more at stake.

"You're a wet dream, babe, with your Harry Potter undies and those sexy-as-fuck stockings. You're a hot nerd." Placing his knees on the bed, he moves up until his big body is between my legs. "What do you need, Virginia?"

"I want you to take the lead here. So far, every instinct you've had about me has been right. I don't want to have to think about it."

"But—"

Placing a finger over his lips, I say, "I promise I'll tell you if it's too much."

"You will?"

"I promise."

He leans down to kiss my lips softly. *Oh, sweet Baker.* My feelings for him have morphed into something I didn't expect. He kisses down my neck until he reaches my breasts. As soon as I feel his tongue on me, I arch my back. My first instinct is to hold his head in place to keep him there, but I don't want to hinder him.

Baker licks and sucks on my right breast, then my left. At times, he nibbles and bites. I would never have guessed that would feel as good as it does, but I'm learning new things thanks to this man. I'm so turned on just from this, but I need more.

"Baker?"

"Yeah? What do you need, Virginia?"

"You. More."

He gives me more. He gives each breast one last lick and begins working his way south. Nervously, I start to wiggle away. Grasping my hips, Baker attempts to keep me in place as his lips move down my body. His fingers slide into the lace of my Harry Potter's. I feel them being tugged down my legs and then off.

In a husky voice, Baker moans, "You're dripping. I love that you're this wet for me, Virginia."

I watch his head move down and do my best to push my legs together. No one has ever done that to me before. I'm not sure I want it now.

His strong hands move to my knees and gently push my legs apart. "You told me you wanted me to take the lead. Right?"

I nod.

"Well, then let me do it, okay? I'm going to make you feel good. Trust me?"

I nod, then moan the second I feel him swipe his tongue over my clit. When he practically growls, "Mm, so sweet," I nearly lose my mind. His tongue moves lower and slides all the way through me from back to front. I tense up.

"Virginia? What's wrong?"

"It's, uh, strange."

"Strange good or strange bad?"

"Good?" Using his big finger, he pushes it into me as he sucks and licks. *Hell.* "Oh, that's good, Baker. Don't stop, please."

He continues to work me with his mouth and finger while his other hand slides up my belly, back to my breasts. When he suddenly pinches my nipple, I launch myself upward. "Oh God, Baker." He begins to work fast, applying more pressure with his tongue and his fingers until I lose control and explode. I'm shaking from the orgasm. My center is pulsing, throbbing around his fingers. *Holy hell.*

Baker moves his body up until his rock hardness is pressing into me. Kissing me, I taste what he just tasted. It's not terrible; it's just a little weird. Now he's giving me sweet kisses all around my mouth and the tip of my nose. I hope he's not finished, because I don't want to stop. Taking a deep breath, I draw courage from the fact that I know Baker doesn't want me to do anything until I'm ready. There's no pressure. It's the opposite. Maybe he doesn't want to pop my, um, hymen.

"Baker? I'm ready to... you know."

"Virginia, we don't need to do that yet. Don't rush it. I don't want you to feel pressured."

"I don't. At all. I'm starting to think you don't want to do it, though."

His head pops up suddenly. Our eyes meet. "What the hell are you talking about? I can't wait to do it. My cock is weeping, it's so ready."

Phew. I thought he was going to pull a Dave. Remember him? Dave the Douche? Ugh, why am I thinking about him right now? "Then let's do it. I'm ready."

"If you're sure." He sits up on both knees and reaches for something.

When a drawer slides open, I look down in time to watch him tear open a condom package. He places it on the tip of his long shaft and slowly rolls it down. He leans back to the drawer and brings out a tube of something. "What's that?"

"Lube. I don't want to hurt you."

"Oh. Okay." He is big. Huge. I know it's going to hurt. *Courage*.

He rubs a small amount of the lube onto the condom and smears it all over the tip.

Oh God. This is it. It's happening. I'd like to tell you I feel a little regret, but that's the last thing on my mind. I'm thinking how happy I am that it's Baker here with me and not someone like Dave. Dave didn't deserve to share this with me.

Baker moves his big body between my legs. When his face is above mine, he looks into my eyes and whispers, "You sure about this?"

"I'm sure."

He kisses me so sweetly and deeply I nearly cry. When he uses his hand to place himself right against my motherland, I stiffen.

"Relax, Virginia. I'll go slow. Just relax."

I take a deep breath and nod. My body relaxes as I feel him press into me. There's pressure there, sure, but it doesn't hurt. When he stops, I ask, "Are you all the way in?"

"Uh, no. That's just the tip."

"Just the tip?" I squeak.

"Do you want me to stop, Virginia?"

"No. No. Keep going."

He presses into me again, a little faster this time, and I'm happily surprised at the sensation. It feels okay. Yeah, it's—"Oh, fuck!"

"Sorry. Sorry, Virginia. *Damn it!* I thought it'd be best if I just went for it. I'm not moving until you say it's okay."

Panting out breaths like ladies do when they're giving birth, I nod. The breathing works. In no time the pain that shot through me is gone. Now all I feel is Baker inside of me and on top of me. He's surrounding me with his weight and warmth.

When the pain is gone, I nod. "I'm good. It doesn't hurt anymore."

"You sure?"

"I'm sure."

Baker kisses my lips quickly and begins to pull himself back.

I wince a little, but as he slowly pushes back in, I moan. "Oh, wow. Th-that feels good."

Baker responds like he's in pain. "I know."

Am I hurting him? "Baker? Are you okay?"

"Great. The best," he says, wincing. He's definitely not great.

"Baker, if you don't like it—"

"Fuck, babe. I love it. You're so tight I'm just trying to hold on long enough for you to come. I'm just trying to keep it together."

"Oh. Oh!" I moan. He's moved a little bit, and now he's hitting a new part of me. "Can you go faster. Please?"

"Oh, hell yes." He pumps into me harder than before, then out. "Holy fuck, Virginia."

I'm going to take that as a good thing. "I kn-know. Don't stop. Harder!"

He continues to pump into me, thrusting his hips so hard the bed moves. It's good. It's amazing. It's—"Baker!" I screech. I feel myself clenching around him like my body is trying to hang on to him.

"Oh, Christ," he mutters as he thrusts even harder. "Sweet fucking pussy, V. The sweetest."

He mumbles more dirty words in my ear, which only makes me more turned on. I begin to move my hips with him, meeting him when he thrusts into me. I'm so close, it's my turn to do some dirty talking. "Oh, fuck. Baker. Fuck me. Harder. You feel so good. Your cock—" My orgasm suddenly hits. "Oh, God!"

"Fuck," he moans. He's stopped moving and his hips are pressed tightly against my body. "Damn." Panting a little, he looks down at me from above and moves a piece of hair off my face. "You okay?"

"Yeah, I'm good." I lift my head to kiss his lips. "Very good. Thank you, Baker."

Chuckling, he kisses me one more time before he pulls out. "Don't thank me, V."

"Why not?"

"Because." He stands up and slides the condom off. There's blood. "I wasn't doing you a favor. I was sealing the deal."

"Sealing the deal?"

Tying the condom into a knot, he tosses it into a trash can near the bed. He crawls back in bed and snuggles close, wrapping his arms around me and pulling until I'm practically on top of him. "Sealing the deal between you and me."

"We have a deal?"

"Yeah. Of course we have a deal. It's official now."

I blink at him waiting for the rest.

"You're mine, and I'm yours."

"I'm yours?"

"Yeah, and I'm yours."

"You're mine?"

He chuckles while kissing my forehead. "Yeah, V. We're the real deal."

It's okay. He doesn't have to say the word for me to understand that, for Baker, this means we're in a relationship. A *real* one. Maybe *the* one. It hasn't escaped me how much my feelings for him have grown since he finally pulled his head out of his ass. It's been fast and furious.

I kiss his nose, then his mouth. Sighing, I lay my head on his shoulder. "We're the real deal."

I fall asleep in his arms with a smile on my face.

Best. Night. Ever.

CHAPTER 39

I'M awoken in the middle of the night by kisses and warm hands touching me. I moan hoarsely at all of the sensations he pulls from my body. "Baker," I whisper.

"I fucking love waking up with you in my bed, V."

"Me too." Especially if he wakes me up like this.

As he latches onto my breast, I turn my head. His clock is blinking bright red numbers next to me, and I realize I'm late. "Baker! I'm late!"

"Late for what?"

"Work! I was supposed to be there five minutes ago." I jump out of bed in search of my phone. "Luckily, I don't have to open." Naked as the day I was born except for those damn stockings, I run down the steps two at a time in search of my purse. "Aha!" I say, nabbing it from the kitchen counter.

I quickly find JJ's number and hit Call.

"You're late!" he shouts through the phone.

"I know. Sorry. I'm at Baker's. I'll be there in a second."

"Nah, we're good. Take your time. Be here before the rush."

"I will. Thanks, JJ."

The rush for coffee at the Bean usually starts at seven thirty.

That gives me an hour. I'm calculating the amount of time it'll take me to get home, shower, change, and get to work when big warm arms wrap around my naked body.

"Eek!" I squeak. "I'm naked!" I attempt to pull away from him so I can grab something to cover myself. I scan the room for anything that would work, a blanket, a doily, *anything*.

"I love that you're naked in my house. We should institute Naked Thursdays immediately. Oh, and Naked Fridays and Saturdays. And—"

Giggling, I reply, "I get it. You want a lot of naked days."

"Absolutely. Every day is naked day at our house."

Our house?

"V, you need to bring some clothes over here. I'll clear out a drawer for you and some space in my closet. That way you can sleep over and not have to worry about going home before work."

"Um. Okay." *Wow, that seems like a gigantic step.* "Are you sure?" Am *I* sure?

"Of course I'm sure." His warm lips touch my neck, and I settle into him. His lips move from just behind my ear down my naked shoulder. My body is thrumming. His erection is pressed against my back.

"Baker, I need to get home to change and shower."

"Let's shower here. There's room for an army in my shower."

I remember its multiple showerheads. "Okay. But no fooling around. I'm going to be late as it is."

"Scout's honor," he says, holding his hand up in front of me.

"You were a Scout?"

"Nah. But I promise to be good."

He lied. His intentions in the shower were less than honorable.

"You'd have made a terrible Scout," I mutter as I lick my way down his body. He's already given me one orgasm with his fingers and was going for another one with his tongue when I stopped him. "No. My turn." I sit on the bench built into the shower and reach for him.

"Oh, fuck, Virginia. I love your hands on me."

I remember what he told me the first time we were, uh, intimate, about the way he likes me to use my hands. He's rock hard, and I see fluid on the end of him. I pull him closer using my hands on his thighs. When he's directly in front of me, I look up at him and swipe the end with my tongue. His moan is so loud the inside of the shower feels like it's vibrating. I do it again, this time with my hand wrapped around him. Sliding it up and down, twisting as I go, I lick again.

"Fuck, Virginia."

I take that as a good sign, because I've never done this before. I grip him a little harder as I lick all around the head of his cock. I'm not going to lie, saying "cock" is not easy for me, but being with Baker, knowing he wants to have sex with me, is giving me more confidence.

"Look at me when you suck my big cock, babe."

Oh, hell. Can a girl come from dirty talk alone? I peer up and moan with my mouth around him.

"Fuck, you suck me so good."

I'm encouraged by his words and begin to work faster, pumping his shaft as I lick and then suck him into my mouth. I don't think I'll be able to take him very far, but it must be far enough because he's cursing each time I do it. He slides his hand into my hair, and I now understand why people like to do this kind of thing.

Baker's hips are moving back and forth with me. "Oh hell. Let go. I'm going to come, V." He backs away from me until I'm out of his mouth. I continue to use my hand on him until he releases a guttural sound. "Oh, Jesus. Yeah." I watch him ejaculate, his head thrown back. It's fascinating. There's quite a bit of it. Some of it hits the wall of the shower, some the floor, and a little bit lands on my chest.

Smirking, he picks up the drop on my chest with his finger and holds it in front of my mouth.

I latch on to his finger, sucking as I blink up at him. Salty.

"Fuck. You're so sexy, Virginia."

"I know." I stand up and kiss his lips. "I've gotta get to work. JJ's going to kill me."

"Let me get some towels. Can you just wear your dress from last night?"

"Yeah." I don't want to, but I've only got ten minutes to get to work now.

I finally get to work way over an hour after I was originally supposed to. The Coffee Bean is busy with a line of four or five deep. Half the tables are filled with students doing last-minute work on their computers or just trying to wake up for the day ahead.

"Sorry. Sorry. Sorry," I say, running past JJ working the register.

"Hurry up, girl. Clock in. These people are turning rabid." He winks at the next guy in line and whispers conspiratorially, "Not you, hon."

I toss my things into the break room, clock in, and grab my apron. "Where do you want me?"

"Restock the sugar station, and then help Jackson," says JJ as he rings up a customer.

I get to work, keeping busy right through my morning break. I'd like to volunteer to stay an extra hour to make up for my late start. "Hey, JJ?"

"Yeah, hon?"

"I can skip my afternoon class."

"No. Don't skip class. I'll find a way for you to make it up to me. Don't you worry," JJ says as he wipes down the counter. "Oh, I know how you can make it up to me." He taps his chin. "Since Jackson's gone for the day, you can cover for me so I can run over to that gorgeous little shoe store that just opened up. I won't be gone long."

"Sure. No problem. Sounds good."

"Awesome sauce! Be right back!"

I mumble an affirmative to him as he prances out the door. Yep, he pranced.

Sighing, I head into the back room to get the ladder. I've been meaning to clean the display shelves. I might as well do it now since we're kinda dead with only a few people hanging out, drinking their brews. I set the ladder up in front of the tall display shelves that showcase our coffee accessories and step up until I'm high enough to reach the top shelf. I absently dust and rearrange the coffee cups and travel mugs as a figure approaches me from the left. I recognize her. She's been sitting at the table in the corner nursing a café mocha for about an hour.

"May I help you?"

"Probably not," she snaps. "I just came to see who has her hooks in my son."

"Your son?" Is she referring to me? "You mean Baker?"

"That's the one. My precious boy," she pouts. She inspects me, starting at my shoes. Her eyes travel upward, stopping briefly at my middle. "You're not who I picture my son with."

Uh-oh. Here we go. "No? Why not?" *Okay, why in the hell did I ask her that?*

"For one, you're quite fat, aren't you?"

"Okay. Sure." I shrug. I'm plump. I don't like that F-word, though. I try not to use it. I peer down at her since I'm still at the top of the ladder and can't help noticing she's dressed for high tea with the queen. When she walked in, I saw her wearing a fur coat that looked real. *Poor little animals.* Now that she's shed the layer of helpless dead animals, I see she's in all white: white sweater, white slacks, white heels, and white blonde hair that's styled into a complicated sort of swirl on the top of her head.

She's staring at me, blinking slowly like I'm the most boring thing she's ever seen. "You're wearing your outfit from last night? I assume that means you're fucking my son."

That startles me. It was completely unexpected and inappropriate. I mean, how would she know what I was wearing last night unless she's like a stalker or something? "That's none of your business, ma'am."

"Call me Dawn. On second thought, why bother? You won't be around long enough to know my name."

"I won't?"

"No. You won't. Baker isn't the kind of guy to stick with the same woman for very long—especially an unattractive fat girl. I think he's got some sort of sex addiction, what with the way he bounces from girl to girl to girl." She looks at her long red fingernails, then back up at me. "And no doubt you're just a money-grubbing whore. What are you planning to do? Get knocked up so he has to pay you off with *our* money?"

I'm stunned. I think I know why Baker doesn't like his mom very much. She's a bitch on wheels. "Ma'am, with all due respect, you don't know what the hell you're talking about. You need to leave." I point to the door, but she doesn't move.

"Excuse me? You don't think I know *my son?*" she says, patting her chest to emphasize.

"I don't—"

"That's right. You *don't*! You don't know a thing, you little cunt."

"Ma'am! I—"

The woman reaches out and grasps hold of the ladder, pushing on it with each word as she says, "Stop. Calling. Me. Ma'am." On that final word, she tries to push the ladder, but another set of hands pulls her back, stopping her momentum.

I swing my arms around, twirling them frantically backward in an attempt to stop the inevitable. Squeezing my eyes shut, I prepare for the fall, but instead I'm held firm by big warm hands. "Baker?"

He guides me down the steps on the ladder until I'm sure-footed again, then turns to the woman. "What the fuck, Mom? What are you doing here?"

"I, uh...."

"Virginia?"

I look over at the source of the new voice, then blink.

"Was this woman assaulting you?"

"Mom?" I haven't seen my mom for well over a month, ever since I found out about Dad's letters. In that time, I've only really communicated with her via text or email, and that's only if I absolutely had to. "What're you doing here?"

Ignoring my question, she asks one of her own. "Why is this woman trying to hurt you?"

"It's Baker's mom. I think she's insane." I look over at Baker to make sure I haven't said something that would upset him.

He shrugs.

"What?" she screeches. "You little bitch. I'm not insane." Lunging for me, she continues her rant. "I'm gonna—"

"You're going to leave before I call the police," Baker growls as he rubs his hands roughly over his face, then runs them both angrily through his hair.

"Too late," my mom says, placing her phone to her ear.

Dawn isn't having any of that and lunges for my mom.

Baker moves swiftly to place his body between my mom and Dawn before she can get to her, shouting, "Jesus, Mom. Calm down!"

I watch in slow motion as Dawn reaches out and takes a swipe at Baker's face. Now I know how he got those cuts on his face. Now it's my turn to help. I leap forward and wrap my arms around Dawn's waist, holding her in place as Baker grabs her wrists and prevents her from clawing him again.

Sirens whistle in the background as the two of us attempt to hold her in place.

"Let me go!" Dawn squeals, squirming in my arms.

"Why are you here, Mom?" Baker's voice sounds strained, stressed.

"Cupcake," Dawn whines. "I was just trying to help you."

"Help me how, Mother? By hurting the only other person besides Granna that I love?"

Love? Did Baker say *love?*

"Y-you love her?" Dawn spits. "She's a money-grubbing whore. She's just trying to get knocked up, trying to take *my* money." Her voice is at an all-time high, several octaves above average.

"I think she needs to be sedated," says my mom as she comes up behind me. "And some psychiatric help."

"I do not, you fucking cunt!"

The door flies open and four of Ames's finest run into the shop. Luckily, no guns are drawn, but one of them has his night-stick out at the ready. I'd love to tell him to go for it and give the crazy lady a whack, but that's wrong. Right?

They quickly take over, cuffing Dawn behind her back and pushing her onto the ground face first. One of the cops stays with her, another talks to Baker, and the third officer questions my mom and me.

While all this is in progress, JJ races in holding two large shopping bags. "What the kryptonite happened? I was gone for like five minutes, and while I'm gone the SWAT team races in here like there's a hostage situation! Someone please tell me what's going on."

That's exactly what I needed. I needed me some JJ. I start to giggle, then giggle some more until I'm bent in half holding my stomach. God, he's hilarious. A breath of fresh air, for sure.

An officer approaches JJ. "Sir, I'm going to have to ask you to step back."

"But, Officer, I'm the manager here. I just stepped out for a moment. Is my Virginia okay?"

I manage to stop giggling long enough to say, "I'm fine, JJ. We're all fine. It's going to be fine." What? Too many "fines"?

A cop is pulling Dawn up off the ground and starting to lead her out the door to the patrol car parked outside. "The fuck it is," she mutters. "I'll be back to get my money, you ungrateful asshole."

Baker stands completely still, his mouth closed in a tight straight line as they escort her out. He looks to his right, gazing out the window as they place her in the squad car. Once she's securely inside the vehicle, Baker turns to me. "You okay, V?"

"Yeah. I'm okay."

"Good. Then, uh, I'll be back. I need a minute."

"Okay. Take your time."

He walks out the door and takes a left, heading in the opposite direction of the police cars. I hope he comes back. We need to talk—about love.

I look around the place and sigh, then peer down at myself and see my hands are shaking. That scene with Baker's mom is something I'll not soon forget.

When my mom steps next to me, she rubs her palm up and down my back. It should be soothing but the second her hand touches me, I stiffen. I'm not ready to see her. I may never be ready to see her. "Mom. Why are you here?"

Reaching into her bag, she pulls out a large bundle of letters. "I gave up hoping you'd talk to me on the phone. I also know you're not coming home for a while, so I wanted to hand deliver these."

I reach out with both hands to take them. There has to be several hundred letters bundled together. I'm at a loss for words. What *can* I say? "Thanks."

"There's nothing I can say to make you understand, but my frame of mind was a little warped. Your dad broke me."

"I know, Mom. But this"—I hold up the bundle of letters —"was wrong on so many levels."

"I know. I'm sorry. I hope you and your dad can work things out. You deserve to have both parents in your life. I know he loves you very much. You were always his little peanut." A tear slides down her cheek. "I was so wrong, honey."

"Yeah, you were." I sniffle. "I could have had all that time with him."

"I know." She stares down at her hands. "Well, now you can make up that time. I get why you're going to visit him for the holidays. He deserves to have you there. God, I'm sorry." She wipes away several tears from her cheeks. "I know it's going to take time for you to forgive me. I'll be patient. When you're ready to talk, I'll be there."

I nod. I'm not ready to make plans to talk. Not yet.

As she turns to leave, she puts her hand on my shoulder. "Oh, and Baker?"

"Yeah?"

"He's a stone-cold fox."

That surprises me, and a giggle erupts that I can't control. "That he is."

"Is he good to you? Nice to you? Does he treat you with respect?"

"Yeah, Mom. He's great." *He's perfect.*

"I'm not sure how I feel about his mom. Oh, wait... I do know. I hate her."

I laugh a little more. "She's not in his life. She just showed up for some reason. He hasn't told me much yet, but I'm sure he will now."

"Well, be safe. She won't be in jail for long, so watch your back. I'll kick her ass if she hurts you, angel."

"I know. So will Baker."

"I believe that." Leaning down, Mom kisses my cheek. "I'll be ready to talk when you are, Virginia. I'm also going to call your dad. I owe him an apology."

I arch my brow.

"Several apologies."

I look at my mom, probably the first time in my life I've really looked at her. I know she's human. Humans make mistakes. Hers just happened to be a whopper of one.

"Fine. Several hundred apologies. I'll call him."

"Good. I'm glad. It's been long enough. Maybe you could start dating—" Maybe if she dated, she'd be able to move on with the rest of her life. She deserves love.

"No. I'm not ready for that again, sweetie. Maybe someday."

I stand up and hug her. "See you later, Mom."

I watch her leave the coffee shop just as Baker reaches the door. Mom stops to speak to him. Nodding, Baker hugs her. Seeing the two of them together, hugging, gives me an odd tingling feeling down my spine, like a weight just lifted off me, leaving me feeling light. Happy. Free.

Baker

WHEN DID my life become a real-life episode of *Jerry Springer*? Oh, I know. The minute my mom showed her overly Botoxed face. I've never been close to her, but she's never been this far out of control, this unstable. Sure, she's always been obsessed with money, but there's got to be more to this than she's letting on.

I tug my phone out of my back pocket and hit Call. It rings three times. "Granna?"

"Baker? What's wrong?"

I could argue with her, tell her there's nothing wrong, but I'm sure she can hear it in my voice. "Mom just showed up at Virginia's job. She, uh, was about to push her off a ladder, but I stepped in just in time.

"Oh my God."

"She kept going on and on about the money. What's going on with her? Why is she so desperate for this money? She's unhinged."

"She's always wanted the money."

"Yeah, but this... it doesn't add up. Is it just because I inherited the first part of my trust?"

"Maybe. Where is she now?"

"In police custody."

"Oh, dear. Did it escalate?"

"Oh yeah. Virginia's mom was there too. Mom tried to claw everyone's eyes out."

"Maybe the police could trim those suckers down. They should be considered a deadly weapon."

I chuckle because I refuse to cry. "Is there a way to find out if there's more to this than just her being crazy and greedy? Maybe she's got gambling debts or into drugs, perhaps?"

"I'll call our attorney. He may be able to find out. Is Virginia okay?"

"Yeah, she's fine. Spooked a little bit." *I hope she doesn't see this as a problem between us.* Maybe she won't understand that my mom isn't part of the package. "Damn it. I should have told her about Mom."

"Baker, it's fine. That girl loves you. She'll stick. Just tell her everything now."

"You think she loves me?" Because I pretty much told her I loved her earlier. I wonder if she caught that.

"I do."

I hope she's right. "All right. Call me later?"

"I will. I'll let you know what the attorney finds out. But Baker?"

"Yeah?"

"I'm sure it's just about your money. She never got over the fact that your father didn't get his inheritance."

"I know. I guess I was just hoping—"

"That she wasn't this bad?"

"Yeah. I want to believe she had some redeeming qualities."

"She does. She had you. She gave us you, Baker. For that, I need to thank her. Maybe I will. Maybe I'll give her some money.

If she promised to leave you alone, I'd give her everything I had."

"No, Granna. That's your nest egg."

Chuckling, Granna sighs. "That's *some* nest egg. It'll be yours someday, sweetheart."

"Don't remind me."

"Now, see? That's what makes you so special. You actually love me for me, not for my money."

"Of course I love you for you. I'd be lost without you."

"Well, maybe before."

"Before what?"

"Before Virginia. Now you've got two of us."

I do. I have two amazing women in my corner. "I do. You're right. Love you, Granna."

"Love you more, baby boy."

❦

I FIND Virginia standing in the same spot she was in when I left to get some air. I move until I'm in front of her, as close as I can get without touching her. Looking down, I see she's got something in her hand. Bundled-up letters? Pointing to them, I ask, "What're those?"

"Letters."

"Oh, uh, are you sending them or...?"

"It's a long story, but I'll give you the gist." She stands up on her tiptoes and wraps her arms around my neck. "They're from my dad. Every letter he ever wrote to me when I was a kid."

"Your mom saved them for you?"

"Sort of. She never showed them to me in the first place. She kept them from me, told me my dad didn't care about me. For years I thought he didn't love me. It broke my heart that he never remembered my birthday, holidays, or even my graduation. But it was all a lie."

I move in closer, wrapping my arms around her back. "What was? How?" I kiss the top of her head, listening.

"Everything. Dad sent me letters and cards and money, but Mom hid them from me. The only reason I found out about them was because I called my dad a couple months ago to borrow some money. That's when he told me he'd been putting some away for me my entire life."

"So, when he was at your place...?"

"It was the first time I'd seen him in years. We're working on our relationship."

"Well, it makes sense, then."

She rests her cheek on my chest. I hold her tighter.

"What makes sense?"

"As your mom was leaving, she told me to be there for you. You were going to need me."

"I do need you, Baker."

"I need you too, V." *More than you'll ever know.* I bring my hand up to touch her pretty face, my finger tracing from her cheek down her neck. Damn, she's so soft. I kiss the top of her head again and give her bottom a little pat with my free hand as I pull away from her. "You ready to go?"

"Yeah. I'm ready."

"I'll take you to class and pick you up, and then we'll go to your place so you can pack a bag. We need to talk tonight, and I'd rather do it at my place, so we can be alone. We can order in some food."

"That sounds nice. It's been a pretty stressful and emotional couple of days. I'd love to skip my classes this afternoon, but that will only add to my stress. Do you have practice this afternoon?"

"No, we lifted weights this morning. I went in after I dropped you off here." I left her here to deal with my crazy mother. Damn, I feel like shit. I look down, then to my left. I can't look at her. This is all my fault. "I'm sorry about my mom, V."

Her lips turn up into a small smile while her eyes are sweet, sincere. She's looking at me not with pity, not with anger. I swear it's with love. "I know. It's not your fault, baby."

God, I love when she calls me that. "She's unstable."

"You think?" She smirks.

"Yeah, I think. I'll tell you everything tonight. I'm sorry I didn't tell you about her sooner. You'd have been better prepared if I had."

"Yeah. Maybe."

She leads me by the hand to the break room to get her things. Clocking out, she stops to tell the very exuberant JJ that she's leaving.

"Oh, I forgot to tell you, no slumber party tonight, boo," JJ coos. "I've got a hot date with Jackson."

"Rain check?" she asks.

"Of course. Rain check. We'll make it an epic slumber bash!"

"Sounds perfect." She kisses JJ on the cheek and pulls me out the door.

What the fuck just happened? A slumber party? "Hang on, Virginia. You're having a slumber party with another man?"

"It's JJ."

Like that alone explains it. "He's gay, right?"

"Uh, yeah."

"Okay. You can have a slumber party."

She stops in her tracks, jamming her fists on her hips and arching her brow. "You're giving me permission?"

I know what that means, but I wait to see what she does next.

"You know, Baker, I don't need your permission. I can have a slumber party with whomever I choose."

"The fuck you can, Virginia."

"Don't you start that macho bullshit with me, Baker Stark." She stops talking and stares up at me. "What's your middle name?"

"Keith."

She starts over, and it makes me want to laugh. "Don't you

start that macho bullshit with me, Baker Keith Stark! Oh yeah. That was much better."

Chuckling, I wrap my arms around her again. "I'm sorry. I overstepped. You may have slumber parties with gay men and girl-friends."

"Baker," she growls.

"Seriously, Virginia. You don't expect me to let the woman I love *slumber* with another guy, do you?"

"The woman you l-l-love?"

I know I said it before, but shit just got real now. "Yeah, V. I love you."

"Baker?"

"Yeah."

"I love you too."

"I know."

Laughing, she slaps my chest. "You do not!"

"Yeah I do. Granna told me."

"How did she know?"

"Oh, you might as well learn this now. Granna knows *everything.*"

Giggling, Virginia leans up and kisses my lips. "I love you, Baker Keith Stark."

"I love you, Virginia..."

"Melody Murray."

"I love you, Virginia Melody Murray. It sounds like a song." *But it's not as pretty as Virginia Melody Stark. Now that sounds pretty fucking beautiful.*

Oh Jesus. What happened to me? A month or two ago, I was perfectly happy to hook up with random chicks as needed. Now I'm planning my wedding?

I'm so totally fucked.

CHAPTER 41

"Oh my God, Baker." It's Sunday. Baker and I are hanging out at his house. I'm sitting cross-legged on the floor, working on my kissing research. Of course, he's watching football while stretched out on the sofa above me, looking all sexy and manly.

"What?"

"Did you know the world record for the longest kiss is fifty-eight hours, thirty-five minutes, and fifty-eight seconds?"

"Wow. Cool," he says distractedly. Apparently his team is behind.

"Could you imagine kissing me for that long, Baker?"

His head quickly swivels to look at me, expression serious. "Fuck yeah. I'd kiss you forever if I had the chance."

Aw, that was so sweet. "Baker," I whisper. "You're the sweetest guy in the entire world." I see him blush and want to hug him, so I do, sliding up to my knees and crawling to him. "So, you know what that means?"

"What?"

"That you're not only the world's greatest goalie, you're also the sweetest guy in the entire world and the best boyfriend ever."

Baker smirks and gives me a lazy Sunday morning kind of kiss.

The kind of kiss that leads to other things. Other things that aren't so lazy.

I move away from him before I grab him and take him upstairs. Crawling back to my spot with my books and papers, I look back at him. "Later, babe. I've got to get this damn research done." I pick up the information about the world-record kiss. Reading more about it, I choke. "Oh, Baker. You may change your mind about that sixty-hour kiss-fest."

"Why?"

"Well, for one, the rules are insane."

"Read them to me."

"Okay. Listen to this." I begin reading from the *Guinness Book of World Records*. "The rules. If you want to break a record that is published in a record book or governed by an international authority, there may be other or additional rules. So here goes... 'The kiss must be continuous, and the lips must be touching at all times. If the lips part, the couple is immediately disqualified. Contestants must be over the age of consent in the country the event is being held. The couple must be awake at all times. The contestants must stand during the attempt and cannot be propped together by any aids such as pillows, cushions, or people. No rest breaks are allowed. Incontinence pads or adult nappies/diapers are not allowed.'" I stop reading and look over at Baker. His mouth is agape. I continue. "'Couples must not leave the venue during their attempt.'" I look up again to see Baker's reaction.

"So, they can't take pee breaks?" he says with a look of horror on his face.

"Apparently not."

"I guess they probably get dehydrated, so peeing isn't necessary."

"Only an athlete would consider dehydration an issue." I giggle.

He shrugs. "It sounds like it'd be tough to break the record."

Baker slides off the couch and kneels next to it. Placing his hands on the floor, he crawls toward me on his hands and knees. My panties melt at the sight. He's almost catlike. From only a few feet away, I can see his eyes darken, his pupils dilating. Damn, he's hot. When he stops in front of me, he sits back on his feet as his hand makes its way beneath the front of my big Iowa State sweatshirt. As it moves up, he stops at the place where my bra would be if I were wearing one.

"No bra, babe?"

"It's Sunday."

His palm moves down over my belly and into my comfy yoga pants. "Fuck. No panties?"

"I need to do laundry."

Leaning in to me, he snuggles against my neck. With a kiss and a lick, he says, "You naughty, naughty girl."

"Baker," I whine. "I've got research...."

"This *is* research." He lifts me by the waist and places me directly on his lap. He's hard already. Jeez, the man is a machine—a sex machine.

I straddle his legs and wiggle against his lap until I get everything just where I want it. I don't waste time using my hands to pull his lips to mine. Baker's hands find their way beneath my sweatshirt again, heading straight to my nipples where he tweaks and pinches. When I wiggle around a little more, he growls, "Someone needs to sit still."

It's only taken him five minutes to make me this needy. "I can't sit still."

Before I know it, Baker is up on his feet, my sweatshirt has been tossed to parts unknown, and he's pushed down my yoga pants to reveal my surprise.

"You shaved," he says huskily.

"I did. I read it heightens, uh, the sensations."

"Fuck yeah." He lifts me up and sets me down on the couch, then kneels on the ground so his body is between my legs. Staring at my, uh, bareness, Baker doesn't even speak; he doesn't need to. I see the desire on his face. The man is so sexy like this.

"Lick me, Baker." I've gotten a little brazen and a lot more confident about myself. Knowing he thinks my body is the hottest thing in the world helps a great deal.

"Say it again, V. Talk dirty to me."

"Lick me, babe. Lick my pussy."

"Oh, fuck yeah." Diving in like his life depends on it, Baker does just that.

God, I love Sundays.

CHAPTER 42

Baker

A LOT HAS HAPPENED in the last few weeks. My relationship with Virginia has gone from zero to sixty, for one, and I think I'm okay with that. Of course, there have been points where the intensity of my feelings has required that I stop and think. I've had thoughts like *Is this really what I want?* and *Are we moving too fast?* Each time I question myself, I look over at her in her nerdy reading glasses and messy bun, and I smile because she's so beautiful like that. She's nothing like I imagined she'd be, you know? The girl I'd fall in love with. To be honest, I don't think I imagined anyone making it this far. BV, or Before Virginia, my only goal was to just hook up with girls to get a little release now and then. Since the deal at the coffee shop with my mom, V and I have been inseparable. We've spent every night together that we could. I've had some away games that kept me out of her bed for a night or two, but otherwise, we have our own brand of slumber parties every night.

The guys on the team keep giving me shit about being "pussy

whipped" and referring to Virginia as the "ole ball-n-chain." It's okay; I don't mind. Besides, they're giving Tig just as much shit. He's just as enamored with Peach as I am with Virginia. We both just smile knowingly at each other. Luckily, Tig and I still hang out at practice and games; otherwise, I'd probably never see him. I suppose that's what happens when relationships get serious. I wouldn't change anything, though, so there's no reason to get upset with the dicks on the team; they just don't get it—yet.

WE'RE ABOUT to enter our first holiday season with Thanksgiving in five days, and I'm a little unsure what to do about it. I want to drive her to her dad's for the holidays, but I know their relationship is fragile right now. While I don't want to interfere, I also don't want my girl renting a car and being on the road alone for that long. Call me whatever you want—controlling, domineering, bossy—but I want to protect her, keep her safe. I can't help it. I know the best course of action is just to ask if I can go with her since I don't think she's going to ask me. She'll assume I want to spend it with Granna. I need to prove to her that I want to be with her, and I'll do it tonight.

We're at my place tonight after spending a couple days at her apartment because Peach and Tig were on a romantic weekend getaway. It was a nice change of scenery for us, but I prefer my place. I know where everything is in my kitchen, and since I'm cooking tonight, it hasn't taken me twice as long to get shit done. Hell, it took me ten minutes and a search through every cupboard at her place just to find a skillet. For the record, the women only have one, and it's about six inches wide. Trying to make stir-fry in that tiny thing was impossible. I step into her bedroom and see Virginia lying on her stomach, papers and books spread out around her as she works on her research. While she has until May to finish up the project, she's struggling to find the point to her research on kissing. She'll figure it out. All I need to do is encourage her and support her. Granna's advice.

"Babe?"

"Yeah," she responds absently.

"Dinner's ready."

"Okay."

"And, uh, while we eat, can we talk about the holidays?"

"Sure." She still hasn't looked up at me.

I'm going to keep going. I can't wait. "I'd like to drive you to your dad's for Thanksgiving."

She finally looks up at me, blinking. "Uh, Dad's coming here to get me."

"Since when?"

"Since he told me he didn't want me driving alone or renting a car."

"Babe, I want to take you." Okay, that sounded a little whiny, but damn it, I want to go with her.

Sighing, she sets down the book and papers she's holding and slides off her bed, which causes her shirt to slide up and reveal lots of pale, soft skin. Uh-oh. All she fucking has to do is shit like that and my dick twitches. I need a little internal monologue here: *Baker, this isn't about sex.* When she gets to me, she peers up at me with concern in her eyes. Damn, I don't want her concerned.

Placing her hands on my chest, she says, "I know you would have taken me, but I want this first holiday to be about my dad and me. I know Tina will be there, but that's different. She'll stay out of our way and—"

"*I* would stay out of your way." Defensive much, Bake?

"Baker, you know how I feel about you. I'd love to spend our first Thanksgiving together, but my dad and I need this time. You know I've read all of his letters, right?"

I nod.

She blinks and looks up at the ceiling. I know she's fighting back tears when she does that. She's had a hard time with everything, especially after reading the letters her mother finally relinquished. Some of the early ones sounded desperate while others were angry and a little mean. The last letters were more resigned and came less often. It felt like he'd given up, and I think that hurt her more than anything else. She told me she understood where all of his emotions came from, but it was hard for her to read them, especially all at once. After reading them all, she called her dad and they talked for hours—literally hours. When she emerged from her bedroom afterward, her eyes were red from crying, but she was smiling. The only concern I've had is the fact that she's been extra quiet ever since. When I've mentioned it, she just shrugs and tells me she's got a lot on her mind. I hope that doesn't include ending things with me.

Fuck. What if it does?

"Your dad doesn't need to do that. I can drive you and stay in a hotel and—"

"No."

"No?"

"No. I love you so much for wanting to keep me safe, Baker. I just need to do this my way this time."

Sitting down on her bed, I rub my face with both hands, then run them through my hair. I need a haircut. It's almost to my shoulders now. "Fine."

"You're angry with me?"

"No." *Yes.*

She gives me a shrug, and that hurts right in the middle of my chest. She doesn't care? When she slides onto my lap and wraps her arms around my neck, my heart hurts less. "Baker, I love you. I'm going to be sad you're not with me, but this is how it's going to be for Thanksgiving. Will you drive me there for Christmas?"

Ah, the proverbial olive branch. "What about Granna?"

"Well, what if we spent Christmas with my dad and New

Year's with Granna? Next year we can switch everything up to make it fair. Do you think she'd be okay with that?"

"Next year?" My brow arches.

"Oh, uh," she says tentatively. "I just assumed."

"No! I just liked the sound of it. That you're invested in this thing between us as much as I am."

"Of course I am, dork."

"I'm not a dork," I say, pinching her ass. "You're a dork with those silly, sexy glasses and that messy, sexy hair."

"So, you think I'm sexy?" she whispers shyly.

"You know I do," I whisper back.

"Thanks, Baker." Leaning in, she kisses me softly.

I deepen the kiss, sliding my hand up into her tangled hairdo. I bump her glasses off-kilter with my nose, but neither of us gives two shits. I reach up and take the glasses off, tossing them onto her nightstand, then use my upper body to pull her closer. "Straddle me, V."

"Baker?"

"Uh-huh," I say, kissing her throat.

"I think you're sexy too."

"Yeah?" As I kiss and suck on her neck, I slide my palm past the waistband of her stretchy yoga pant things, straight into her panties. I palm her pussy with my hand, sinking one finger through her slit. "You're wet?"

"When you're around, Baker. Constantly."

"Good to know." Sliding off my lap, she shimmies out of her yoga pants and kicks them off to the side. I stand, pushing my sweats down to the middle of my thighs. My cock is hard and dripping with precum. I watch as she places her right knee on the bed next to my left hip. She repeats the same on the other side, causing her legs to spread wide above me. "God, you're beautiful like this, V."

"Thanks." She slides her hand down her stomach until she's touching herself.

That's new. *Oh, fuck.* "Touch yourself. Let me see you make yourself come."

Her face turns a pretty shade of pink, but she does as I ask. Swirling her finger around and around her clit, she begins to move her pelvis with each twirl.

Mesmerized by the sight of her, I wrap my hand around myself and slowly pump up and down. "This is the fucking hottest thing I've ever seen, Virginia."

"Uh-huh." She's moving her hand faster and faster.

I decide to help her along. "Keep doing what you're doing." I lean forward, pressing my middle finger into her, then begin to pump in and out with her movement.

"Oh shit, Baker. I'm gonna come. Don't st-stop."

"I won't." I add a second finger, and just as I start to feel her core constrict, I pull my hand out quickly and push in my cock in its place, plunging deep inside of her. She screams, and I let out a guttural moan. "The fucking best, V." Nothing feels like this. Nothing has ever felt like this. It's like... *oh, fuck.* I quickly pull out. "I forgot a condom, hang on."

I start to lift her off my lap, but she places a hand on my shoulder. "It's okay. I'm on the pill."

"Since when?"

"Tenth grade."

"Tenth grade? I thought you were a virgin when we—"

"I was!" She looks hurt.

"I didn't mean that the way it sounded."

"Lots of girls are on birth control pills for other things, Baker. It helps with our cramps and regulates our period."

"Sorry. I guess I didn't realize."

"So, I'm covered," she says with a slight smile.

I look from her face down to her pussy. It's tempting, but.... I lift her up and off me so I can walk over to my sweats to extract my wallet. I pull out a condom, tear it open, and slide it down my cock. When I turn to walk back to her, to say I'm shocked at what I see is an understatement.

"What're you doing?"

She places a foot back into her yoga pants, then blinks up at me. "You don't trust me."

"What? Yes, of course I trust you."

"No, you don't, or you wouldn't have just put on a condom after I told you I was on the pill."

"I trust you. It's just that the pill is only 99.9 percent effective." Besides, my mom's words are rolling around in my head and I don't know why. *"She's a money-grubbing whore. She's just trying to get knocked up."*

She's staring at me now. "So, you're worried about the 0.1 percent chance of me getting pregnant?" Placing her hands on her hips, she adds, "Or is it that you don't believe me when I say I'm on the pill?"

"I, uh. I believe you. I just want to be careful. The last thing I need is for you to get knocked up, V." She flinches at my words, and I'm not sure why. Does she want a kid or something? "I'm not ready for a kid, Virginia. I may never be." I've seen firsthand what happens when a couple has a kid when they don't want one.

"The last thing *you* need," she says, bending down to pick up her book bag, "is for me to get knocked up?" Unhappy. She's definitely unhappy. "For your information, *Bake*"—she spits my name out like she's mad at me—"it takes two people to 'get knocked up.'" She uses air quotes to emphasize the last three words.

"I know. I just meant—"

"You meant that you don't want me to get pregnant and what? Trap you?"

She's got her book bag packed, and now she's slipping on her furry boots.

"What are you doing?" I ask.

"I'm going to the library. There's a book... I need to do research there."

"You're lying," I spit.

Her eyes grow large and then turn into little angry slits as a scowl appears on her pretty face. "Yeah, I'm a liar and a whore who wants to get knocked up and trap you into a loveless marriage. Jesus, Baker. You sound like your mom now."

My mom? She just had to throw my mom in my face. Luckily, we haven't seen Mom since the incident at the coffee shop. She took off after being released from jail. Somehow, Granna's attorney found out that she wasn't on the run from some drug lord and didn't have gambling debts. That's good news, I guess. The bad news, from what I understand, is she honestly thinks she's entitled to this money, and her feelings of resentment have been festering for a long time. When I suggested I talk to her and possibly give her some of my money, Granna said that I'm "absolutely not to give her a cent" and that she'd "take care of it." It's not like I'm ever going to spend a million dollars. Hell, that's only the first disbursement. I'm getting another one when I turn twenty-seven, then one at thirty, and the final bulk of my inheritance when I turn thirty-five. In all I'm due to inherit just under seven million dollars. So yeah, how the fuck am I ever going to spend all of that? In the end, I promised Granna I'd let her take care of it, but if Mom shows up again, I'll do something about it.

I'm pulled from my thoughts when I hear the front door slam shut. "What the fuck, Virginia?" I run to the door, opening it to a gust of chilly air. Peering down the driveway, I see she's practically running. "Virginia!" I yell.

She stops and turns back, walking toward me until she's at the bottom of my front steps. "Baker, I love you, but sometimes love isn't enough."

Love isn't enough? What the fuck is she talking about? "Look, I'm sorry."

She blinks up at me, tears clinging to her lashes, then looks back down at the ground.

"Did you hear me? I said I was sorry."

"I know. I heard you." She's still not looking at me.

"No, V, I'm *really* sorry. I should never have made you feel like I didn't trust you. It's just my history with my parents and their unwanted pregnancy is still fresh in my mind all these years later."

"But *we* aren't your parents, Baker. It's not fair to compare me to your mom. I'm not her."

"I know. You're the complete opposite of her." *Obviously*.

She looks up at me again. "You never want to have kids?"

"I don't know." I'm being honest. I don't know.

"Well, I do. I want at least three someday. If you don't, then we should probably just end things."

"End things? Why?"

"We want different things. It'll never work if I want them and you don't. We'll both end up hurt and resentful."

"Wow, you're serious? You're willing to just give up on me?"

"I'm not giving up on you."

"The hell you aren't. You're giving up on us just because I may or may not want kids with you someday. I'm only twenty-fucking-two, Virginia."

She takes the three steps up the stairs and reaches out, touching my arm. "I think we should take some time to think about this. It's been pretty fast and intense with us. When I get back from my dad's, we can talk."

"You're fucking breaking up with me?"

"No. I think we both need time to think about what we really want."

"So, if I tell you I want ten kids, we're going to be golden? Is that it?"

"No. I don't want you to tell me something just because it's what I want to hear. You deserve to be happy, Baker, and if having kids will make you unhappy, then maybe I'm not the one for you."

"Just because I don't want to knock you up, you're out of here?"

"No! Jesus, Baker." Several tears start to roll down her cheeks. "You're not being fair."

"*Me? I'm* not fucking fair? You won't even give me the courtesy of *trying* to understand my point of view on this shit. Instead, you run off while accusing me of the 'not trusting you' bullshit." Sure, I say it in a faux bitchy female voice. That's not going to win me points with her.

"Well, on that note, I think I'll head out. See ya," she says, stomping down the steps.

"V, I didn't mean it."

She lifts her middle finger in the air as she marches down my driveway.

I want to laugh or maybe cry; I'm not sure which because damn, she just flipped me the bird. "Virginia," I whine. "Come back. Let's talk about this."

She keeps walking. My first instinct is to go after her. She's not wearing a damn coat again. I could make sure she's warm, give her a ride home, but I don't. I just stand there on my front steps, freezing my balls off and wondering what the hell just happened. Oh, I remember, she broke the fuck up with me because she wants a fucking kid.

"Jesus, she drives me fucking crazy." And not in a good way this time.

Fine. Fuck her.

CHAPTER 43

MY DAD ARRIVES at my place late Tuesday night, and we're on the road bright and early on Wednesday morning heading to his house. He must know something's wrong, because he keeps asking me vague questions about classes, my friends, and Baker.

On one of our weekly calls since this whole thing with Baker started, I told Dad that Baker and I were dating. He patted himself on the back for predicting that would happen. I think he also liked the fact that he was getting to hear about a part of my life that I'm not sharing with anyone else. Not even Peach. She's been very caught up with Tig, and since Tig and Baker are close, best friends, I opted not to tell her about the latest drama. That's not fair to Tig or Peach. Besides, if she knew, she'd kick Baker's ass.

On the ride to Illinois, I spill everything about the argument we had over children. "Dad, I just don't want him to feel like he has to have kids, a family, if he doesn't want that. I also don't want this to come between us later on."

"Okay. Let me ask you this. I know he loves you, but do you love him?"

"I do." I sniffle as quietly as possible, but I know he heard me.

"Oh, sweetheart. This will all work out. I promise you."

"How do you know that?"

"Let me tell you a little something about men."

"Oh no." I laugh a little.

"Now, now. Let me say this. Men are simple creatures."

I blink but say nothing.

"No, seriously. We are simple. If you feed us, kiss us, love us, and praise us, we'll be happy men."

I roll my eyes when he calls men "simple." Men aren't simple. They're more complicated than a Rubik's Cube. "Dad...."

"Let me tell you what I think Baker is doing right now."

Oh, I want to hear this. I've thought about Baker almost every minute since I stormed out of his place on Sunday. I've checked my phone about a thousand times for messages or missed calls, but there's been nothing. Granted, I haven't written or called him either. I'm not ready to make the first move.

"What's he doing?" *Please don't say he's out picking up another girl. Please don't say he's—*

"He's wallowing in self-pity right about now."

"Baker's not like that. He's very confident. I'm sure he's out with his friends, meeting someone new." On that last word, I start to cry. "He'll find someone new, Dad." *Someone who doesn't want to have kids. Someone he can trust.*

"Sweetie, don't be surprised when you get back to find a shell of the man you left on Sunday."

"What are you talking about?"

"He's not going to take this well. I know I only met him the once, but you need to go see him as soon as you get home."

"Should I be worried?"

Shrugging, Dad says, "Maybe. I think you need to hear him out."

"I did."

"Not really. He's obviously got some serious qualms about

fatherhood. Let him tell you what those are, and perhaps you can work things out."

"I guess I can do that."

"Just trust me, honey."

"Okay, Dad. Thanks for the advice."

"You're welcome. I'm sorry you're going through this, but I'm not gonna lie, I love being able to talk to you about your life like this." Dad's voice gets shaky. When I hear him sniffle, I look over at him and see his eyes are a little shiny.

"I'm glad I can talk to you about it too, Daddy."

Since we've been talking, I've mostly called him Dad. Occasionally I use my old term of endearment, Daddy, but I've noticed when I do call him that, he gets emotional. Like how I heard him sniffle just now. He pulls the car over at the next exit to wipe his eyes. "I'm... I've missed you so much, Virginia. There's been a hole in my life without you."

"Oh, Daddy. Mine too." We wrap our arms around each other, hugging.

When we're finally on the road again, I take some time to think about Baker and his request to drive me home. I would have loved a road trip with Baker, but I'm glad Dad picked me up so we could talk. This has been cathartic.

"Okay, we're almost home." Dad smiles, eyes focused on the road ahead. "Twenty more minutes or so."

"Good. I'm hungry."

"Tina's got a feast ready for us when we get there, but it's nothing compared to Thanksgiving dinner."

"So, you and Tina are good?"

"Very. We're very good. She's my best friend."

"Oh, that's so cool. I'm happy for you both."

"It just wasn't meant to be for your mom and me."

"I know."

"She called me, you know?"

"She said she was going to."

"We talked for over an hour. She also sent me a box."

"A box?"

"Yep. Filled with things about you. School pictures, videos, class projects, newspaper articles—you name it."

"Really?"

"Yep. I pulled out the school pictures to hang on the wall, but I thought it'd be fun for you and me to go through the rest of it together, so you can tell me about everything."

Damn it all to hell. I'm crying again. "I'd love that, Daddy." *So much.*

THE FIVE DAYS I spent with my dad and Tina were perfect. It was just the three of us most of the time, but Thanksgiving Day, the house was filled with family I hadn't seen in years, along with some of Tina's family, who were all gracious and kind to me.

On Friday and Saturday, it was just Dad and me. Tina decided to visit her sister for the weekend in another suburb of Chicago, claiming she was going Christmas shopping. Since she wouldn't be back before Dad and I returned to Iowa, we said our goodbyes as Dad placed her overnight bag in the back of her car. She wrapped her arms around me and held on tight. When she let me go, her eyes were ringed with wetness. "I've loved having you here, Virginia. Your dad hasn't been this happy in years. It fills my heart when he's happy. I'd do anything for him, Virginia. I hope you know that."

"I do. I'm sorry."

"None of the past was your fault, so let's focus on the future, okay? No good will come of rehashing that old stuff."

"I agree."

Dad and I wave as Tina's car drives away. Back in the house, we spend my last two days talking, drinking wine, and going through the box Mom sent. It is awesome. Of course, we cry a lot, but we laugh a lot too.

The ride back to Iowa is quiet until we start planning our Christmas together. We'd started out early Sunday morning so I could get back in time to unpack and prepare myself for classes on Monday. "I invited Baker to come home with me, but that was before."

"That's fine. I'll plan on him coming unless I hear otherwise. Sound good, peanut?"

"Sounds good."

After Dad carries my bags up to my apartment, we hug quickly. Neither of us wants to say goodbye. "I love you, peanut."

"I love you too." I squeeze him extra hard and pat his back at the same time. "I'm so happy we found each other again." I wipe my nose and sniffle at the same time.

"You know how happy I am about this. I promise I won't ever let you go without a fight again. I shouldn't have—"

"No. What happened is in the past, like Tina said. Let's focus on the future. Let's focus on Christmas together."

"Good. That's good. I'll need a list from you. A long, long list. I owe you for so many years."

I put my hands on my hips, sniffling again. "What'd I just say, Dad? Focus on the future. And I need a list from you and Tina too."

"Fine." He chuckles, turning toward the door. "I'm leaving before I blubber like a fool." With a squeaky voice, he adds, "I love you, Virginia."

"Me too. Text me when you get home so I know you're safe."

He laughs. "Now who's the parent?"

"Hey, I don't have to be a parent to worry. Drive safe, Daddy."

Choked up again, he nods and is out the door before he sees my tears. Happy tears.

Taking in a deep breath, I release it and let my shoulders relax. I'm going to unpack and get ready for a new week.

At five o'clock on Sunday night, I somehow find myself standing on Baker's front porch. *Why am I here again?* Oh, I remember. On the drive back, Dad suggested I get settled and then talk to Baker. At the time, I scoffed at the idea internally. Why should I talk to him? Baker hasn't tried to call or text me. He doesn't care about me.

Before I knock, I can't help noticing there's loud music playing inside, which makes me nervous to ring the bell. Is he having a party? It sure sounds like he's having a good time without me. Hesitating, I suck in a deep breath for courage and press his doorbell. I doubt anyone will hear it over the music anyway. I press it again, and just as I'm about to turn and walk down the steps in a clean getaway, the door is wrenched open.

Turning back to face the door, I'm shocked at the sight before me. "Baker? What's wrong?"

He's standing in the doorway wearing only a pair of dirty sweatpants. Nothing else. His hair is sticking out in all different directions and looks like it hasn't been washed in days. The beard on his chin tells me he hasn't bothered shaving either.

"Baker?" I ask again.

"What the fuck do you want?"

"I, uh, I wanted to—"

"You what? You wanted to pick up your shit? Well, I've boxed it up for you." He turns away from me, bending at the waist. When he stands, he's holding a large cardboard box. Stepping over the threshold, he drops the box down unceremoniously to the concrete step in front of me. "There. That's everything."

There's a bunch of stuff rolling around in the box and in my mind. I can tell he's drunk. Like really drunk. And from the looks of him, I'd guess he's been drunk for more than just today. He's not showered or shaved for days, and I think Dad was right. Baker didn't take anything that happened last weekend well.

"Baker, I—"

"I, I, I. It's all about you," he snaps. "Well, guess what? I don't give a flying fuck about you. Now just take your shit and go." He slams the door in my face.

I blink a few times, trying to get a grip on everything that just happened. What do I do now? Take my stuff and leave or knock again?

CHAPTER 44

Baker

As soon as I slam the door, I stumble back to my couch and
face-plant. I remain sprawled there until I hear the doorbell ring
again. It's chimed continually since I threw her shit on the front
porch.

"Jesus, leave me the fuck alone," I yell at the top of my lungs.

When the bell rings again, I know she must not have heard
me. I'm going to have to just tell her to her face, but I don't want
to see her face. She looked so pretty. So soft. Shaking off the
lovey-dovey bullshit running through my head, I stomp to the
front door and yank it so hard it nearly comes off its hinges. "I
said go away!"

"No."

"No? Why the fuck not?"

"Because."

"Because why?"

"I think we need to talk, Baker Keith Stark."

Oh no she didn't. She said all three of my names. She's just thrown down. "Well, you listen to me, Virginia Melody Stark."

"Murray."

"Huh?"

"Murray. Virginia Melody Murray. You called me Stark."

"No I didn't." *Did I?* I wobble on my feet a little bit but grab the doorframe before she notices. Confession. I'm still a little drunk from yesterday... and the day before... and the day before that. Sure, I've been on a little bender. I needed it to get through the fucking holiday, okay?

"You did. I'll show you. I recorded it."

"The fuck you did." *Did she? I didn't even see her do it.*

"Let me in and I'll show it to you."

"Fuck! Fine!" I yank on the door, holding it open with my arm to create an arch that makes it necessary for her to walk beneath it. Her box of shit is still sitting out on the porch. Shit! I'd better grab it and bring it inside. Not that anyone would steal it in *this* neighborhood, but it's better to be safe than sorry.

With the box in my arms, I step back into my house and see Virginia sitting on my couch with her legs tucked underneath her plump little ass. Damn, I love that ass. *No, Baker! You can't let her get to you.* I step over to my stereo equipment and hit Off. Ah, quiet.

"Don't get comfortable. You're just here to...." *Oh, fuck. Why did I let her in again?*

"To show you the recording."

"Right. That."

Tripping on the edge of my rug, I fall onto the sofa but just a little. I'm able to recover quickly. Looking at her again, I see her attention isn't on me. She's gazing over the mess all around my living room. There are beer cans, a half-empty whiskey bottle, several pizza boxes, and lots and lots of empty potato chip bags. Yeah, I pigged out. So what?

"Did you, uh, have a party or something?"

"Or something."

Sighing, she pulls her phone out of her pocket.

I lean in close and breathe in. She smells so fucking good and sweet. Like her sweetness is coming out of her pores.

She turns her head enough so we're not eye-to-eye. God, she's got pretty eyes. "Are you sniffing me?"

"No."

"You were. You were sniffing me."

"I was not. Now, are you going to show me that, uh, thing?"

"No."

"No?"

"There's nothing to show you. I just used it as a ploy to get into your house."

"You lied?" *Again.*

"No, I didn't lie. I just wasn't truthful."

"Same difference." *Fucking semantics.*

"I wanted to come in because I missed you."

"Ha! I know you didn't miss me."

"Yes I did. I missed you. *A lot.*"

"If you had missed me, you would have called or something."

"Did you miss me?"

"No." *God, yes, I missed the shit out of you.*

"Now who's lying?"

"I'm not a fucking liar."

"Neither am I. I've always been truthful with you, Baker."

"Whatever. I think you should go."

She takes in a large gulp of air. "Okay. If you never want to see me again, I'll leave."

What'd she just say? If I never want to see her again? Is she leaving? Forever? "I, uh, I didn't say that."

"Yes you did."

"No I didn't. I'm just not in the mood to talk right now."

"Oh?" She leans in to me until our lips are barely an inch apart. "What are you in the mood for?"

I breathe in again. My dick is a fucking traitor. I want her so much right now. Hell, the second I saw her on my porch in her little winter coat and that stupid hat with the furry ball on top, I wanted to rip it from her body and fuck her raw. I force myself to sit back as far away from her lips as I can.

She stands up, holding her hand out for me to... what? To do what? Shake? "All right. I guess this is goodbye."

I grab the bottle of Jack Daniels I've been nursing for a couple of days. "You know the way out."

"I sure do." Her boots make a cute clomping noise as she walks to the door.

When it clicks open, it hits me. I can't let her go. I won't let her go. She came here to talk, to work things out, and I've been nothing but a dick. In the past five days, all I've done is think about her. Out of the five days, it only took me the first hour to decide I'd have a fucking van full of kids with her because one, she'd be an amazing mother, and two, she'd look beautiful all big and round with my children.

I jump off the couch, tripping on the same rug, and shout, "Wait!"

"What? You want to be sure I've got my box?" she says, holding up the large box. "Well, I've got it."

"No," I say, taking long strides to get to her before she steps out into the cold.

"Then what?"

"This." I grab the box from her hands and toss it to the floor. Sliding my hands into her hair, I pull her to me and kiss her like my life depends on it, because it does. I kiss her like she's the only woman I'm ever going to kiss again, because she is. And I kiss her like I'd be lost without her, because I would be. I kiss her lips, her nose, and her cheek. I kiss her eyes and her neck, all the while saying everything I've wanted to say since Sunday. "I love you so much. I hate thinking of my life without you. I want babies with you—lots and lots of babies. Just not yet. After graduate school, when we're settled somewhere. I want you in my bed every fucking night, V. I want to grow old with you."

Virginia isn't talking. She's kissing me back with as much love and passion as me. "I love you too. I missed you so much. I wanted to call you, but you were so angry."

"I know. I'm sorry," I say into her ear before I bite the lobe. "I need to fuck you, V. I need you so much."

"I want you too, but I think we should talk first."

"What? Why?" I whine.

"Because, Baker, I want to understand your point of view on all of this. I wasn't fair to you when I gave you that ultimatum. My dad told me I needed to give you the benefit of the doubt."

"Can't we talk after?"

When I hear her giggle, I know I'm going to be okay. "No. Let's sober you up, get some food in you, and talk. We've got all night to make love."

"Make love?"

"Yeah, Baker. I want to make love with you."

Oh fuck. Shit just got real.

"Do you want that too?"

I want that too. I love her. "I do."

When she kisses me softly and swipes her tongue over my bottom lip, I growl, "Jesus, V. You drive me so crazy."

She laughs as she walks back into my living room, grabbing empty bottles and pizza boxes as she goes. Her laughter fills my house as much as it fills me up.

Turning to me, she winks. "I know, babe. I know."

CHAPTER 45

Baker. Six months later.

"I did it, Baker!"

"You finished it? Your amazing research study on kissing? Congratulations! I knew you could do it. Oh, and you're welcome, by the way."

"Oh yes, Baker, thank you for being the inspiration behind my research," she deadpans.

"No problem. I was happy to be part of your in-depth study."

"Anyway, it's finished, and Dr. Kellogg is so pleased he plans to publish it."

"That's great, babe. That'll look great on your grad school application." In the end, she decided to call her senior thesis "Modern Love: A Millennial's Guide to Kissing." It's clever and insightful and all her.

"Dr. Kellogg already told me he'd help me with all of that. With you already accepted into the physical therapy program and working for the Iowa State athletic department, we're pretty set for the next two years, aren't we?"

It'll take both of us two years to get our graduate degrees. I wouldn't mind going on to work on a PhD after that, but we'll see. I've got other things to think about for now. "Well, we're *almost* set. There are a few loose ends."

"Loose ends? I've already told Peach I'm moving in with you at the end of the semester. She was happy for us but even happier for herself since Tig is going to move in and take my place. It forced his hand."

"Nah, he wanted to live with her. He was just playing hard to get."

"Why does he do that to her? He kept Peach hanging for weeks before he bedded her."

"Bedded her?" I chuckle. "You say the goofiest shit."

"Whatevs."

"Okay, back to the topic at hand." I pull her by the hand until her legs hit the sofa. She plops down while I continue to stand in front of her.

"What topic?" she asks, peering up at me.

"Loose ends."

"What loose ends?" she asks with her hands on her sassy hips.

I kneel down in front of her, pulling out Granna's engagement ring. It's a pretty sizeable rock. It's probably going to dwarf Virginia's little finger. Granna said it is over three karats and a bunch of other shit about cut and clarity. It was overwhelming. "To be safe," she wrote out the description of the ring so I could show it to Virginia after I proposed.

"B-B-Baker? What are you d-d-doing?"

"Tying up our loose end." Clearing my throat, I attempt to recite the proposal I've practiced in my head for a month. "Virginia, I love you. You drive me crazy. I want you to keep driving me crazy for the rest of my life. Marry me? Please? After graduate school if you want to wait, or now?" Okay, so it wasn't quite as eloquent as I rehearsed, but I did it without passing out. *Winner.*

Scooting up to the edge of the sofa, she touches my face. "Yes, Baker. I'll marry you... now, if you want."

"I *want*." I definitely want. "So, that's a yes?"

"Absolutely! That's a great big *yes*!"

She kisses me with tongue and everything. Hottest proposal ever. Damn, I love being engaged. Before she can take it to the next level, the door to my kitchen opens and our people start to flood into the living room.

She must not notice our company, too busy looking down at the ring that fits her little finger perfectly. "This ring is too much, Baker."

"It was Granna's. She asked me if I'd like to give it to you, and I said yes."

"It's amazing. If she's sure."

"She's positive," says Granna from the doorway to the kitchen.

"Oh, you're here!" V squeaks.

"So am I," says Peach as she walks toward us holding two champagne flutes in one hand and a bottle in the other. "Please tell me you said yes, Virginia."

"Peach! Of course I did."

I look over and see the smiling faces of Tig, Granna, and her boyfriend, Tommy, waiting for the all clear before they move into the room.

"She said yes! I can't wait to go dress shopping!" Granna shouts, holding up her empty glass.

"Me too!" Peach agrees. "I've got a million ideas for you!"

"Of course you do." Virginia smirks. Turning to me, she says, "I can't wait to tell my dad... and my mom."

"We will. We can call your dad and Tina later tonight, and when they come for commencement, we'll go out and celebrate. We can go visit your mom and tell her next week if you want." Her dad already knows because I called to ask him permission for her hand. I'll tell her about that later.

"That's a good plan, Baker. Thanks."

We watch as Peach moves around the room, pouring champagne for everyone.

"I'd like to propose a toast," says Granna, holding up her champagne flute.

With a whisper, Virginia asks, "You were pretty confident I'd say yes, weren't you?"

"I was, yes."

Rolling her eyes, she steps up onto her tiptoes, lips close enough to taste. "Baker Stark, you drive me crazy."

"Glad to hear it, babe. Glad to hear it."

APPENDIX: SURVEY A (FOR HETEROSEXUAL MALE PARTICIPANTS)

Appendix: Survey A (For Male Heterosexual Participants)

Sex Survey

About You

Mark your responses with an "x" when applicable.

What Is your Gender?

__Male

__Female

__Other (please specify):

What is your age?

__18-19

__20-21

__22-23

__24+

What is your college major?

What year in college?

    ___Freshman

    ___Sophomore

    ___Junior

    ___Senior

    ___Graduate Student

    ___Doctoral Student

    ___Other. (Please specify):

Personal Relationships

The next questions relate to your personal relationships and sex life. If you feel uncomfortable you may press "Submit" now. Thank you for your time. Mark your responses with an "x" when applicable.

If no, how many sexual partners have you had in the past?

Are you now or have you ever been in a long-term relationship?

(For the purposes of this survey, long term relationship is defined as 6 months or longer.)

    ___Yes

    ___No

If yes, how long was/were your relationship(s)?

Sex Life

The following questions relate to your sex life. Please respond truthfully. Beware! Graphic terminology used. Mark your responses with an "x".

Are you a virgin?

___Yes
___No
If no, at what age did you lose your virginity?

Would you sleep with a virgin in a one-night-stand?
___Yes
___No

Would you sleep with a virgin if you saw them as a potential life partner?
___Yes
___No

Would you wait until marriage if your partner requested it?
___Yes
___No
Would you consider a long-term relationship with a person who slept with you on the first date?
___Yes
___No

⊗⧉⊗

Attraction

The following questions relate to attraction. Please answer honestly.
Mark your responses with an "x".

Favorite hair color of potential sexual-partner.
___Blonde/blond
___Brunette
___Redhead
___Black
___Color as in purple, green, etc.

___Other (please specify):

Hair style of potential sexual partner.
    ___Very short, pixie haircut
    ___Short, chin length, straight
    ___Short, chine length curly or wavy
    ___Medium, shoulder length, straight
    ___Medium, shoulder length, curly or wavy
    ___Long, strong
    ___Long, curly or wavy
    ___Other. (Please specify):

Body type preferred of potential sexual partner.
    ___Ultra-thin (waif)
    ___Thin
    ___Average
    ___Athletic
    ___Curvy/ voluptuous
    ___Full-figured
    ___Any, I'm not picky
    ___Other. (Please specify):

Body Parts: Rank your favorite body parts in order of favorite (1) to least favorite (10).
    _____ Face
    _____ Eyes
    _____ Legs
    _____ Breasts
    _____ Ass/Butt/Behind/Bottom
    _____ Arms
    _____ Hands
    _____ Teeth/Mouth
    _____ Feet
    _____ Smile

Physical height
____Short (5'5" or less)
____Average (5'6"-5'8")
____Tall (5-9" or above)
____It doesn't matter as long as she's not taller than me.
____Doesn't matter.

৩৶৩

Personality Traits (What is important to you?)
Mark how you feel about each Trait below with an "x".

Faithful

____Not Important
____Somewhat Important
____Important
____Extremely Important

Confident

____Not Important
____Somewhat Important
____Important
____Extremely Important

Dependable/Trustworthy

____Not Important
____Somewhat Important
____Important
____Extremely Important

Kind

__Not Important
__Somewhat Important
__Important
__Extremely Important

Moral Integrity

__Not Important
__Somewhat Important
__Important
__Extremely Important

Good mother to future (or current) offspring

__Not Important
__Somewhat Important
__Important
__Extremely Important

Sense of humor

__Not Important
__Somewhat Important
__Important
__Extremely Important

Intelligent

__Not Important
__Somewhat Important
__Important
__Extremely Important

Passionate

___Not Important
___Somewhat Important
___Important
___Extremely Important

Generous

___Not Important
___Somewhat Important
___Important
___Extremely Important

Good listener

___Not Important
___Somewhat Important
___Important
___Extremely Important

Romantic

___Not Important
___Somewhat Important
___Important
___Extremely Important

Good in bed

___Not Important
___Somewhat Important
___Important
___Extremely Important

Good kisser

___Not Important
___Somewhat Important
___Important
___Extremely Important

Can cook/bake

___Not Important
___Somewhat Important
___Important
___Extremely Important

Good earning potential

___Not Important
___Somewhat Important
___Important
___Extremely Important

Good sense of style / clothing

___Not Important
___Somewhat Important
___Important
___Extremely Important

Physically fit / active

___Not Important
___Somewhat Important
___Important
___Extremely Important

College major / Career minded

___Not Important
___Somewhat Important
___Important
___Extremely Important

Have earned or will earn a college degree

___Not Important
___Somewhat Important
___Important
___Extremely Important

❧

First Impressions
When you first meet someone, what characteristic(s) make you want to
learn more about them? Mark your responses with an "x".

General appearance / body type.

___Not Important
___Somewhat Important
___Important
___Extremely Important

Personality

___Not Important
___Somewhat Important
___Important
___Extremely Important

Speaking voice

___Not Important
___Somewhat Important
___Important
___Extremely Important

Their ability to flirt

___Not Important
___Somewhat Important
___Important
___Extremely Important

Clothing / style

___Not Important
___Somewhat Important
___Important
___Extremely Important

Manners

___Not Important
___Somewhat Important
___Important
___Extremely Important

How the interact with you and/or your group (if applicable).

___Not Important
___Somewhat Important
___Important
___Extremely Important

❧

Body Parts: Rank your favorite personality type order of favorite (1) to least favorite (8).

______ Introverted / shy
______ Extroverted/outgoing
______ Bubbly/Silly
______ Happy-go-lucky
______ Solemn/angsty
______ Academic/nerdy
______ Dominant/opinionated
______ Type-A, Anal retentive, uptight

❧

In the past 60 days, which of the following dating sites, apps, or social media have you logged into to search for potential sexual partners?

Please mark all that apply with an "x".

___*Tinder*
___*Ashley Madison*
___*Diskreet*
___*Feeld*
___*Happn*
___*Whiplr*
___*Blendr*
___*Down*
___*eHarmony*
___*Match*
___*OkCupid*
___*Baboo*
___*Bumble*
___*Facebook*

___*Snapchat*
___*Instagram*
___None
___Other. (Please specify):

❧

Other

Mark your responses with an "x" when applicable.

Dirty Talk: Do you like dirty talk during sex?
   ___Yes, but only if it's me doing the talking.
   ___Yes, but only if it's my partner doing the talking
   ___Yes, if we both talk dirty.
   ___No.

If no, why not?

Do you masturbate?
   (And frequency, if applicable)
   ___Yes, once in a while
   ___Yes, once per week
   ___Yes, several times per week
   ___Yes, daily
   ___Yes, multiple times per day
   ___Yes, can't keep track
   ___No
   If no, why not?

❧

Tell us how you feel about each of these sexual positions using the options (right).

Missionary
___No Way
___I'll try it, once.
___Whatever. I'm just happy I'm getting laid.
___Tried it. Liked it. I'd do it again.
___Personal Favorite

From behind (doggy style)
___No Way
___I'll try it, once.
___Whatever. I'm just happy I'm getting laid.
___Tried it. Liked it. I'd do it again.
___Personal Favorite

Cowgirl (partner on top)
___No Way
___I'll try it, once.
___Whatever. I'm just happy I'm getting laid.
___Tried it. Liked it. I'd do it again.
___Personal Favorite

Reversal Cowgirl
___No Way
___I'll try it, once.
___Whatever. I'm just happy I'm getting laid.
___Tried it. Liked it. I'd do it again.
___Personal Favorite

Anal
___No Way
___I'll try it, once.
___Whatever. I'm just happy I'm getting laid.
___Tried it. Liked it. I'd do it again.
___Personal Favorite

Standing up (against hard surface)
___No Way
___I'll try it, once.
___Whatever. I'm just happy I'm getting laid.
___Tried it. Liked it. I'd do it again.
___Personal Favorite

Other. (Please specify here):

❧

Stereotypes.
Which do you prefer? Rank the following from favorite (1) to least favorite (10)
_____ The Cheerleader
_____ The Sexy Librarian
_____ The Tomboy
_____ The Girl Next Door
_____ The Trophy Girlfriend/Wife
_____ The Marrying Kind / Take Home to Mom
_____ The Bad Girl
_____ The Nerd
_____ The Porn Star
_____ None. I don't like stereotypes.

❧

Help!
I need additional volunteers for a more in-depth study. If you would be willing to do a one-on-one interview, please fill out the information below. If you are chosen to participate, you will receive a $5.00 gift card to the Coffee Bean. Participants will be chosen at random and will be contacted within the next two weeks to set up a time to meet.

Thank you for taking this survey!

Name:
Cell Number:
Email Address:
Best time to reach you:

ACKNOWLEDGMENTS

Thank you to Hot Tree Editing for editing this book from start to finish.

And an extra special thank you to Becky at Hot Tree Promotions for your advice, expertise, and your positivity.

And for my beta readers.
Thank you so much for your time and feedback!

ABOUT THE AUTHOR

How did it all start? Well, I love reading and one day I was searching for a book. A book about a certain type of woman and a specific kind of man and I couldn't find it so, I wrote it. I called it Game Changer and it couldn't have been a more appropriate title. It changed my life in many ways. While my real job is teaching young people, my fun job is conjuring up characters and situations to write about.

My goal, as a writer, is to write stories that relate to all of us, to make readers laugh and maybe cry sometimes. I hope my readers can escape into a fantasy, one that's actually possible. Sure, some of the stories could be dubbed "Insta-love" stories but that's okay. I fell in love with my husband pretty damn fast and with my daughter the second I saw her. So, it's a thing, I swear.

Please Follow Me on these social media sites. Following on BookBub to learn about special book deals.

I love hearing from you!

facebook.com/authorkaytmiller

twitter.com/kaytmiller1

instagram.com/kaytmiller1

bookbub.com/profile/kayt-miller

THANK YOU!

Thank you so much for reading Virginia and Baker's story! When I start a story, it begins with an outline, notes, and lots of crazy thoughts running through my head. When I actually start writing, the characters take over, leading me through the story like they're holding my hand—guiding me. The process is exciting and cathartic. With that said, I hope you enjoy the story.

If you did, please go to my website, www.kaytmiller.com, and join my newsletter so you can be the first to know what's coming up next. And...

And remember...Please, leave a review!

Thank you!

SNEAK PEEK: ONE OF A KIND
BY KAYT MILLER

Chapter 1

Happy Frigging New Year

"Yo! Mac. Hottie at three o'clock," my best friend says as she approaches me.

Looking to my right, I scan the crowd. "I don't see any hotties."

"No, I said *three* o'clock," Lauren clarified, annoyed. "Don't make me point. It's bad manners."

"I know. I looked at three o'clock and saw only Father Time." Seriously, there's a guy dressed up as Father Time. Ah, New Year's Eve in Chicago. It brings out the crazies.

"No, dork, *my* three o'clock."

"That would be my *nine* o'clock, not my three o'clock."

"Crap, girl, just look to the right."

"Wait, my right or your right?" Lauren can be so confusing.

"Jesus, now he's gone. You missed him. He was your dream man."

"Ooh, you mean he looked like Jason Momoa?" I look frantically around the room.

"What? No. Jason Momoa is your dream man?"

"Uh… yeah. After *Game of Thrones*, he's *everyone's* dream man. Ooh, did you know he's the new Aquaman? I can't flipping wait to see that movie. The man is a god."

"Well, this guy was hot, and he was actually *here*," Lauren says, rolling her eyes. Even in the best of times, the girl barely puts up with me. She continues, "He's got blond hair, and he had that faux-hawk fade haircut that's so in right now. Plus, he had on nerd glasses."

"Holy shite. I love me some faux-hawk. Add the nerd spectacles, and I can feel it in my pantaloons, *giiirrrl*. Gimme. Where is he?"

Lauren giggles. "God, you're such a dork. Spectacles? Pantaloons? Where do you come up with that stuff?"

"I read a lot of Regency-era romances."

"You mean Regency erotica. You're a pervert," she deadpans.

I let out a surprised giggle. *Lauren, Lauren, Lauren.* "It's not erotica. It's *romance*. Sure, there are some naughty little debutantes types in the books and even some wicked rakes, but it's all in good fun."

"Whatevs. I'm going back to Blake. He'll be lost without me."

I snort, rather unattractively, I'm sure. But the truth is, she's right. Blake is her husband of almost a year, and he would literally be lost without her. I'm not sure the man can choose his own clothes, to be honest. I think she chooses his outfit for the next day and sets it all out before they go to bed. It works for them, and I guess there's nothing wrong with it. He adores her and she him, no matter how creepy their love seems to me.

Now that I'm on my own again, I decide to move around the ballroom with eyes peeled for the mysterious "hottie at three o'clock." While I do, I do my best to put this into perspective. Even if I find him, Mr. Hottie would not be interested in me. There's nothing extraordinary about MacKenzie Blue Parker. I'm just your average woman with an average face and a larger-than-average ass, but who *does* have an interesting middle name.

"Thank you, Mom," I say softly, looking up toward heaven. I'm not sure why she used a color for my middle name. When I asked Pops about it, he just said she was whimsical. I love that he used that word to describe my mom. I don't remember a lot about her, but I do remember that she was pretty and lots of fun.

I squeeze through the throng, turning by body this way and that, saying "excuse me," "pardon me," and "oh, I'm sorry my ass knocked your drink out of your hand." After all that, I'm grumpy, my feet hurt, my head hurts, and I'm still hungry even after nibbling on the delightful spread they've got here. I'm trying to look on the bright side but *ugh*, New Year's Eve sucks.

Are you wondering why my feelings about such an optimistic holiday have taken a nose dive? Personal history. Yep, personal history tells me New Year's Eve is a night filled with loneliness, sore feet, and worst of all, shattered expectations. I'm referring specifically to the promised kiss at midnight that never seems to happen—at least not for me. *Why did I let Lauren talk me into coming to this fancy-schmancy party tonight?* Oh, I remember. It's because I'm a sucker for my best friend's charms. I'm a grown-ass woman. You'd think I could turn her down, but Lauren Jacobs-Warner practically guaranteed that I'd have the time of my life tonight *and* I'd get a kiss at midnight.

I don't know why I let her do this to me time and time again. Yeah, my dress is fabulous. I actually feel sort of pretty in it. Pretty but pained. I've been thrust into fashion purgatory with four-inch heels and a too-tight Spanx undergarment. Ugh. I seriously think the people that invented Spanx are sadists—not to mention strange. I mean, who says "undergarment"? No offense, Spanx Incorporated, or whatever you call your business.

To be honest, I'd rather be home watching Netflix and eating junk food. That's my usual activity on holidays like this one, but my best friend sweet-talked me into this. I told her I didn't have the appropriate clothes for this part. I even modeled my best outfit, a pair of black leggings and sparkly top. But that wouldn't do for my friend, the little socialite. So she gave me a dress, an old one of hers that she "didn't really like." I don't believe her for a second. I mean, how could she not *love* this dress? This dress is *Ah. Maze. Ing.*

Imagine a dress that Audrey Hepburn might wear in *Breakfast at Tiffany's*. It's black with a delicate lace overlay. Beneath the lace overlay is a satin dress with a sweetheart bodice. The lace top has a boat neck that is open to my shoulder. Simply put, it's spectacular. Itchy, but spectacular. Oh, and it's got pockets. It's perfection. It has three-quarter sleeves and a flirty skirt that's lined with tulle so that it flares out at the waist and stops right above my knee in a 1950s style. It's a flattering silhouette, because it hides my larger-than-average rump. The truth is, that's the only reason this dress fits me, because Lauren's got a perfect bod. She's five-feet-eight with an hourglass figure in perfect proportion. I'd be jealous if I didn't adore her. But I do, so I'm not.

To ensure I'd attend this little shindig, Lauren even provided me with a date—her cousin, Frederick. He's not really my type, though. Not that I have a type. I haven't even had an actual boyfriend, per se, so maybe *type* is the wrong word. I have book boyfriends, sure. Television and movie boyfriends, of course, but nothing in the flesh. Yeah, so *type* is the wrong word. Perhaps I should just say he's not my dream man. He's short, only an inch or two taller than my five-feet-five-inches. He's also a tad doughy. I know that's not at all nice to say since I'm a bit doughy myself. But he's got a paunch on him like a sixty-year-old man, and he's only in his thirties. He's a little too young to have the dad bod, if you ask me.

Too judgy? If so, I'm sorry. I'm sure Freddy is a great guy.

He seems nice enough, though. I've met him at a couple of the Jacobses' family gatherings. The Jacobses are rich as Croesus. That's what Pops used to call rich people. It fits. He's rolling in it. So, this is more *his* kind of party, not mine. Lauren means well— she really does. But I'm so *not* this girl. I'm a starving artist. Figuratively. Not literally. No, *literally*, I live off of forty-cent packages of ramen noodles and macaroni and cheese in the blue box, so, no, I've got lots of carb-induced meat on my bones.

Case in point. Right this minute I'm surrounded by hundreds of rich people, famous people, important people, and politicians. I think I saw the governor a few minutes ago. We're in a huge ballroom in one of the five-star hotels in downtown Chicago. The ballroom is practically the size of a football field. Above me are the most spectacular chandeliers I've ever seen. They're enormous and appear to be dripping with jewels. The way they glitter and sparkle makes the entire space feel like a scene from a fairy tale. Because I'm no princess, and this place is so beyond anything I've ever seen, it makes me feel self-conscious.

Everyone is dressed in tuxedos and beautiful gowns or cocktail dresses like mine. Thankfully, I don't look completely out of place here. Waiters and waitresses dressed in penguin suits are walking around with trays of finger foods and flutes of champagne. There's a relatively large orchestra sitting off in the far corner near the huge dance floor. Several couples are already out there cutting a rug; not the kind of dancing I'm used to. This is fancy, grown-up, ballroom dancing, not the grind-your-ass-into-the-guy-behind-you dancing that I've done at clubs. No matter, I won't be dancing tonight unless I want to make a complete fool of myself.

As my eyes scan the room, I notice the long table filled with endless amounts of food and delectable-looking desserts, and my stomach rumbles. *Of course, I'm hungry.* In the center of the table is a giant ice sculpture of a swan. If it were sitting on the floor, it would probably stand taller than me. The swan's neck is bent down as though it's ready to take a bite out of all of the deliciousness below it. The main bar is nearby, while other smaller bar stations are located throughout the ballroom. Deciding a drink is in order, I cross my fingers that it's an open bar. I brought a little money with me, but I'd rather save that in case I need a taxi home.

Walking to the bar, I look to my right and spot Lauren standing with her husband, Blake. I recognize the people they're with as old family friends. I scan the other way in search of my "date." *Now, where did he go?* I spot him standing near the bar with a group of guys. They're in a small circle, and each man has his phone in his hands, texting.

I walk toward Frederick in the hopes that he'll be fun tonight. He hasn't proven to be much of a date thus far, but he *is* doing me a favor, I guess. I'm sure Lauren had to coerce him into bringing me. I move to stand next to him and wait for him to notice me. Should I tap him on the shoulder so he knows I'm here? Do I stand and wait for Frederick to ask me to dance or if I'd like a drink? I decide to do my best to be a good date. I wait. And wait. And wait. Nearly ten minutes pass, and Frederick does nothing but text and talk to his buddies. None of the guys even look at me. It's annoying. What? *Am I hideous?* I don't think I'm that tragic-looking. I've got cool hair that's naturally reddish-auburn and cut bluntly just past my shoulders. I've also got the ends tipped with blue tonight, like my middle name. It's only temporary color, but I'm an artist; we artists need to have funky hair at special events. It's the law. I giggle, which draws several pairs of eyes to me. Oh, *now* Frederick notices me.

"You okay?" he asks. He doesn't make eye contact with me, and before I can respond, he's back to his phone. I hear him mutter to his buddies, "Chick is weird." The men chuckle at that little slight, and that's it? That's all I get? Whatever.

"Asshole," I grumble as I start to move around the room again. I can keep *myself* entertained. I'm used to doing things alone. That's probably why I hate stuff like this. I'm much better on my own, in my own world, in my own head. There's nothing wrong with being alone. It's being lonely that sucks.

www.ingramcontent.com/pod-product-compliance
Lightning Source LLC
Chambersburg PA
CBHW031619100726
47898CB00006B/1862